TERMINATED

COAST GUARD RECON BOOK 5

LORI MATTHEWS

ABOUT TERMINATED

From the bestselling author of the Callahan Security Series.

Meet Cain Maddox of the US Coast Guard's TEAM RECON. As in reconstructed. As in broken and needs fixing.

The sole survivor of a deadly IED attack that killed his best friend, for the last year, Cain has been recovering physically and mentally, thanks to his assignment to Team RECON. Now feeling better than he has in months, it only takes the latest op to turn his world upside down.

On a personal vendetta of revenge on her brother's killer in Iraq, Harlow Moretti has made taking down Silverstone Group her life's mission. But now the mercenary group is onto her, and a potentially fatal mistake leaves her life hanging in the balance.

Harlow barely escapes a locked and sinking cargo container. But she thanks her lucky stars a bit too soon as she comes face to face with Cain Maddox, the man who'd point-blank refused to help her with her quest. Cain cannot believe that Harlow has spent all this time chasing the murderous thugs. Even though she's his dead best friend's sister, and he shouldn't want her, she's the one weakness he can't shake. It's only a matter of time before Silverstone comes after their cargo and Cain knows they will stop at nothing to retrieve it, including killing Harlow. He'll protect her at all costs, even if it means losing his heart.

This one is for my fans. I cannot tell you how grateful I am that you read my books. You have made my dreams come true.

ACKNOWLEDGMENTS

A huge thank you to Joseph D'Elia (Lieutenant, USCG) who is always willing to answer all my questions and then turn a blind eye when I manipulate the answers just a wee bit to suit my own needs. I couldn't have created Team RECON without his help. Any mistakes are my own.

Thank you doesn't cover it when it comes to my rock star editors, Corinne DeMaadg and Heidi Senesac. They are truly the most patient people. Thanks also goes out to my cover artist, Llewellen Designs for making my story come alive: my virtual assistant, Susan Poirier and my FaceBook guru, Amanda Robinson. My personal cheer squad which I could not survive without: Janna MacGregor, Suzanne Burke, Stacey Wilk, Kimberley Ash and Tiara Inserto. My husband and my children who make me laugh every day. And to you, the reader. Your emails and posts mean the world to me. The fact that you read my stories is the greatest gift ever. Thank you.

PROLOGUE

2007 Iraq

"Are you sure this is the right call?" The soldier glanced nervously down the tunnel. Roman Vance didn't normally question his superior officer, but this…this was different.

Lieutenant Asher Foley's eyes were black as night and his face was burnt from the Iraqi sun. His dark hair was badly in need of a cut, and he was in desperate need of a shave. Foley was in excellent shape as any Army Ranger should be, but he was covered in a layer of dirt that made him look more like he lived on the street rather than in uniform.

He glared at Vance. "It's not like we can just waltz this out of Iraq at the moment. It should be fine here for a while. Once things calm down, we'll move it." He leaned forward so he was mere inches from Vance's face. "Remember, this is not a sprint, but a marathon. This is the beginning for us, not the end. In a few months when we get out, we're gonna build a business, and this is going to help us. So don't worry, but more importantly, don't fuck this up."

While Foley walked over to check on the other men who were rearranging the pallets in the tunnel, Vance backed up and leaned against the tunnel wall. He didn't want to be here. They had it all within their grasp, but his superior officer and soon to be boss when he mustered out was willing to put it off. But for how long? When would it cool down enough to move their prize?

Vance wasn't known for his patience. He respected Foley, but the truth was, burying the whole mess was making him nervous. If it was found, they would lose their entire future. If it wasn't found but they couldn't get it out of the country, their future plans would be erased like writing in sand during high tide. He was trying to remain calm, but all he kept thinking about was if he died before they could extricate the prize, he would miss out. And he hated missing out.

Foley came back. "They're finished. Everything is in place. You know what to do." He nodded at Vance and walked over to the rope ladder. He climbed out of the tunnel without a backward glance, confident that his subordinate would carry out his orders.

As he was instructed to do, Vance waited until Foley was gone and then went over to the four Iraqis they'd hired to move the pallets into the tunnel. They were resting and drinking bottles of water. It was hot, tiring work. They deserved a break.

Vance raised his machine gun and, with a loud burst of fire, shot every single man. Then he walked to the rope ladder. He glanced over at the pallets. It was killing him that he had to leave all of this behind. He was even tempted to take some of the cargo with him, but if Foley ever found out, he would be a dead man.

He ground his teeth and climbed out of the tunnel. It would only be a couple of months. He could hang on for that long, couldn't he?

CHAPTER ONE

2022 Iraq

Harlow Moretti angled the binoculars so they wouldn't reflect the sunlight as she lay down behind the outcropping of rocks. The sun was hot, and she wiped the sweat from her forehead before it could drip into her eyes. Her hair was tied back in a bun to keep her neck cool but it wasn't working. The heat was getting to her. The hijab she had worn to blend in was lying in the dirt beside her, as was the black abaya. Why women in the middle east chose black to wear every day was a mystery to her. The shops in the cities had all these colorful dresses, but all the women chose black or brown. Not only was it drab, but it was hot as hell.

She scanned the area. It was just another quasi-abandoned village, but it was on the outskirts of Mosul, and with the way the rebuilding was going, it wouldn't be long before this, like many other abandoned villages, would be gobbled up and incorporated into the city.

Currently, six men hovered in the shade of two dilapidated clay buildings. The two houses, or that was what she assumed they were by the shape and size of them, had long since ceased to provide any real shelter. The roof on one on the right had caved in, and the other one was missing doors and the far wall had collapsed, making the roof sag.

The village had most likely been abandoned during the war and left for nature to reclaim. The dirt track the houses were on was short and stopped where the road turned left, away from Harlow. There were more old buildings behind the dilapidated houses with an old water well in between them. It must have been a community well at some point in the past but it was probably dried up by now.

Her senses were heightened. It made no sense. There didn't appear to be a thing of interest about these buildings as far as Harlow could see. So why were the men here?

Harlow adjusted her hips so she was resting more comfortably on the ground and once again silently thanked her brother for teaching her survival skills as he'd called them. How to shoot, use the right equipment like binoculars to watch her quarry, how to build a fire and survive in the woods. He'd been talking about hunting animals to eat and surviving being lost in the woods. The desert was different and her targets were human but the principles were the same. If there was one thing she'd learned in the last six months of following Roman Vance, it was that what he did and where he went didn't always make sense. Well, not yet anyway.

She reached back and grabbed a water bottle out of her pack. She kept at least a six-pack at all times, along with snacks and power bars. She drank deeply from the bottle and then put it back. She picked up her field glasses again and focused in on the men below.

Vance was resting in the shade. He was lying on an old door that had been put up on clay blocks, presumably to make a table. His men were scattered around the area, lounging in whatever shade they could find. They all looked like they had nothing better to do than take an afternoon nap. It wasn't true, of course. They were all on their guard. One false move, and they'd spring up and kill whoever threatened them.

She'd almost fallen for their trick once. In the very beginning when she didn't know any better. She had approached Vance with the intent of shooting him through the heart. At the last moment, a man stepped out of the shadows and went for Vance before she could get a shot off. Vance's men killed the assailant in the blink of an eye.

Harlow readjusted her hips again. The ground was hard, and she was tired. The cargo pants she wore were the color of sand so she would blend in, but she longed for a pair of shorts. Still, she didn't take her eyes off what was happening below. She said a prayer for the unknown assailant who'd died that night, all those months ago. She felt she owed him some sort of debt. He'd inadvertently saved her life.

A sound reached her ears. Engines. She turned her head. Dust kicked up behind three large trucks heading into the abandoned village. They had shipping containers on the back of them. The first one drove past and then reversed until it was jammed into the space between the two houses. The other two trucks parked on the street.

Harlow shifted so she could see a bit better and refocused her binoculars. Vance was talking to the driver of the truck, whom she recognized. He was one of the Silverstone guys that Vance often worked with. Hugo something? She couldn't remember his last name, or maybe she'd never heard it. He was of average height and build. His gut was hanging over his belt a bit more than was good for his line of work. Not too many people wanted to hire overweight military contractors.

Vance turned and waved to his crew. Five men emerged from the shade of the hut and started messing with the well.

They were smashing the stones with a sledgehammer and then pulling them apart. Then they seemed to be pushing the dirt aside and pulling up boards. Why the hell would they bother with that? Unless…they'd put something down there.

Harlow cursed under her breath. She needed a better vantage point. Lowering the binoculars, she took another look around the area. There was nowhere else that provided enough cover to keep her hidden. Moving now was a huge risk anyway. She was stuck where she was.

She scuttled back a bit and then moved to the other side of the rock outcropping. She settled on her belly again and refocused her field glasses. The men had destroyed the top of the well, leaving a pile of smashed stones and debris off to the right and it looked like they widened the hole. Maybe it wasn't really a well. The hole had to be ten feet by ten feet. No well is that big.

Finally, about a half hour later, they began to hoist something out of the hole. It took them a few minutes, but they managed with the help of a winch from the truck. It was a big square block, maybe six feet by six feet by three feet high, bound by what looked like Cling Wrap. What the hell was it?

She tried to focus in on the block, but the angle was bad and the sun's glare off the plastic didn't help. Vance walked over to the square and pulled on a piece of the loose plastic. Something fell out. It was about the size of a brick, but it was the wrong color. The brick appeared greyish green, but it was hard to tell with the angle of the sun. It wasn't the normal dull red-orange associated with bricks, that was plainly visible. Also, the edges weren't ridged. It looked like it was something wrapped in plastic. Drugs? Was Vance running drugs? It wouldn't surprise her. Nothing this man did would surprise her at this point.

He stooped to pick up the brick-shaped object. He pointed at the hole it had fallen out of, and one of the men brought over duct tape and covered the hole. Vance then turned in her direction. She was focusing in on what was in his hands, but a man walked out of the shade of the building on the right and went over to stand in front of Vance, blocking her view. *Asher Foley.* Top dog at Silverstone. Foley and Vance stayed that way for a few minutes talking. By the time the conversation was over, Vance's hands were empty.

"Fuck." What could it be? Drugs. It had to be drugs, didn't it? That was *a lot* of heroin if that's what it was. She had no clue what the street value of all that would be. Could Vance be transporting drugs via shipping containers without anyone knowing? Possibly. If he had the right connections. Still, it seemed a bit dangerous and not his style. If she'd learned one thing following Vance all these months, it was that he was careful.

And what was Asher Foley doing here? He didn't come to Iraq much. She'd only seen him once before. If he was here, did that mean something big was going on? These large, wrapped cubes they were bringing out of the ground certainly qualified as a major development.

The men brought up ten pallets of wrapped cubes. Taking another swig of water, Harlow sighed. She knew she should consider herself lucky. Vance could have easily discovered she'd been following him over these last months and had her killed. She had often wondered why he didn't notice her but then at one point, she realized that she didn't register as a threat with Vance or any of his men. They only reacted to what they perceived as threats, namely, big strong men. If she stayed quietly in the background and looked like all the other aid workers, he'd never notice her.

That realization felt like an insult on one level, but she accepted it. It was better to be ignored than to be found and killed. Her moment would come. Vance would know she was a threat. She would make certain of it.

CHAPTER TWO

Twelve Hours Later

"Don't move," the voice behind her demanded.

Harlow held her breath and tried not to panic. Her brain worked frantically to come up with an excuse as to why she was in the container. "Um, I—"

"Shut it. Put your hands in the air and turn around slowly."

Harlow did as she was told and was immediately blinded by a flashlight beam in her eyes. Then there was another one and another. That wasn't good. What the hell could she say to get out of this mess? She couldn't come up with anything. All she heard was her parents' voices in her head. *One day, Harlow, your impetuous nature is going to get you in trouble.* Not to mention a very big, very loud *I told you so*.

"What do we have here?" a voice said, and one flashlight broke away from the rest. The beam moved forward followed by the scrape of boots on the metal floor. She couldn't make out the face of the man holding it, but she knew the voice and it sent chills down her spine. James Daughtry. By all accounts, he was one of the cruelest men on the planet.

"What are you doing in this container?" he demanded.

Harlow still couldn't come up with any kind of reasonable explanation, so she remained silent. Her stomach plummeted, and sweat broke out between her shoulder blades.

Daughtry turned his head slightly. "Finish closing up the other containers," he called over his shoulder. "I'm gonna be busy here for a little while." The other flashlights moved away.

Maybe if she knocked the flashlight out of his hand, she might have a chance to at least make a break for it. She had tensed to spring when Daughtry turned the flashlight away slightly so she could see the gun in his other hand.

So much for that plan.

She was well and truly screwed.

Her heart ramped up like an airline engine. There was no escape. After six months of following Roman Vance and his men, looking for a way to bring them down, her own stupidity had turned the tables on her, and now *she* was the one going down. Permanently.

"I'm gonna ask you one more time," Daughtry snarled. "What are you doing in here?"

"I-I thought this was my stuff. I'm shipping some stuff home, and I thought this was my container. I must have gotten the number wrong."

Daughtry threw his head back and laughed. "That is the shittiest excuse I've ever heard. Not even a good try." He moved forward again so he was only a few feet away. "You're not bad, sweetheart. Nice tits and a nice round ass. I think we should have some fun."

She could see his face now, and she knew that look. Her stomach rolled. She was going to be ill. Daughtry was going to rape her and then kill her. Could she get to her backpack?

Her gun was in there. She glanced toward the corner she'd left it in. Too far. No way she'd reach that before Daughtry shot her. Her mouth went dry, and her hands started to shake. "N-no. I j-just got the wrong container. I'll go."

Daughtry's voice got hard. "Who are you? Who sent you here?"

Acting the innocent, Harlow made her eyes as wide as possible, which wasn't hard at that moment, and shook her head. "N-no one. I just got lost."

He took another step forward and backhanded her with his flashlight. She fell over the side of a pallet and saw stars. His evil chuckle iced her blood. "Don't fucking lie to me. I will make you hurt in ways you can't imagine. Who sent you?" he demanded.

She tried to straighten up, but she was too dizzy. Her cheek throbbed. "I…" She couldn't get any words out. There was shuffling behind her, and suddenly he had her by the hair and pulled her to her feet. Then a knife pressed on her neck. She'd seen what he could do with that knife firsthand a couple of months ago. He'd left a woman alive but permanently disfigured.

"You're gonna tell me what I want to know, or I'm gonna slit your throat." When his stale breath hit her cheek, the urge to retch nearly overpowered her.

She swallowed the rising bile and tried to think, but her mind had gone blank at the sight of the knife.

"No?" Daughtry chuckled. "You're a feisty one. I like that. You and me are gonna have some fun before you die."

The knife disappeared. She heard the sounds of him undoing his belt buckle and then his zipper. Her mouth went dry, and she swallowed convulsively. A cold sweat broke out on her skin. There had to be a way out of this. *There had to be.*

She flailed around, trying to hit him, but his grip on her

hair was too tight and she couldn't get enough power behind her hits. She kicked backward but he dodged her feet and gave her hair another painful jerk for her effort.

Daughtry started to undo her cargo pants. She clawed at his hand, trying to pry it away, but he yanked hard on her hair again. "Try that again, bitch, and I'll slit your throat. I don't mind fucking a warm corpse."

All the air left her lungs. This was not how she wanted to die.

Suddenly a cell phone went off. Daughtry cursed and threw her forward onto the pallet again. He stepped back. She glanced over her shoulder, but the gun was already in his hand again.

"Daughtry," he said. Then silence. "Yes, Vance, they're ready to go. Just closing them up now." More silence. "Fine, I'll check. The other two ships are being loaded now. We should get it all out of Tel Aviv tonight." He rang off.

Harlow straightened, preparing to fight. She whirled around, but Daughtry had already stepped out of range. He was still holding the gun. He tucked his phone in his pocket and started doing up his pants. "Fuck. I hate to miss out on some fun, but duty calls." He turned and started walking away.

Harlow started after him. "What are you going to do with me?"

"Nothing. Absolutely nothing. By the time this container gets to the other side, you'll be dead."

The container door slammed closed.

Harlow's knees went weak. "No!" she yelled as she lunged forward, hitting the door with her fists. She heard the lock snap into place. She pounded some more, but it was no use. No one was coming.

"This is not good," she mumbled to herself as she paced back and forth in the container. How the hell was she going to get out of this one? She took a deep breath and then another and another. She realized she was starting to hyperventilate. She needed to calm down and check out her surroundings. Maybe there was another way out.

She picked up her cell phone. No bars, of course. She was in what equated to a Faraday cage. Totally surrounded by metal. No signal would get through that. She turned on her phone's flashlight which provided some light and searched all around the container. "Shit, shit, shit." The light was strong, but it wasn't bright enough to reach the corners. Were there holes in the corrugated metal or not? Was she going to suffocate in here?

She tried to stop herself from panicking, but that just psyched her out more. She was sure she was using way too much oxygen. Waving the phone around, she frantically searched for holes in the walls and ceiling. Nothing. Her stomach cramped as sweat poured down her back. What the fuck had she been thinking coming in here?

The walls surrounding her undulated as a wave of dizziness crashed through her. She stopped and leaned against the side of a large pallet. Bending at the waist, she rested her head near her knees. *Pull yourself together.* Normally, she was much more in control than this, but too many days with little sleep had left her head fuzzy, and now she'd made the biggest mistake. She forced herself to calm down. Her cheek still throbbed, so she used the pain to focus her brain.

Finally feeling a bit better, Harlow picked up her phone again and studied the container. She aimed the flashlight into the corners again. In the back right corner, there might be a small hole, but it was hard to tell. She moved the light slowly along the seam where the roof met the wall, from the back of the container toward the front. About two-thirds of the way down, there was a depression, and in the dent was a fist sized hole.

"Thank you, Jesus," she muttered. She sucked in more oxygen and tried to get her body to relax. If this had been daytime, she'd have noticed the hole right away, but since it was the middle of the night, it was pitch black outside as well as in.

Harlow leaned against one of the pallets again. She wanted to scream. It was her own damn fault she was trapped in this container. She had thought she was being so smart. She'd followed Vance and his trucks all day, waiting for an opportunity to see what it was that he was moving. She figured it had to be drugs, but she wanted confirmation before she alerted any authorities.

She'd spent the last six months tracking Vance and his people in an attempt to find something big that would send them to prison, or preferably, to a CIA black site and thrown in a hole, never to be heard from again. He was the reason her brother was dead, he and his boss, Asher Foley, head of Silverstone Group, and they had to pay for that.

Then, out of the blue, Vance and his men ventured into the Iraqi desert, picked up these pallets and stored them in these containers. She'd followed them as they drove the trucks to Tel Aviv. She figured this had to be it. It was her own fault for getting too excited and not thinking clearly. If only she'd been more patient. Instead, she had snuck into one of the containers when the guard had walked away. Then didn't that fucker come back, and with Daughtry? She shuddered again. She should have known he wouldn't go far with it unlocked. She just thought she'd have time to get in and get out before anyone noticed. *Stupid.*

She could keep trying to get someone's attention by pounding on the metal, but in all likelihood, the noise would have attracted one of Vance's people, and they'd probably just shoot her. She remembered the look on Daughtry's face and shivered. He would have raped her if his cell hadn't gone off, and he still would have left her in here to die. *Monster.* She should have just walked up to Vance and shot him dead, which was her original plan. Then she wouldn't be in this mess. But no, she had to get ambitious and decide to take down the whole Silverstone Group.

She ran her hands over her face. Well, since she was here, she might as well see what all the fuss was about. She picked up her cell again and tried to peer through the plastic wrap. There were four large pallets in the container, and each one was wrapped in many layers of plastic.

Harlow moved around to the other side of the pallet closest to the wall of the container and pulled out her knife. She placed her cell phone on the top so the flashlight hung over the edge. Now her hands were free to slit the plastic. She reached in and tried to pull out some of the contents. It didn't budge. She grabbed her phone and shined the light through the hole she'd made.

"Son of a bitch," she murmured. She tore at the plastic, managing to make a big enough hole to grab a wad of the contents and pull it out. Money. American dollar bills. Hundred-dollar bills in large stacks. Four pallets of hundred-dollar bills. She knew there were three containers. "Jesus," she mumbled and promptly fell on her butt. She couldn't do the math, but this wasn't small potatoes. There had to be millions here.

Sitting there stunned into silence, a sound reached her ears, machinery of some kind. It was getting louder. She glanced at her watch. It was just after two a.m. The docks worked twenty-four hours a day. The machinery might cover the sound of her gun that was in her backpack. If she'd only had that out when Daughtry had found her. But how would it have helped? It wasn't like she could shoot him and live. The others would have shot her in an instant. But now, she could possibly shoot off the lock from the inside and get out. If—and it was a big if—Daughtry and his men weren't close by. Had they left after securing the container, or were they still lurking around outside?

She wished there was some way for her to see around the outside of the container, but the hole wasn't big enough to stick her phone through without cutting her hand to bits and, knowing her luck, she'd drop the phone. She got up and searched the rest of the container. There were other small holes, but nothing major and no way out.

The machinery noise was getting louder. Harlow leaned against the pallet of money and started to laugh. Why was it when she finally had money, she had no way to spend it, and when she had everything in the world to buy, she had no money? Life's little ironies.

The container clanged, and Harlow started. What the hell? The machinery was so loud, it must be just outside. When the container started to jolt and sway, she grabbed her cell phone before it could slide away from her. *Shit*! Someone was picking up the container.

"Oh, my God," Harlow groaned as she braced herself between two pallets. That's what Daughtry had meant. They were loading the containers on different ships and shipping them out. The pallets stayed in place as the container swayed. At least they were tied down so they couldn't crush her.

She swallowed hard and tried not to puke. If she was going to be stuck in here for a while, then smelling puke was not going to help. The swaying continued for what seemed like an eternity, and then suddenly there was a loud clang as the container dropped and the swaying stopped. Harlow blinked into the darkness.

Light was now coming in through the hole in the wall. On her tiptoes, she tried to see out of the hole, but at five-feet-four inches, she was too short. She got on top of the nearest pallet and then put her hands on the wall on either side of the hole. She leaned over and peered outside.

It took her a second to comprehend what she was seeing. She was on a ship. The smell of the Mediterranean hit her nose. The container wasn't on the deck but on other containers. At least that's what she surmised from looking out the hole. She was up in the air. Her gut rolled just thinking about it. She hated heights.

So much for shooting her way out. If she shot the door now, she had no way of getting down. Of course, she could make a lot of noise and someone might eventually hear her, but then would she be safe, or were Vance's men on board?

She glanced at the money. There was no way in hell Roman Vance was going to leave millions of dollars unattended on a ship. His men were on board for sure but if there were multiple ships as Daughtry's phone call implied then maybe Vance wasn't here. At the very least, Daughtry would be on this cargo ship, wouldn't he? Maybe not, but someone from Vance's world would be for sure. She sat back on the pallet, dangling her legs over the side. Now what the hell was she supposed to do?

She turned on her cell phone flashlight again and went over to the corner where she'd dropped her backpack when she'd first entered the container. Opening it up, she discovered that she had six bottles of water, four energy bars, and a falafel sandwich. She'd stocked up when Vance's trucks had stopped for gas. There was also a pair of binoculars, some sunscreen, and her gun.

The water and food were helpful—the rest, who knew? She grabbed her backpack and went over to sit on the pallet again. There was more light by the hole, and she wanted to save her cell phone battery for as long as she could, not that she could make a call. Plus, who would she call? She was out here on her own.

Her friends all thought she was out of her mind. She'd given up her job as a dental hygienist in a busy practice to travel to Iraq and find out the truth about her brother's death. Her co-workers didn't think it was worth risking her own life to find answers. Nor did her friends from the stables. She loved to ride and kept her horse with some close friends, Gale and John Lindsey but they thought she was just not dealing with her grief. Gale wanted her to take some time off and join them on the horseshow circuit. "A change is as good as a rest," she said.

But they all didn't know the whole truth. Finding out what happened to Perry gave her focus. It gave her a goal. It made her heart pound and provided a reason to get up in the morning. She actually hated being a dental hygienist. Although it didn't seem so bad at the moment.

Her parents even thought she was crazy. They loved Perry, her brother, but they didn't feel the need for answers like she did. They had accepted what the Navy had told them and tried to move on with their lives.

But she couldn't. It didn't make sense. Why would her brother die in the middle of the desert when he was supposed to be doing exercises in the Persian Gulf? How could he be killed by an IED when the area he was driving through was a friendly zone? Why would no one answer her questions? And worse, why did everyone look guilty when she asked about her brother's death?

She'd been right, though. It had taken months of legwork and dating a certain captain that had access to the files before she found what she was looking for. She did feel badly about using Gavin. He'd been sweet and loving during their time together. And she'd made noise about not wanting to get too serious about anyone. She'd lost count of the number of times she'd said, *this is just for fun, right*? Truth was, she had needed his security clearance. It had taken weeks for her to figure out where to look for the information and then even longer to get Gavin's password. In all fairness to him, she'd done her utmost to make him feel like she cared. And she did find she'd cared about him. She'd been a good girlfriend to him even if she was in the relationship for all the wrong reasons.

Once she had the information she needed, she slowly disentangled herself from Gavin. To this day, he thought he had dumped *her*. That was fine. She never wanted to hurt him. Hurting people wasn't something she ever wanted to do. Gavin was engaged the last she'd heard, so it seemed to have worked out for him.

She, on the other hand, was still looking for answers. The file was thin, but it did explain that they were on their way to the port when the IED went off under their vehicle. They were chasing down a lead in regard to U.S. currency that had been sent to Iraq and then had gone missing. Roman Vance had been a person of interest in that investigation.

Surprise. "I found the money, Perry," she whispered. Or rather, the money had found her. Now she just had to figure out if she could get out of this mess to let someone know. "It was Vance, Perry. You guys were on the right track," she murmured softly.

It was why they had to die. She was sure of it. As soon as she'd seen Vance's name in the file, she knew he was the reason her brother was dead.

The sole survivor, Cain Maddox, wouldn't talk to her about what happened. He had told her it was classified. He wasn't wrong, but she had a right to know, goddammit. Perry was her brother! Cain had been temporarily appointed to her brother's team joint training exercises. Cain had a background in explosives and coming from the Coast Guard, he also knew all about boarding vessels. He was with Perry's team to learn more detailed skills in certain areas. At least that's what Perry had said. He wouldn't elaborate further because it was classified. In truth she had been surprised she'd gotten that much out of him, and they'd all become real close while on assignment. She smiled at the memory of hanging out with her brother and his teammates when they'd been Stateside on leave.

And then, one day, they were all gone—except Cain, and he might as well have been since he was most certainly struggling. He had cut her out of his life completely at the moment she needed him close. All because of one little kiss.

They were both hurting and had met for a drink at the bar where Perry and the team had hung out. They'd had a couple of beers, and then in the parking lot, he'd kissed her. Or she'd kissed him. He sort of panicked. He said he couldn't date Perry's sister. It wasn't right.

And that was it. They'd spoken on the phone a few times after that, mostly him trying to convince her to stop chasing what happened to Perry, but even those calls stopped after a while.

The man was just too extreme. Her brother wouldn't have cared if they'd dated. Well, maybe he would have, but he'd know better than to stick his nose in where it didn't belong. Okay, that wasn't true either. Perry would have pitched a fit because she was his little sister, but he also would've gotten over it. He'd really liked Cain.

Harlow pulled out the sandwich and ate it. It wouldn't last without a refrigerator, so she might as well enjoy her last meal. She sighed. It was warm in the container at the moment, but it would get cooler as the night progressed. She might have to cover herself in the plastic wrap if she got too cold.

She flopped back on the pallet of money. If someone had told her one day she would sleep on millions of dollars, this scenario never would have entered her mind. She knew deep down that she was in serious trouble. She was stuck in a container somewhere above the deck of a large cargo ship. The only way out was down. If she did get out of the container, it would only be a temporary reprieve because Vance and his men would no doubt kill her. She knew their secret.

Her parents and Cain were right. She should have stuck to cleaning people's teeth. Being a dental hygienist wasn't the worst job in the world. It sure as hell was preferable to being trapped in a shipping container when not a soul on the planet knew where she was. Except Daughtry, which was no help since he was the one who locked her in.

When there was another loud clang, she jerked upright. Were they moving her again? No, the container didn't move. They must have dropped another container on top of hers. At least she wasn't at the top of the pile. That could easily be sixty feet above the deck.

Exhaustion overwhelmed her, and she flopped back down again. Tears pricked the back of her eyelids. It was all so much. She'd been running on adrenaline for months, only to wind up here. *Stupid.* She put an arm over her eyes. She might as well sleep. There was nothing else to do at the moment. Putting off the inevitable seemed as good an idea as any.

CHAPTER THREE

Harlow rested against the side of the pallet and stared at the last sip of water in her last bottle. She'd managed to last six days by her count, but she was considerably weaker now, and unless she did something soon, she would die in the container. Maybe she should have done something days ago but, in reality, it was likely it wouldn't make a difference. She'd either die in the container or die when Daughtry or some other member of Vance's team discovered her inside.

On the other hand, maybe just maybe, she could get one of the crew of the ship to help her. But, she was a stowaway in a container and that would bring up all kinds of questions. The kinds of things Vance and his people would not want brought up. There was no way Vance let this shipment go without his people on board. They wouldn't let her off the ship alive. After following these people for months, she could guarantee it.

Stupid. It was the only word that described the horrible situation she'd gotten herself into. If she'd just waited, she wouldn't be in this mess. She could have found out where the container was going and met it on the other side. No, she had to take the bull by the horns, and now she was either going to die in the container or die when Vance's men found her.

Thunder rolled overhead. More rain. It had rained a few times since she'd been in the container. Once it blew in sideways, so she was able to capture a bit of water from the hole, but not enough to really make a difference. Who knew if that would happen again? She sighed and struggled to her feet. The minuscule world she'd existed in for six days gave a sickening lurch as dizziness rocked her. She steadied herself on the pallet.

This was ridiculous. She was done. She needed help, or at least she needed to die in a more dignified manner. Croaking in a container filled with money was just all kinds of wrong. Harlow went over and grabbed her gun out of her backpack and laid it on top of a pallet. Then she turned and stuffed several wads of cash into it. Then she added a few more. If by some miracle she managed to get out and Vance's men didn't kill her, it might come in handy. Closing the pack, she put it on her back. And if she didn't make it, well then, maybe some lucky soul would find it and have a better life.

Her heart broke for her parents. Perry had always been their favorite, but they'd loved her, too, and this would be another hit for them. She let out a sob at the thought that she would bring them so much pain again.

The thunder crashed, and the ship rolled in the waves. She'd gotten used to the rolling of the ship, but it had gotten much worse over the last few days. They were probably far out to sea by now. Combined with the stormy conditions, the ship constantly pitched back and forth. She'd looked out the hole in the side of the container but all she could see were other containers.

Harlow stood in front of the door. If she shot through where the lock was, surely, she'd be able to blow it off. Then what? She guessed she was either in the second or third container up from the deck. Of course, she could be wrong and be in the tenth container up, at which point opening the door wasn't really gonna help. She'd be a splat on the deck if she jumped. But honestly, although it was hard to tell, she thought she wasn't that high up. She knew there were at least two more containers on top of her so at least she wasn't at the very top. *If.* And that was only if the containers were stacked from the deck.

If it was one of those ships that loaded from down inside the hull all the way up then she was screwed. She knew she was above the side of the ship because she'd seen the harbor in Tel Aviv when she'd looked out the hole before they loaded up containers next to her which meant she was way the hell up there. Nope, she decided. She just couldn't be that high up with no hope of getting out alive.

Going back to the first scenario. *If* she was in the second container from the deck, then the fall wasn't bad. The container she was in was about eight feet tall, so that would mean she'd be just a little over eight feet from the deck. Assuming she had sufficient strength and she could hang from the edge to drop, she'd only be about two feet from the ground. *If* she was in the third container up, then it was a different story. She'd be about twelve feet up. She didn't want to think about that. It was all down to the *ifs.*

By the loud cracks of thunder, immediately followed by bright flashes of lightning, the storm must be just overhead. The roll of the ship also seemed to have changed. It was sluggish or something. She had to stand on an angle to be upright. Did that mean the ship was listing? Her gun slid across the top of the pallet. There was some loud crashing and clanging. It sounded like containers banging together. She dropped into a squat and put her arms over her head out of sheer reflex.

The crashing and clanging stopped but suddenly, an alarm blared. This wasn't good. *Shit.* It was now or never. She stood and reached across the now angled pallet to grab her gun.

Harlow said a small prayer and then took aim. She fired three shots in rapid succession. Then she pushed on the door with one hand. Nothing. She took a step back and fired again as the thunder crashed.

She put her gun in her backpack and pushed hard on the door. There was a bit of give. She stepped back and hit it harder this time with her shoulder. When the left side swung open, she had to grab on to the right side to steady herself. She looked out.

The rain was coming down in sheets and slanted almost horizontally, so it was hard to see, but the sound of the alarm was much louder and she looked to the right. The stack of containers that used to be there had vanished. She blinked. Was she hallucinating? When she'd looked out the hole just earlier, there were containers next to her. Now there was nothing.

She looked down and realized two things. One, the containers that had been next to hers were on the edge of the ship, and now they were in the water. The ship was tilting. They were going down. And two, she was in the larger type of cargo ship. The deck was far, far below her.

Her heart slammed against her rib cage while her stomach rolled. There was no way she was climbing out of the container. The drop would kill her even before the ship sank. She leaned against a pallet and sucked in air. Was it better to jump and die by being a splat on the deck than drowning? *Fucking hell.* She started to hyperventilate. The groaning of the ship brought her to her senses. There had to be another way.

She walked out to the opening again. In her panic, she

hadn't taken in the full scene around her. The container she was in, was definitely way up there. Looking up, there were still about three more above her so maybe she was seventy feet up, give or take a few feet. Looking around Harlow struggled to keep her breathing even. Her throat seemed to be closing over.

Don't panic. Panic kills. That was what her brother used to say. She gripped the edge of the doorway and calmed her breathing.

There was a stairwell directly in front of her container. It was too far out to reach but if she ran and jumped she might be able to grab onto the railing and pull herself over onto the stairwell. It was slightly below her so she should have a good chance at catching the top rung but if she missed there were two more before she'd miss altogether.

Glancing around, she immediately realized this was her best option. The stairwell was maybe eight feet away. Maybe more but the rain was going to make the railing slippery. She glanced at the deck below. It was a long fucking way down. And there were no givens about her waning strength. Being locked in a container with minimal calories had weakened her. If she missed, she was dead. If she reached it, but couldn't hold on, she was dead. Then again if she stayed here, she was most certainly dead. The ship rolled again. The alarm continued to blare. It was now or never.

She slung the straps of her pack over her shoulder and pulled them tight. Then Harlow backed up the length of the container. There was a straight line between the pallets. She was going to have to run up and take a flying leap. She readied herself, taking a few deep breaths. A surge of adrenaline boosted her strength. *Let's hope it's enough.* She let out one last breath and then took off. She ran and then took a flying leap when she hit the end of the container, but the ship rolled throwing her off balance. She careened over the edge but didn't have enough power to reach the handrail.

She crashed against the bottom rung of the railing catching it in both hands and then as her arms took her full weight along with the weight of the backpack, her right hand slipped off. She screamed as she dangled over the deck below. Her lungs stopped working. Icy fingers closed over her throat. *Don't panic.* Perry's voice rang in her ears.

Her left hand was slipping off the wet metal bar. She was not going to die this way. She gritted her teeth and swung her right hand upward, grabbing the railing again. Pulling as hard as she could, she managed to wrap her arm around the bar and then get her feet onto the edge of the platform. She stood, steadied herself, and then climbed over the railing to the stairwell landing. Her knees gave out and she ended up sitting on the floor, leaning against the inside of the railing, catching her breath.

Her arms hurt but other than that she was fine. She'd made it. "Thanks, Perry," she said aloud. There was a sudden loud groan from the containers next to her. The sound of metal on metal and loud snapping had her on her feet and heading down the stairs in seconds.

"Hey!" she heard a voice and looked down the stairwell. A man in a uniform was coming up. He was wearing a life jacket and a hard hat. "What are you doing here? You need to be on the starboard side by the lifeboat."

"I—"

"And where's your life jacket?"

It was hard to see him clearly, but he had dark hair and a scar on his chin.

She blinked and shrugged.

He cursed. "Follow me. Did you see anyone else?"

Harlow shook her head.

The man turned and headed back down the stairwell. He

glanced over his shoulder to make sure Harlow was following him. She had to move quickly to keep up. He led her through a maze of walkways on the outside of the ship until they came to another stairwell.

Then he went digging in a bin about ten feet away. Pulling out a life vest, he staggered back to her and put it over her head. "Stay here in line," he shouted over the storm. "They'll get you on the life raft." He looked worried and didn't sound remotely confident in what he said.

Harlow merely nodded and glanced up the stairwell. There was a line of people wearing life preservers. She moved over to stand behind an older woman who was wearing a white chef's outfit under her life jacket. Harlow took off her backpack to put her life vest on properly and then attempted to put her pack back on. It fit oddly with the life jacket, but she wasn't giving up her gun. Nor the money.

The people in line held onto the stair railing, keeping their legs braced wide. She followed suit. It was hard to keep her balance with the listing of the ship and the driving rain. Her legs and arms were on fire. She heard loud voices over the sound of the rain. Looking up through the middle of the stairwell she caught a glimpse of two men.

One was tall with dark blond hair. He was well built. The other man was stouter with dark hair.

She couldn't follow their argument. They weren't speaking in English.

"They argue about us." The woman ahead of her in line said. "There are too many of us for the lifeboat."

Well fuck. Harlow nodded her thanks not trusting herself to speak.

It was one of those conundrum questions that were always asked in the hypothetical. *Do you overload a lifeboat, quite possibly causing it to sink and thereby killing everyone on board, or do you fill it to capacity and leave those who don't fit to die?*

"Isn't there another lifeboat?" she asked the woman. Her voice was raspy and Harlow wasn't sure the woman heard her at first.

"The containers. They fell into the water. They damaged the other lifeboat. This is the only one left."

Harlow wanted to cry. She was exhausted, weak, hungry, and just fed up. She slumped against the railing. The woman awkwardly patted her shoulder.

There was another loud groan from the ship and the men stopped arguing. The line of people moved suddenly. Harlow climbed upward and finally reached the landing where the tall blond helped her into the lifeboat.

The boat looked like one of those toys kids use in their bathtubs. It was white on the bottom and the top was bright orange. It was facing downward. The inside was jammed full of people. They lined both inside benches and they were all sitting at an odd angle trying to keep from crushing the person next to them but it was useless. The angle of the boat was too steep and there were too many people. There was no room for her to sit. Several people were already on the floor. She looked around and the woman that was in front of her in line moved over very slightly and Harlow crowded down onto the bench. She could only get one butt cheek on, but it was better than nothing.

"Brace yourselves," the blond said in a heavy accent and then he turned and closed the door. He lumbered to the front of the lifeboat.

Harlow grabbed onto some straps that were hanging behind her and tried to brace her feet. The boat suddenly shot forward and then slammed into the water. Harlow was tossed all around and landed half on the woman next to her.

She immediately apologized as soon as she regained her breath. The woman just shook her head.

Everyone adjusted as best they could and then sat in silence. The officer who'd given her the life vest asked if everyone was okay. A few people had bumps and bruises but otherwise they were all okay.

"Now what?" Harlow asked.

The officer looked at her. "Now we wait. Hopefully someone will come rescue us."

"Hopefully?" she squeaked.

He shrugged. "We're in the middle of the Atlantic Ocean."

Harlow leaned back against the side of the lifeboat. She ground her teeth. She didn't just spend six days locked in a container to finally get out but die in a lifeboat in the middle of the Atlantic. She just couldn't. That was her last thought before she passed out.

CHAPTER FOUR

Cain Maddox looked in the mirror and studied his reflection. His long wavy hair hung down to his jawline, framing his tanned face. He'd had his thick black hair undercut so the bottom was short and the top was long enough to put in a ponytail. It was his pushback against Coast Guard regulations. He'd started wearing his hair like this in Panama. Being part of an elite team meant he could get away with small shit like that.

His father was a different story. Was it worth the hassle his father was about to dole out? Maybe he should find a barber and get it cut. He glanced at his watch. Not enough time. Plus he'd then have to explain the change to his teammates. They'd never let him get away without an explanation.

He sighed as he brushed the curls back and secured it in a short ponytail. Taking a step back, he took in his appearance in the full-length mirror. Dressed in a gray pinstripe lightweight suit with a white shirt, he looked like a hedge fund investor rather than a Coast Guard Special Ops team member. Good. He wanted to keep as low a profile as possible.

The shirt and the blazer pulled slightly across his back and chest. He'd been working out more lately and had increased his muscle mass, but the pants fit him perfectly. He looked good. Though, trepidation rocketed through him. It was always that way when dealing with his father.

He glanced at his watch again. It was time to go, and yet he stood, looking around his apartment. It had been his refuge of late, and he enjoyed living there. It was a penthouse apartment in a luxury building in Miami. He had a one-hundred-and-eighty-degree view of the Atlantic in front of him. He loved it. It was soothing to sit and look at the water.

The apartment itself was modern with concrete floors and exposed ductwork. The huge, combined living, dining, and kitchen areas made up half the apartment, while a separate but equally large bedroom with a massive bath-room encompassed the rest of the floorplan. He'd loved the place the moment he'd walked in, but he looked at it now with a growing sense of dread. He'd never invited his team-mates up. They knew the building because they'd picked him up before but he just didn't want to have to explain how he could have the apartment on his Coast Guard salary.

His father owned the building, or at least this apartment. Cain didn't ask too many questions. Questions would get him in deeper, and he didn't want to be any more indoctri-nated into his father's world. Just living here had obligated him on some level.

He never should have accepted his father's invitation to use the place but, in truth, he just didn't have the energy to fight against it. Pushing back against his father required a lot of effort, and it was always a hard dance. He'd been feeling run-down when they'd hit Miami, and the idea of having a place that was fully furnished and move-in ready had been appealing. Then he saw the place, and he'd just said "yes" without really thinking. That was probably why his father insisted he see it.

He sighed and straightened his shoulders. It was time to pay the piper. He'd asked for help a few times lately, and his father had obliged. Now he had to pay his respects. There was always a price to pay. Cain walked across the apartment and grabbed his Glock off the counter. He never went anywhere without it. After tucking it in his shoulder holster, he adjusted his suit jacket and then hit the elevator button. He was as ready as he'd ever be.

Thirty minutes later, he walked into a Mediterranean restaurant in South Beach. The man at the door gave him a nod. Cain loved this restaurant. The food was exceptional, but the reason his father chose the place was because it was also hidden from the street by overgrown tropical greenery. No one could see in the windows. Which was fine by Cain. It was possible for him to sit and eat a meal with his father without the world noticing.

Or so he told himself. If he were honest, he'd admit that the higher-ups at Homeland must know who his father was. Probably the FBI, too. His team didn't, though, and that weighed on him. They should know the truth.

The restaurant was empty, which was to be expected. His father always rented out the whole place when they met. The man in question sat chatting with several of his men at a back table. He looked up as Cain walked across the room, and his face broke out into a large smile. "Giancarlo." He got to his feet.

Cain nodded. *Giancarlo.* Just hearing that name always made him break out into a sweat. "Father," he said as he approached the table.

Suddenly, his father disappeared from view when a great hulk of a man moved to stand in front of Cain. "Tiny" was what they called him. Tiny's job was to search him for weapons. Cain resented it but understood. Tiny, the four men in the restaurant, and the five others outside were tasked with keeping his father safe. It wasn't an easy job, and they had to be vigilant even with Cain, the man's own son.

Cain lifted his arms. "Tiny," he said. "Shoulder holster under my left arm. No ankle pistol this time."

Tiny nodded. He grabbed Cain's gun and then stepped out of the way. Cain moved over to stand directly in front of his father. His own green eyes looked back at him.

"Giancarlo, you are looking good." His father leaned in and gave him a big hug before kissing him on each cheek. "The hair, though. What is with men and ponytails? It's all the rage in Europe. It's not good. Get it cut."

Cain ignored his father's comment. "You are looking good as well." And it was true. His father's black hair was now salt and pepper, and there were more lines on his face, but his eyes were bright and exuded intelligence. He was still in fighting shape with the merest of a belly starting. His hug had been bone-crushing as it always was. Salvatore Ricci didn't look to be in his mid-sixties. He appeared to be at least ten years younger.

"Sit, sit." His father gestured toward the table, and they both sat. His father stared at him. "Seeing you does my heart good. It's been too long." He waved away his security team, leaving the two of them alone in the back of the restaurant.

Cain merely nodded. What was he supposed to say? He didn't miss his father, nor did he feel any real affection for the man. He'd given up on that years ago. "How have you been?"

"I've been fine. Life is good. Better for seeing you. You look healthy. You've been working out more. You're bigger than you used to be." His father studied him. "Is everything good? How is the apartment?"

"Things are good. The apartment is great." Cain struggled

to think of something else to say. They had little in common. "How are Lucia and Sofia?"

"Your sisters are doing well. Sofia is getting married." His father gestured to a waiter, and a splash of red wine was poured into a glass in front of him.

"Tell her congratulations for me." Cain waited for his father to taste the wine and give his approval. His sisters hated his guts, but he at least tried to appear to care about them.

Salvatore nodded to the waiter, and the man filled both glasses and disappeared. "Tell her yourself. You are invited to the wedding. It's next month."

Cain froze. *How the hell was he going to get out of this one?* The last thing his sister wanted was her bastard brother at her wedding, and he had no interest in attending a Ricci wedding. His face and name would be known across the world in a matter of minutes on both sides of the law. He decided saying nothing was the best response.

"Giancarlo?"

Cain's gaze locked with his father's. Here it was. The lecture and then the moment when his father exacted the price for the help he'd provided. Cain had asked for help from his father's people when Elias's family was caught up in the whole Santiago mess. He'd asked for assistance a couple of times. He knew then that he'd pay in the future, but he hadn't hesitated. Family was everything. He believed that. And his teammates were his family. The man sitting in front of him might have contributed the sperm used in creating him, but he'd had no part in raising him other than supplying the money.

"Father." Cain sat back calmly and took a sip of his wine. He portrayed confidence he didn't feel. He hated that his father could still wind him up. Make him feel nervous and unsettled. He was quite possibly the only thing on earth that could.

Okay, maybe not the only thing. Harlow Moretti's smiling face flashed in his mind. *She* always had him off-kilter. He gave himself a mental shake. His father was studying him, and he would not give in to the temptation to fidget or show any weakness.

"Giancarlo, I have watched you these last years. You have done well. You survived when many would not."

Cain didn't flinch at the mention of his former team-mates all dying. It still ate at him, but there was no need for his father to know that.

"You have established yourself in your chosen profession, and you have excelled. You are one of the best. I expected no less. You have invested your money well and you make shrewd business decisions."

Jesus. His father was following his finances? He should have guessed.

"So, it is puzzling to me why you reached out to me for assistance and jeopardized all of this. You could have found other methods or people to help you."

He felt the weight of his father's stare. His gut rolled as he tried to brace himself for what was to come.

His father took a sip of red wine. "The only conclusion I could come to is you, in your own way, are trying to reach out to me. Giancarlo, you are always welcome in the family. You do not need to create a problem to get my attention. You always have it."

Cain blinked. *What?* "Er, no. No. No. I legitimately needed help. I wasn't reaching out." Sweat trickled down between his shoulder blades.

His father cocked an eyebrow.

"Seriously," Cain said. "One of my teammates got

involved with the Street Aces and Santiago. I needed backup to watch his house while we were…involved in other things."

The corner of his father's mouth twitched, and Cain quickly realized his father was laughing at him. "Hilarious," he growled.

"Giancarlo, you make it so easy to bust your chops. I cannot help it." His father was belly-laughing now.

Cain wanted to be angry but, honestly, the laughter had broken the tension. He smiled. "Fair enough."

"Let's eat." His father signaled the waiter, and the first of many courses arrived on the table.

Cain ate well and chatted with his father about inane things. Sports, the weather, the olive orchards, and the vineyards in Italy. It was nice to just have a relaxed meal for a change.

When coffee was served, Salvatore leaned forward. "Giancarlo, we do have to get serious for a moment."

Cain's stomach knotted. They'd been having a good time until then. "Okay." Cain braced himself again.

"Your sister Sophia's wedding—"

"I'm not going." Maybe it was the wine or the relaxed conversation, but whatever it was, it was too late to take those words back now. He pressed on. "I know she doesn't want me there, so there's no point in making the bride miserable on her wedding day."

Salvatore smiled. "If it were only that issue, I would be happy." He shook his head. "You are right. Sophia and Lucia do not—are not your biggest fans. They feel much jealousy toward you."

Cain frowned. "Why in the hell would they be jealous of me? They were the ones that got to spend time with you. I was never in the picture." He knew he'd made an error immediately. The statement had come out of his mouth before he thought to stop it. "I'm—"

Salvatore's face clouded over, and he held up his hands for silence. Cain was a strong man who was not afraid of much, but taking on his father wasn't something he really wanted to do. It was a lose-lose for him no matter what.

"You know the reason behind that. I have made that clear. I have also made it clear that any time you wanted, you could call or reach out to me."

That was true as far as it went, but it didn't go far enough. Cain was inclined to let it go, but something in his father's eyes made him reconsider. Maybe now was the moment for truth.

"That's not quite true, Papa." He used the affectionate term to soften the words. "I did call many times as a child. I reached out on more than one occasion, only to be told you were busy. You couldn't attend my baseball games. You were out of town for my graduation. You couldn't possibly be expected to attend my induction ceremony to the Coast Guard. Again and again, the answer was 'no.' You sent money instead." Cain shrugged. "The girls were your world. I was just your...dirty little secret." There. He'd said it. The thing that he'd always felt but never put words to. It was time.

His father's face turned hard. Those green eyes that were so familiar glittered with anger. "That is not true."

Something perverse in Cain wouldn't let him stop. "Yes, it is. We're both adults. It's time to tell the truth. You were otherwise occupied when it came to me. It hurt then, but I'm over it. Your lack of attention helped make me what I am today, and I am good with that."

Salvatore's hands trembled. His face turned red. His breaths came in sharp, short puffs.

Cain sat back and waited for the blast that was about to come.

"You were never ignored!" his father roared. "You had everything you needed!" Salvatore hit the table with his fist.

Cain leaned forward and said in a quiet voice, "Except you. My mother was dead along with my brother. I was raised by my aunt and uncle, who barely tolerated me. To have you in my life would have made all the difference." Cain shrugged. "You had other obligations. That's the way life goes."

He stood. He was suddenly tired of all the games, of the undercurrents, of trying to please his father in little ways that didn't cost him too much. He was done. "Father, it was nice to see you. I enjoyed dinner, but there's really no need to continue the charade. I am too old, or maybe too burnt out, to want to bother anymore. I will move out of the apartment by the end of the month. You need not make these trips anymore. Take care of yourself."

Cain offered him a nod and then turned and walked away. He caught a glimpse of his father's face in the mirror above the bar. The old man's face had turned white, and his eyes blinked rapidly. Cain tried not to laugh. No one had ever walked out on Salvatore Ricci before, at least, no one had lived to tell about it. Having one of the most powerful mafia dons in the world as a father meant all sorts of things, not one of them was good.

Cain was done. Let the chips fall where they may.

Two hours later, Cain had finished packing up all of his stuff. There wasn't much. He was used to moving every few years, so he traveled light. His plan was to check into a hotel by the beach for a few weeks while he found a place to live. Maybe he'd see if Elias's building had any apartments for rent. He didn't really want to live with all the old people, but the views were great, and he might score a rooftop garden.

His phone pinged, and he snatched it from the table. "Shit," he mumbled. His plans had to go on hold. Nick wanted everyone to meet down at the heliport. They were flying out to meet up with a cutter. Something was definitely up. They usually would do major planning first.

He turned and picked up the duffel bag at his feet. He needed to change into his tactical gear. Ten minutes later, all changed and ready to go, he grabbed his cell off the table and headed toward the elevator. It dinged before he pushed the button. It was a private elevator only for his apartment. No one was supposed to have access except him or if the doorman in the lobby called up and asked permission. Someone had called the elevator down to the ground floor.

His father. *Fuck.* The man probably had keys for the elevator. He didn't have time for this. Cain stepped back and to the side. He drew his weapon from his holster and pointed it at the elevator door. He couldn't be too careful.

With another ding, the elevator doors opened, and Tiny made a move to step out until he saw Cain with his gun pointed at him. Tiny raised his hands and cleared his throat. "Your father wishes to speak with you."

Cain snorted. "Well, he'll have to wait. I have to go to work." He holstered his weapon and got on the elevator. He hit the button for the lobby. Tiny reached over and hit the button for the parking garage.

"I'm afraid I'm going to have to insist." When Tiny turned slightly, Cain saw that he had a gun in his hand.

"You've got to be fucking kidding me." Cain glared at the man. "I have to go to work. My father will have to wait. When I'm back, I will see him."

Tiny shrugged. "Mr. Ricci doesn't like to wait."

Cain turned so he was facing forward. He put his hand

on his gun again. "Well, he's going to fucking well have to. I am going to do my job." He looked over at Tiny. "And you're going to let me because I'm telling you right now, it won't end well for you."

Again, Tiny gave a small shrug. The elevator doors opened at the lobby. Cain started to move out of the elevator when a little blond girl, about four years old, walked in. "Is it this one, Mommy?" Cain froze. He didn't want the kid to get hit in the crossfire. He quickly glanced over and realized that Tiny had hidden the gun behind his bulk so the little girl couldn't see it.

"No! No, sweetie," her mother said and reached into the elevator, grabbing the little girl's hand. When she glanced up and saw Cain in his tactical gear and Tiny looking like the Incredible Hulk, her smile died. She quickly pulled her daughter out of the carriage. "Ours is over here." As soon as the little girl disappeared, Cain started out of the elevator, but the doors closed again.

He glared at Tiny. "You seriously don't think you're going to take me to my father now, do you?"

Tiny remained silent. Cain readied himself to react as soon as the doors opened. The elevator dinged, and Cain started to pivot only to see there were three more of his father's men standing outside of the elevator. *Fucking hell.* He didn't want to shoot any of these guys, but they weren't making this easy.

Tiny gestured with his gun for Cain to exit the elevator. The three men in the parking garage backed up but kept their weapons trained on him.

Cain stepped out and headed toward the black SUV that was parked next to his vehicle. "Tiny," he said, "I'll give you one last chance to fuck right off. I don't want to hurt anyone, but I have to go to work. My team is counting on me."

"You can go to work after you see your father." Tiny

walked behind Cain with one other guy, who would look big next to anyone else besides Tiny. The other two were on each side of him.

Cain's cell went off. He took it out of his pocket, ignoring the men beside him. Elias. Shit. Since Cain spent the first month or more after they'd moved to Miami picking Elias up, Elias wanted to return the favor. The text said Elias was upstairs, waiting at the curb. He put the cell back in his pocket and quickly ran various scenarios in his head. He knew these men didn't want to hurt him so that gave him the advantage, but he didn't want to hurt them either. This was just so fucking stupid. Leave it to his father to throw a temper tantrum and demand his presence.

When they reached the back of the black SUV, Cain turned to face them. "Tiny, gentlemen, I know you're doing what you are paid to do, but this is just fucking stupid. I have to go to work. If my father is so desperate to see me, then I will call him as soon as I get back from this op. It should be later tonight."

He moved away from the SUV toward his own truck, only to be blocked by two men. Tiny was behind him. "Giancarlo, you have to come with us."

Cain turned and faced Tiny once more. He knew chances were good he could take at least three of them out before the fourth one shot him, but he didn't want to go down that path. That way was insanity. But he couldn't not show up at the dock either. When he started moving toward his truck again, Tiny raised his gun, as did the other men. Cain stopped and raised his hands. Was he really going to go with these men now? *Nope. Just no.*

His cell went off again. "I really have to go." He pushed forward, and one of the men on his left grabbed his arm. Cain whirled around and peeled the guy's hand off his arm and then twisted it behind the man's back. Holding the man in place, he said, "I really don't want to hurt any of you, but I will if I have to." He looked at Tiny. "Tell my old man I'll call him later."

He used the guy as a shield and started moving toward his truck. Then he stopped. They'd probably sabotaged his truck just in case. Tiny had proven to be a thorough guy. He dragged his captive toward the stairwell. Tiny and the other men still had their guns drawn. They were fanning out around him. He could still take them out, possibly, but it probably wouldn't go down as well. He could shoot two from the angle he had but that still left one. If the guy he was using as protection was fast enough, he might get away.

Tiny was directly opposite of Cain. "You are wasting time," he said. "The faster we go, the quicker you can come back. We must leave now. Your father is waiting. No more games." He raised his gun.

Elias came out from behind a parked car and put his Glock against the back of Tiny's head. "You're gonna put that down. You guys, too."

The men all froze. Cain tried not to smile as relief pumped through his veins. He had no doubt he could have survived the encounter, but shooting his father's men would be a nightmare. The fact that Tiny seemed okay to shoot him was more than a little disconcerting. His father must really be pissed.

"You heard the man," Cain said. "Drop your weapons, gentlemen." He looked over at Tiny. The man glared at him but gave him a small nod. The men all put their weapons away. Cain thought about taking the guns, but rubbing salt in the wound didn't seem like a wise move. He didn't want to make this into a war with his father.

Cain nodded toward Elias and then the stairs. Elias kept his gun trained on Tiny and made his way over to stand beside Cain. "You okay?" he asked in a quiet voice.

Cain nodded. "Okay, Tiny, I will call when I am finished." He let the guy go with a shove, and he and Elias hit the staircase. They were out in the lobby ten seconds later. Cain led the way across to the entrance. Elias's truck was parked right outside. Cain climbed into the passenger seat, and Elias slid behind the wheel. He fired up the truck and sped away just as the doors burst open and Tiny and his guys spilled onto the sidewalk. Elias didn't slow as he careened around the corner. "You wanna tell me why a pile of guys who look like they're from a Godfather movie were trying to kidnap you in the parking garage?"

"No."

Elias nodded. "So, I guess telling me why you're going to call them later is out as well."

Cain remained silent then asked, "Exactly. How did you know where to find me?"

"When you didn't respond to my text or my calls, I went inside. There was a woman in the lobby, holding the hand of a little girl. Mom, I guess, was complaining to security about a guy in military gear and another huge guy in the elevator. She thought she saw a gun. She told the guy behind the desk the elevator was going down. I thought it was probably you, and you might need help. Turns out I was right."

"Thanks."

"No problem." Elias made a turn and got onto the highway. "I do have to wonder, though. You could have taken those guys out in a heartbeat. You didn't need me. So why didn't you?"

Cain stayed silent.

"You're gonna have to talk at some point."

He cursed a blue streak in his head. He hated that his worlds were colliding and there wasn't a damn thing he could do about it.

CHAPTER FIVE

Help had been much closer than they'd thought. A few hours later, after the storm had subsided, a Coast Guard vessel appeared. Turns out they were closer to the coast of the U.S. than she'd thought. Harlow had never been so happy in her entire life. She cried with relief. After a long week trapped in the container, wondering if she would even live, and then the ship sinking along with her hopes of survival, it was all too much, and she gave in to the tears. And she wasn't the only one crying. The whole situation was beyond intense and harrowing.

Once they were on board the Coast Guard cutter *Dwayne Jones*, the EMTs gave her the once-over and decided she needed to be kept in bed in the medical area. They hung an IV and started her on fluids. They also got her some bland food and told her to eat a bit at a time.

Harlow had just finished some toast when she heard voices. One of them was the man that had treated her. They called him Doc, not because he was a doctor but because he was older and had apparently seen it all. His real name was

Hector Potter. The other voice she didn't recognize. She was in an area tucked around the corner from the main part of the medical bay so they couldn't see her, nor could she see them.

"So, who is she then?" Doc asked.

"No one knows. I asked the officer she was on the lifeboat with, but he had never seen her before. He assumed she worked in the kitchen, but I asked the staff, and no one knows anything about her."

"A stowaway?"

"I guess. We're gonna have to speak with her at some point. I mean, you just can't hitch a ride on a ship whenever you want. The captain and skeleton crew are being airlifted now. They're still worried the ship may sink. The hole in the hull made by the first group of containers that fell is right at the waterline. During the storm, it was taking on a ton of water, but now the sea is calmer, it might just hold. We'll talk to the captain once he gets here and see if he knows anything about our mystery woman."

Doc sighed. "It makes sense that she's a stowaway. The woman's in far worse condition than anyone else. She's dehydrated and weak from lack of food, liquids, and sleep. She's not going anywhere, so you can wait until tomorrow before you ask her any questions. Give her a chance to relax a bit. She's on edge at the moment. It's written all over her face."

Harlow closed her eyes and swore a blue streak in her head. The few bites of toast she'd managed sat heavy in her stomach. She was going to have to tell them what she'd done. Maybe she could lie and just say she was a backpacker who ran out of money so she sneaked aboard a ship, hoping to get back to the U.S. Was that where the ship was even going? They were likely to ask her how she got on board and where she had stayed on the ship while they were at sea. She couldn't answer any of those questions. She couldn't make it up because she didn't know the ship well enough.

She took a drink of warm water since she suddenly felt cold. What if she told them part of the truth? She got stuck in a container at the pier, and even though she tried to get someone's attention, she couldn't. So she had been stuck in the container until the storm came. She'd have to say that one of the other containers hit hers and it somehow made the door open.

Except for the bullet holes, her explanation should work. Harlow sighed. No disguising those but they would want to know why she waited so long to break out of the container. How was she supposed to tell them that she was just putting off the inevitable in the hopes they would dock somewhere, and she could bust out before any of Vance's men were around. Shit.

She was just going to have to make something up on the fly. It had to be better than telling the whole story. Vance's men had to be on board to guard the container chock full of cash. She hadn't seen them on deck, but she hadn't seen every face in the lifeboat either, since they'd been packed like sardines. Chances were good if she started telling the truth, one of those guys would come looking for her.

On the other hand, that money was sitting in the container, and since the ship hadn't sunk yet, it was evidence. Maybe she should ask to speak to the people in charge and tell them about everything. Maybe they could help her. She drank some more warm water as she contemplated her next move.

Doc came around the corner. "How are you feeling, young lady?" he asked. His eyes crinkled at the corners. He had to be mid-fifties if he was a day, but he had a lovely smile and sparkling brown eyes. The full head of medium brown hair that was graying at the temples didn't hurt him one bit. If she were into older men, she'd definitely ask him out.

"I'm doing okay. Tired." She tried to sound weaker than she felt. She wasn't sure what to do just yet.

He pulled over a stool and sat down next to her bed. "So, I've managed to buy you a day or so, but you're going to have to talk to people eventually. Everyone wants to know who the mystery woman is."

"I—"

He held up his hands and shook his head. "I'm not asking. Not my job. I'm just telling you, the clock is ticking. You're in better shape than I said. A couple of days of rest and eating normally, and you'll be fine."

Harlow swallowed the lump building in her throat. "Thanks, Doc." She appreciated his kindness more than she could say. She sunk a bit further back into her pillows.

"You rest up, and I'll do my best to keep the wolves away from the door for now." He patted her hand and got up from the stool.

"Doc?" she said.

He turned toward her.

"Do you think I could get something more than toast? I'm famished."

He grinned. "I'll see what I can do." He winked and then turned and left.

Harlow closed her eyes. Exhaustion sat like dead weight on her chest. Sleeping on top of a pallet of money wasn't the most comfortable thing. She was always either cold or hot and stiff as all get out. Being in a nice, warm toasty bed with a belly that had food in it was such a luxury that up until now she'd taken for granted. Now it was sheer heaven.

A loud crash woke Harlow with a start. She sat up, staring into space, trying to remember where she was. Right.

The U.S. Coast Guard ship. Her heart hammered against her ribs. What made the crash? Doc came around the corner, pushing a cart. It was covered by what looked like a tablecloth.

"Sorry if I startled you," he said with a smile. "This cart has a wonky wheel, and I keep hitting things."

She took her hand away from her chest. "No worries, Doc. It's all good." She smiled back. "What did you bring me?"

He pushed the cart over beside the bed and pulled off the tablecloth. "Ta da!"

Harlow looked at the cart. "Is that soup?"

"Yes. Chicken noodle. And there's fresh rolls and a salad."

She did her best not to be disappointed. "Yum." There was a plate that was covered by a bowl. "What's that?"

He lifted the bowl. "It's the best part. Molten chocolate cake."

"Ooh. That sounds delicious." Now Harlow wasn't so disappointed. She wanted to dive right in.

"Finish the soup and one roll, and the cake is all yours."

She smiled again. "Deal."

He moved everything onto the tray that went over the bed. "Enjoy, and I will come check on you in a bit."

Harlow pushed herself into a sitting position and picked up a spoon. The food was better than she anticipated, and she gobbled it all, in a hurry to get to the cake, which was divine. Finished and full, she had just sat back when she heard more voices.

"I'm sorry, but the patient needs to rest."

She smiled at the thought of Doc protecting her.

"I'm sorry, Doc, but she can rest later. We have questions, and they can't wait."

This voice was new. This wasn't the guy from earlier, and whoever it was, wasn't going to be put off. She barely had time to wipe her mouth when a group of three men came around the corner and surrounded her bed.

"Ma'am," the man closest to her started, "we need to ask you some questions." He had dark hair cut short and shrewd blue eyes. His face was tanned but serious.

Doc came around the corner. "I must insist you leave her be, gentlemen. She needs her rest."

He turned to Doc. "Sir, your patient was a stowaway on a ship that is under investigation. We need answers. She can rest afterward."

Doc shot her a look, and she gave him a small nod. She might as well get this over with. The men turned back to face her. They were all wearing Coast Guard uniforms and had tactical equipment on, vests, weapons, and ball caps emblazoned with the Coast Guard insignia. Some sort of special operations team, she surmised. They must have found the money.

The dark-haired one was definitely the leader. He crossed his arms over his chest. "So how did you get on board the ship?"

Harlow cleared her throat and fussed with the sheet to buy a little time. If she had been tempted to lie, the look on this man's face was enough to scare that idea right out of her. None of them looked like they would put up with any shit. The blondish guy had a kinder face than the other two, but she didn't want to meet any of them in a dark alley.

She took a deep breath. "I got trapped in a container, and the container was loaded on the ship."

The dark-haired man's eyes bored into her, making her break out in a sweat. "I see. What were you doing in the container?"

She frowned. "I was checking out the contents. I wanted to know what was inside."

"Which container were you in?"

She frowned. "I don't remember the number." *Liar, liar, pants on fire.* She glanced at the other two men, whose eyebrows had shot high on their foreheads. They knew she was lying.

The leader leaned forward slightly. "Let's stop playing games. I want details. Answer the questions fully, or I will have Axe here arrest you." He pointed at the guy with the blond hair.

She wanted to demand, "For what," but the reality was she had broken a few laws getting into the container. She didn't really want to piss these people off. She just wanted to make sure she got Vance. "Okay, look, I was following some people and I saw the containers arrive at the pier. I wanted to see what was in them. There was a guard outside of them. Once he walked away, I went in to check the contents, but he and…some others came back before I had a chance to get out. They locked me in there." She held up her hands. "I know it was stupid." She sighed. "Before I could decide what to do, the container was picked up and loaded onto a ship."

"Do you know how long you were in the container?" the blond man, Axe, asked.

"Yes. I kept track of the days. Six. I had some provisions, but today I ran out, and when the alarm went off on the ship, well, it seemed like it was better to face the wrath of the people on the ship than die in a container."

The man's eyes narrowed. "Who are these people, and why did they lock you in the container? What was in the container?"

She wanted to kick herself. Up until that point, she sounded like she was just nosy. Telling them someone would be mad at her just brought up all kinds of other questions. "Er, I'm not sure?"

Axe snorted. "You spend six days in a container you

sneaked into to see what the contents were, but you didn't check it out. Lady, do we look stupid to you?"

She looked down at her hands. *Shit*. She was going to have to come clean.

The leader asked, "Who on the ship would care about you being in the container? They might report you to the authorities, but why would someone be angry?"

"Er, I don't know. I just assumed."

He stared at her for a minute, lips pressed tightly together. "Bullshit. You need to tell us the truth, or this is not going to go so well for you."

She blinked. "Is that a threat?"

The man barked a laugh. "Lady, that was a promise."

She glared at him but knew he was right. She wasn't going to get out of this without telling the truth. "Fine. I assumed that there were guards on board since the container contained millions worth of US currency."

The third guy was thinner than the other two but just as scary. He finally spoke up, "You chose to stay in the container because you thought what exactly?"

Harlow did her best to remain calm. She'd been an idiot, but this guy didn't have to be so smug. "I thought if I could last until the ship docked and they offloaded the container, I might be able to escape unseen."

"Escape to where? Do you have contacts in Mexico?"

"Mexico? Why in the hell would— Wait, the ship was going to Mexico?"

The man nodded.

Holy shit. She'd had no clue. She'd just assumed they were shipping the money Stateside. It had never occurred to her that she could end up in Mexico. But then she hadn't thought she'd ever end up trapped in a container either. Life was full of surprises.

She cleared her throat again. "Well, obviously, I had no clue what ship I was on or where it was going."

The leader asked, "Why did you want to look in that container?"

There was the sound of footsteps and then a voice said, "Tag, we spoke to the captain and looked at the paperwork. Looks like everything was…" The speaker's voice died out.

Harlow looked up and locked gazes with the one man she did not want to see ever again. "Cain," she breathed.

"Harlow! What the fuck are you doing— Oh, for shit's sake, Harlow, are you still harping on this crap? You were mucking about in Iraq, weren't you? That's where the shipment arrived from."

Harlow's heart rate soared. She had an instant headache, and her hands itched to reach out and strangle the man at the foot of her bed. "Just because you gave up on finding the truth doesn't mean I have to. I did find out who was responsible, and I've been tracking him." She folded her arms across her chest. "And I did it all on my own without anyone's help, thank you very much. You can save your lectures about staying out of trouble."

"All on your own almost got you dead. Trapped in a shipping container. Jesus Christ, Harlow!" Cain was glaring at her now, his brilliant green eyes snapping.

"Would someone like to fill me in here on what's going on?" The dark-haired leader shifted his position to take in both Cain and Harlow.

If there was one thing she'd learned about Cain when he was part of her brother's team, it was that he didn't suffer fools gladly. He had no time for stupidity, which is what he thought the whole thing was. Well, she'd proven him wrong. She'd gotten answers. Answers he didn't have.

She smiled smugly at him. "You're just pissed because I found out the truth and you didn't."

Cain's jaw dropped. "I'm pissed because your brother would kill me right now for not forcing you to stop this madness. You almost died, Harlow. It's not fucking worth that."

She blinked. Bringing up her brother was a low blow. She was doing it for him, but she also knew Cain was right. Her brother would kill her if he knew what she was doing.

"Seriously. Anyone. An explanation please?" The leader's head snapped back and forth between her and Cain.

Cain's gaze did not leave hers as he answered, "This is Harlow Moretti, little sister of Perry Moretti. He was the head of the unit I was training with in Iraq. He—they all died in an IED explosion. Harlow always said there was something fishy about the whole thing so, apparently, she went digging around in Iraq and almost wound up dead in a container full of money destined for Mexico."

"I see." The head guy narrowed his eyes at her. "Okay then. First, let's introduce ourselves. I'm Nick Taggert." He pointed to the blond man. "Axel Cantor." Then he gestured to the guy that came in with Cain, "Elias Mason" and then finally to the guy on the right side of her bed. "Finn Walsh." He turned back to her. "It's nice to meet you, Harlow. We're sorry for your loss."

Harlow swallowed. He was being nice to her, and that threw her completely. "Um, thanks."

Nick smiled at her. "Now, we really do need answers. Let's get some seats and start this conversation all over again. Maybe we can get a few more details this time."

She nodded and watched as they all went in search of seats. Cain just stood at the end of the bed, glaring at her, arms crossed over his chest, a muscle in his jaw popping and ticking. His green eyes glittered with some unreadable emotion. He looked seriously pissed off. He also looked sexy as hell. She'd always thought he was the most gorgeous man she'd ever known, and the months since she'd seen him last hadn't changed that. If anything, he looked better. The pony-tail just added to his all-around sexiness. God help her, she'd been trying to hate this man forever but, somehow, she just never succeeded.

CHAPTER SIX

He wanted to kill her. Just put himself out of his misery by taking her out. She would be the death of him yet. Harlow Moretti was the sassiest, sexiest pain in his ass that ever walked the Earth. The first time he'd seen her in a bar in Virginia Beach, he'd been over to her in seconds to stake his claim. He'd gotten no more than two words out of his mouth when Perry came over and told him she was his little sister. Cain had been crushed. Harlow was off limits permanently. He'd grabbed his beer and moved to the other side of the room for the rest of the night, and many nights after that.

She'd flirted with him and chatted every chance she got, but he'd kept his distance and steered clear no matter how much he wanted her. Then, after the funeral, staring into those big blue eyes of hers, it damn near killed him. He'd hugged her and did his best to support her, but it was so fucking hard. He wanted to take away her pain, but also lose himself in her. He'd weakened one night and met her for a beer. That led to a kiss in the parking lot, which would have led to a weekend in bed if he hadn't felt so fucking guilty. She was Perry's sister. *Off limits.*

Then she'd come to him with this crazy idea that she—that *they*—could find out the truth about what happened. He'd tried to be kind at first and tell her to let it go. In the end, they'd had a huge fight and he'd told her to grow up; her brother was dead, and she needed to get over it. He'd felt horrible for weeks afterward, but he was also hurting, and he couldn't see her again. He'd end up taking her to bed if he did, and he couldn't betray his teammate and friend like that.

"Cain!" Nick tapped his arm. "Get a chair."

Cain grabbed a stool from the other side of the room and rolled it over to the foot of Harlow's bed. He wanted to strangle her for getting into trouble, but he was so relieved that she was alright it was scary. He gave her the once-over. She would die if she knew what she looked like at the moment. Her auburn hair was a curly mess. Her blue eyes had big dark circles underneath them. Her skin was pale, and she'd lost weight. Cain thought she'd never looked better. He'd purposely put her out of his mind but, damn, it was good to see her. Wait, was that a bruise on her right cheek?

"Who hit you?" Cain growled.

Their gazes locked, and her chin actually jutted out.

But before either could say anything more, Nick cut in. "Maybe start at the beginning and tell us the whole story,"

When she shot a nervous glance at Cain, Nick reached out and touched her hand lightly. "Don't worry about him. He'll get over whatever it is. Just fill us in."

Cain frowned. Nick was overstepping. Cain couldn't just "forget" that Harlow had been hurt. Trotting around Iraq and getting into trouble was dangerous. He said nothing, but later, when he had a chance, he would speak to Harlow on his own. There was no way in hell he was going to another Moretti funeral, nor was he gonna face her parents and tell them he'd lost another one of their kids.

"Okay." She drew a lungful of air and released it in a hiss.

"I did some research and discovered that Perry's team had been assigned the task of tracking down the missing money."

"I'm gonna stop you right there," Nick said. "You need to go back further. What missing money, and how did you find out what their assignment was? I'm guessing all this is classified?"

She nodded.

"Elias, go tell Doc to leave and then close the door to the medical center. No one in until we're done."

"You got it." Elias stood up and disappeared. A minute later, he was back. "Done."

Nick turned back to Harlow and nodded.

"My brother, Perry, and his whole team except for Cain —were killed by an IED in Iraq."

"Wait, your brother was with Cain in Iraq?"

"Yes."

"I see," said Nick, his eyebrows raised.

RECON's team leader was savvy; he'd made the connection of how Cain and Harlow knew each other. So did the rest of the team by their expressions and how they shuffled about uncomfortably. They knew of Cain's pain from his past, but they also could empathize, having gone through their own tribulations before being assigned to Team RECON.

Harlow continued, "It was tragic but not unlikely in Iraq, except they weren't in any of the areas where fighting was taking place. They were on the way to Israel to track down a lead on the missing money. That was their assignment."

She took a sip of water. "First, the money. Cain knows more about it than I do, but the gist of it is…in the early to mid-aughts, the US government sent money to Iraq in the form of cash. Lots of it. Billions in fact. The majority of it was squandered on consultants and contractors who didn't do anything, programs that went nowhere, and general overcharging for services. Some of it, however, went missing."

"How much?" Axe asked.

"Eight billion," Cain said.

Axe coughed. "I'm sorry, how much?"

Cain nodded. "Yeah, eight billion just disappeared. There were rumors over the years of where it ended up, but the Department of Defense didn't like to discuss it. Now and again, they'd find a stash and then quietly take it back, but there's still a lot outstanding. Like, at least half of it.

"My assignment was to hang in the Arabian Gulf and do one of those joint extended training exercises with Perry's SEAL team. They were doing boarding exercises and water incursions. We'd been stationed there on and off for about three months."

"Just you?" Nick asked, "Or your whole MSRT unit?"

"Me. My old team was going through some growing pains. The team leader was retiring, and the number two guy had gotten hurt during the last operation. The rest of us were assigned to different groups for the next few months while they sorted out who was going to be the new team leader."

He glanced at Harlow. "Anyway, Perry's team had been searching for this money for months before that, following up rumor after rumor. He thought they were getting closer to finding what he called the mother lode. He had a line on a guy whose father had helped years ago when the money was stolen. The man had been shot and left to die after doing the hard labor, transporting, and stashing the money, but he survived. It was up near Mosul, where the man lived."

Cain ran his hands over his face. He hated talking about this. "Perry's commanding officer told him another rumor had come in, and it was credible. Supposedly, there was money in some small town not far from the Jordanian border. I wasn't supposed to go with them, but Perry figured the risk was low, and it was something different. We were all getting bored with all the waiting we did.

"We were almost at the village when it happened. I had my seatbelt off because I was reaching for water bottles that were in the back of the Jeep. When we hit the IED, it blew me out of the truck. The other guys weren't so lucky. Most died immediately, but I remember hearing some groans and then there was gunfire. Lots of it. After that, no more groans. Whoever it was had killed anyone who was still alive. They only missed me because I landed on the far side of the road in a gully. I couldn't be seen unless you were standing at the edge of the road."

He stopped speaking and swallowed hard. Survivor guilt punched him every time he thought of his teammates. They'd only been together for a short amount of time, but they'd clicked as a team from day one. He'd only had one more week with them before he was due back with the MSRT team in Connecticut. He shook his head. He should have died with them. They were good men. Better than he was. None of them were a mobster's kid.

He smelled the burning fuel and heard those groans in his sleep some nights…

When Elias reached out and squeezed his shoulder, Cain refocused. "The money was never found as far as I know."

Harlow nodded. "That's right. It wasn't until now."

Nick directed his attention to Harlow. "How did you end up in Iraq?" he asked in a quiet voice.

"Well, eight months ago, I went to Cain saying I thought the whole thing was wrong somehow and I wanted to find out more details. I told him I wanted to go to Iraq. He told me to keep my ass home. It was dangerous there, and I wouldn't find any answers. I went anyway, but not before I found out who was behind it all."

Cain narrowed his eyes at Harlow. "What do you mean who was behind it all?"

Harlow glared at him right back. "I figured after hearing your story that there had to be more to it. If I thought that, then the military had to be thinking it as well. So I figured out who would have the right access level to get a look at any investigation that had taken place, and I...pursued him."

"What exactly do you mean by 'pursued'?" Cain growled.

"I dated him. It took longer than I thought it would because I wasn't his type, but I eventually won him over."

Cain thought he was going to puke. Harlow had slept with some officer to get more information about her brother's death. *Fuck.* He'd wanted to strangle her for being so stubborn, and now he wanted to strangle some poor schmuck for falling victim to Harlow's scheme. He grabbed the edge of his stool, letting the metal bite into his hands. The pain helped him focus, clear the angry haze from his head.

"I'm sorry. Did you say you dated some guy to get access to the files?" Finn asked.

"Er, yes," Harlow agreed.

Nick ran a hand through his hair. "Did this man show you the file willingly?"

"God no! He had no idea. I used his credentials and password."

Cain closed his eyes. This was going from bad to worse. "You do realize you just confessed to a serious crime, right? You can't just use someone's password to access top secret Department of Defense files. It's illegal. It could be considered treason."

Harlow frowned. "I guess if you put it that way. It really wasn't that big of a deal. He never knew, and I got the information I wanted."

"Jesus Christ, Harlow," Cain muttered. He was horrified.

No, he was stupefied. Did she really not see the problem with what she had done?

Nick let out a long breath. "Leaving the legalities of this alone for now, what exactly did the file say?"

Harlow took another sip of water. "Well, it said that it had been a setup and the bullets had come from American-made weapons, not the kind the Iraqi's tended to use. It also stated that there were rumors of a group of men hanging out in that area a day or two before the guys arrived. They were mostly Americans, and the locals thought they were up to something, but no one was going to ask too many questions." She paused. "They did come up with a name, though. One of the locals had heard an American call the one who seemed to be in charge... Vance."

All the air got sucked out of Cain's lungs. Roman Vance? The man responsible for Nick's injury? The man who had caused all those deaths in Panama and had tried to kill them? Cain touched his leg where he'd gotten shot on that op. He'd been so lucky there was no lasting damage. Vance was the one who had killed Cain's whole team? His whole body rocked as if he'd been hit. He'd been that close to Vance. Close enough to kill him, and he'd missed. He wouldn't miss again. Not fucking ever. He would hunt that fucker to the ends of the earth.

Nick had frozen in place as well. "Roman Vance?" he said softly.

Harlow nodded. "Yes. It's not a popular name, so I did some poking around and found out that he works for some military contractor company named Silverstone." Harlow asked, "Do you know Vance?"

Cain nodded. "We've had a few run-ins with him. He's a bastard."

"He is," she agreed. "I saw him kill someone once." She clasped her hands in front of her and bit her lip. "Anyway, the file said where he worked so I called up and asked for him. They said he was in Iraq. By the time I got there, he'd left and gone down to South America or something. I hung out for a little more than a week, and he showed up again. I spent the next so many months following him and his men."

Cain was still reeling from the shock of finding out Vance was the man responsible for his teammates' death. He couldn't begin to comprehend how Harlow could follow Vance for months and not be noticed. "How?" was all he managed to get out.

"I'm a dental hygienist. I volunteered with a group of aid workers, helping local kids and adults with their teeth. It gave me a lot of room to move around, and no one asked any questions. To Vance, I was just background noise. Not any kind of a threat. The sort of person he wouldn't notice. I couldn't follow him all the time obviously but I managed to figure out where he spent most of his time so it was really just checking up on him when I could."

Cain was dumbfounded. How someone could not notice Harlow was a mystery to him. Until he'd walked into this room for the first time an hour ago, he'd have sworn he could sense Harlow as long as she was within a hundred meters. He'd always had a physical reaction when she was nearby. He didn't even need to see her to send butterflies into flight in his gut. Not that he would ever admit that to anyone. Ever.

Nick blew out a breath. "So he didn't notice, and you followed him all around Iraq. How did you end up in the container?"

Harlow frowned. "That was my own stupidity, if I'm being honest. I happened to see Vance gather his guys together and then get in their vehicles. Something just seemed…different about it so I grabbed my backpack and took a chance. I followed them out to this abandoned village on the edge of Mosul. He had his crew bring up these pallets from what looked like an old well and load them in containers on the backs of trucks. At the time, I thought it was drugs in the pallets. I followed the trucks to the port in Tel Aviv but even when they offloaded the containers, I couldn't get a clear view, so I went closer. The guard left the container open and walked away for a few minutes. I thought I would have enough time to get in and out without being seen, but he came back with a bunch of other men, including James Daughtry, one of Vance's main guys."

"Daughtry found you in the container?" Nick asked.

Harlow shrugged. "He kept asking me who sent me, but I couldn't tell him anything, so he hit me."

Cain's gut tied itself in knots. A slow rage burned through his veins. *Daughtry hit Harlow.* He'd get Daughtry, and he'd make sure it hurt.

Nick leaned forward. "Then what happened?"

"Daughtry got a phone call and told the guy to lock me in the container. They figured I'd be dead by the time it got to where it was going."

Cain ran a hand over his face. She'd come so damn close to dying. His heart couldn't take much more of this. She had to learn to be more careful. *Fuck.* She needed to just go back home and stay there. He let out a long breath. "Two things," he said. "One, if he was willing to leave you in the container to die, then either him or someone he knows would be on the other end to receive the container and, two, he wasn't worried about customs."

Nick nodded. "I was thinking the same thing."

"Wait," Cain said. "Back up a minute. You said pallets, trucks, containers. How many of each?"

"There were a lot of pallets. I didn't get a count on how many exactly, but more than ten. There were three trucks with containers on the back, and my container, or at least the one I was trapped in, had four pallets in it. Assuming they all had that many, or quite possibly more, there had to be hundreds of millions, if not billions, in US currency. The stack that I pulled out when I was checking the container was in hundreds."

Axe whistled between his teeth. "That's unbelievable."

"Yeah. It's almost hard to fathom," Harlow agreed. "But it's true. You can go check out the containers on the other ship."

Cain glanced at Nick. He didn't realize they hadn't told her.

Nick leaned forward. "That's going to be a bit difficult. The container you were in went over the side. We only know about the money because some bills—well, a lot of bills—were floating on the surface of the water."

Harlow's eyes got big. "When? I mean, how? I…"

"It happened not long after you guys were rescued in the lifeboat. The containers on that side had already started letting go, and with the storm, more of the tie-downs and hooks broke. They lost about half of the containers."

Harlow looked down at her hands. Cain recognized the look. It was finally sinking in how close she'd come to dying. When she blinked, he knew she was fighting tears. Good. He wanted her to feel scared, to feel the horror, because then maybe she wouldn't do anything stupid anymore.

Who was he kidding? This was Harlow. She was always going to do stupid things. It was her personality. Impetuous. Impulsive. Stubborn as hell. And he loved it.

Cain swore silently. When he stood, everyone looked at him. "We need to get moving. We have to find those other ships before they dock somewhere and we lose our chance to get Vance." He gestured toward Harlow. "She needs sleep. It's after midnight. She's been through a lot." That was it. That was all he could say without wanting to strangle her all over again.

Nick stood. "Cain's right. We'll let you get some sleep."

"What about Vance's men? Do you already have them locked up somewhere?" Harlow asked, stifling a yawn.

"What do you mean, Vance's men?" Cain demanded. "I thought you didn't know anything about anyone on the ship. You were supposedly in the container the whole time." He glared at her. Was she lying to him? If so, she'd gotten a hell of a lot better at it.

"I *was* in the container." Her eyes snapped at him. "But you don't think Roman Vance is gonna let all that money go on a ship without an escort, do you? I don't care what the manifest or anyone else says. He had people on that ship. I guarantee it. Just like he didn't put all the money on one ship, Vance isn't an idiot, not by a long shot."

Axe grunted, "She's right. That asshole isn't gonna let all that money travel without someone to keep an eye on it."

Nick nodded. "Axe, you, Finn, and Elias have a look at the crew manifest for the ship that Harlow was on. See if anyone comes up as being suspicious. Talk to not only the captain, but also call whoever owns the ship and get their employee files.

"Cain, you and I are going to see if we can track down those other ships." He turned to Harlow. "You get some rest. We'll talk again soon."

They turned and headed out of the room. Cain resisted the urge to look back at Harlow, but it was damn hard. "What?" he asked. Nick was speaking, but he had no idea what the hell he'd said.

"I asked if you had that kind of money, where in the world would you take it?"

Cain shook his head. "I can't imagine having that kind of money. Dunno enough about moving lots of cash." But he knew someone that did. Someone he owed a visit to. Well, a call would have to do. "I do know someone I can ask."

Nick glanced at him. "Really? You have a gazillionaire friend who might have a clue how to handle that kind of money?"

Cain remained silent. What could he say? "Lend me the satellite phone, and I'll see what I can find out."

Nick gave him a hard look but handed over the phone. "I'll go see if we can get some sort of small office space to work out of. I'll text you where we'll be."

"Wait, Nick. Do you think we should place a guard on Harlow? I mean, if Vance does have people on board, then they might go after her. She's the only one that can tie him directly to the container."

"Good point. I'll get Axe back down there to stand guard until we can get one of the security guys on board to take over."

"Thanks."

Nick clapped him on the back. "She's gonna be fine." He started to walk away but Cain called him back.

"We're fucking going to get Vance. I know you want him for what he did to your back. I want him for Perry and the rest of the team. I told you before I'd help you track him and kill him. If we don't get him now, I'm going to take time off and do it. Roman Vance is not going to live a second longer than absolutely necessary." He'd just stated out loud his intention to kill in cold blood. Nick could probably get him fired just for saying it, but he knew Nick felt the same, or at least Cain thought he did. And he trusted Nick not just as his team leader but because Nick had proven time and time again, he was a true friend and a serious operator.

Nick nodded once to Cain and offered his hand. The men shook on it and then went their separate ways.

Cain headed out to the deck. He found a quiet corner where he could see his surroundings and placed the call. He wasn't worried about waking his father. The man never really slept as far as he could tell.

"It's me, Tiny. I need to speak to him."

Tiny's voice sounded tinny on the phone. "He doesn't want to talk on the phone. He wants to see you in person."

Cain did his best not to sigh. "That's impossible at the moment. I am offshore, using a satellite phone. Not sure when I'll be back in town."

"Then why are you calling?"

He ground his teeth. He hated that there was always this layer between him and his father. It was never just, "Hey son, how are ya doin'?" He had to explain himself to Tiny or Tony or someone. "I need to speak with him."

He felt sure Tiny was about to obfuscate some more when there was some fumbling sounds and his father's voice grated in his ear. "Cain." His voice was cold.

Cain's stomach knotted. His father could do that to him faster than anyone on earth. He always felt like that twelve-year-old boy who just wanted his father's approval. His body reacted like that young boy, too.

He let out a long breath and tried to relax his gut. "I know you're angry, but I need a favor."

"Another favor. You seem to need a lot of help these days. I'm not getting anything in return. Why should I help you?"

"Then don't." Cain had no patience left, and he wasn't going to beg. They were on an unsecured line, so they couldn't really talk freely, and his father was pissed at him. His father calling him by his chosen name, instead of Gian-carlo, always gave him the creeps somehow.

"What do you need?" his father finally asked.

"If someone had a lot of money, like hundreds of millions, where would be the safest place to keep it?"

"A bank," came the short reply.

Cain ground his teeth. It was his own fault. "Sorry. I

wasn't clear. If someone had physical cash of several hundred million, where would they put it so it could be used without drawing attention?"

There was a long silence. "It would depend. The days of secret banking are over. Numbered accounts are dead. It is very difficult to hide money these days."

Cain frowned as he looked around the deck of the cutter. "So, what do people do?"

"Keep it in the open."

"How the hell does that work?"

"There are many ways to do it." His father's voice changed from the growling tone of earlier to more of a university professor. "But in this case, you would form a great many companies and put the money into offshore accounts as seed money for all of these new companies. You can create a list of investors who never really gave you any money, but they did on paper.

"You will have to pay taxes if you're American. There are other countries where you do not have to pay taxes if you live outside that country. You pay local tax only. Sadly, America is not one of those. Unless you renounce your US citizenship, you must pay taxes until you die." His voice sounded slightly bitter.

Cain thought for a moment. "So, if you had millions in US funds, you could break it up and deposit it in many banks in many places under company names. Does that set off alarm bells somewhere?"

"Well, that depends on where you choose. If you aren't American, the US is one of the best tax havens in the world, but yes, they would most likely ask questions. Assuming this money has been obtained illegally, no one is moving it without having some sort of a plan in place. That means they would have connections at a bank. They could set up hedge funds and start investing without causing too many eyebrows to raise if they have the right connections."

"Assuming what you're saying is correct, where is the best spot to do this?"

"There are many places. Not as many as there used to be, but still quite a few. Belize, The Cayman Islands, Singapore, Hong Kong, Georgia, The Seychelles—"

"Jesus," Cain muttered.

"Yes, the list is quite extensive if you are looking for a specific person or group of people. The reality is they will want somewhere with more...flexibility and someone on the inside."

"Why would someone want to go to Mexico with that kind of money?"

His father grunted. "They wouldn't. Not unless they owed the money to the cartels."

"Could they use the cartels to launder the money?"

"It's possible, but chances are excellent the cartel would just shoot them and take the money. No one goes up against these groups on their home turf."

Cain rubbed his face. "So money going to Mexico would be payment to the cartels."

"Yes, that is most likely."

"Shit. So, I guess that means if they lost it, they would still have to pay the drug or gun lords somehow."

His father's voice was quiet. "You are tired."

Cain was caught completely off guard. "Er, yes."

"If you would like, I can make certain inquiries. If it's physical funds in the quantities you are speaking of, it will not have gone unnoticed. Something like that takes time to move. Preparations would have already started even if the money is still in transit."

Cain tried to be cautious. Owing his father for more favors made him nervous. "That would be...helpful."

"Fine. I will make some calls."

"Thank you." Cain's gut knotted tighter. This was not going to end well for him. He knew it in his bones. It was like waiting for the other shoe to drop, and he'd been doing it for years. It was exhausting. He was about to click off the call when he heard his father's voice.

"Cain. We do need to talk when you are back. There are…some things…we need to sort out."

Cain nodded. "I know. I'll reach out when I'm back in the city."

"I will call you on this number if I find out anything useful." Without a goodbye, his father hung up.

CHAPTER SEVEN

Harlow leaned back into her pillows. Doc had turned down the lights on her end of the room and told her to get some sleep. She'd heard him leave soon after. She was exhausted, but her mind raced. Cain fucking Maddox was here on this ship. Her heart gave a little lurch in her chest. She should be pissed at him for not helping her, or at least supportive that she went after the man responsible for killing her brother but, in fact, she was just so damn glad to see him she couldn't conjure any of those feelings for him. He looked tired, but still sexy as hell.

Cain Maddox was the only man she'd ever lusted after from the moment she'd seen him. He'd walked into the bar and ordered a beer. When their gazes locked, he'd come immediately over to her table. She still remembered how her stomach had dropped and her heart thumped hard against her ribs. He'd been the sexiest man she'd ever encountered. If his first words to her had been, "Want to come to my place?" she would have left with him immediately. Those green eyes of his glittered and held secrets in their depths.

Instead, he'd said, "Hello, I'm Cain." But then her

brother had shown up and ruined everything. She'd tried many times after that to get Cain to engage with her, but he always kept her at a safe distance. She was Perry's sister. Off limits. Permanently. She'd thought maybe after Perry died that Cain would ease up, but no. He had stuck to his guns about not dating her. *His loss.* Or so she told herself, but deep down she knew it was hers, too.

She heard a sound and glanced up. It was the man from the cargo ship, the tall one who had been arguing with the other guy about loading the lifeboat. He smiled. "Hey. Sorry to disturb you so late."

"Hey." She frowned. "Can I help you?"

He was taller than she remembered, but she'd been so out of it at that point, she was surprised she recognized him at all. His blond hair was darker than she remembered, and as he drew closer, she realized he was also older than she'd thought.

He walked toward her. "I just wanted to check and see how you are doing." He had spoken another language on the cargo ship, but his English was good, only a slight accent, but one she didn't recognize. He grinned. "You're the mystery girl. Everybody wants to know who you are."

The hair on the back of her neck stood up. Something was off. She quickly decided to lie about her name. "Uh, I'm Dana, and I'm fine. How are you doing?" She glanced to her left at the table beside her. There was nothing on it she could use as a weapon, but her backpack was on the right side of the bed. If she could just get there, she could pull out her gun.

When the blond man advanced toward her, she smiled at him. "Would you please pour me a glass of water? The cups and water are just around the corner next to the desk. It gets so dry in here, and I'm still a bit dehydrated."

He looked unsure for a second, but then, "Of course."

He turned and disappeared around the corner. Harlow immediately rolled off the bed. Doc had given her a hospital gown that she'd tied in the back, but it felt pretty damn flimsy at the moment. She squatted down next to her backpack. She opened it and searched for her gun. It was hard to find thanks to the wads of cash she'd shoved in there. Finally, she pulled it out of the bottom.

"Where'd you go?" the blond man asked as he came back around the corner.

She stood up, holding the gun behind her leg. "Sorry, just looking for my glasses. I thought I left them in my backpack. I'm having trouble sleeping. I thought I might read for a bit." The thing about growing up with Perry was he made sure she could handle herself and she could lie like nobody's business. Well, except to Cain. He always saw through her immediately.

The man held out the hand with the cup in it.

"Just put it on the table. I'll get it in a bit."

"I thought you said you were thirsty?"

She shrugged. "I'll drink it in a bit. I like it at room temperature. Cold water gives me a headache." She offered him a quick smile. "So, on the ship, you were arguing with the other man in another language. What language was that?"

He put down the water. "Afrikaans."

"Oh, did you grow up in South Africa?" She turned ever so slightly so she had a better angle on him and to make herself a narrower target in case he pulled a gun. She knew in her soul that she was not wrong about this guy. He was here to hurt her. All her instincts were screaming at her to get out of there. She glanced around. Her phone was over on the counter, plugged into the wall.

He must have seen her look at it because he moved to the end of the bed, blocking her access to the rest of the room and the phone. "I grew up in all kinds of places, but my family is from South Africa, yes."

"Nice. Never been, but it's on my list. I've always wanted to go on safari."

"Oh, you like to hunt?" he asked as he inched closer.

She shook her head. "No. I hate hunting. Just photography." She'd backed into a corner. Perry would be flipping out if he could see her now. She'd made the wrong move when she glanced at the phone. Of course, if Perry were with her now, he would just shoot the guy and ask questions later.

"I'm sorry. I didn't catch your name…

"Hendrik."

She nodded. She tried to think of something else to say. "Do you have a lot of family still in South Africa?"

Hendrik moved around the end of the bed. "Not anymore. I had a brother, but he died not too long ago. His name was Christo."

"Oh? I'm sorry to hear that." Harlow instinctively backed up, which was a mistake. He knew for sure she was on to him then. In an instant, he had a knife in his hand, and he was coming at her. She backed up against the wall and pulled up her gun. She aimed it center mass. "Wrong weapon," she growled.

Hendrik froze. He narrowed his eyes. "You won't shoot me."

Harlow just stared at him. "Yes, I will."

He backed up a step and raised his hands as if to say he was surrendering, but he still had the knife in his right hand. It was a switchblade, long and thin, very deadly, and she had no doubt he knew how to use it.

"Why do you want to kill me?" she demanded. If she could keep him talking, maybe she wouldn't have to pull the trigger. Doc should be back to check on her soon, shouldn't he? It wasn't that she couldn't do it. She just didn't want to.

He smiled at her. "You know too much. My orders are to kill you."

"Orders? Who ordered you? Who have you been in touch with?" She kept her gun trained on him.

He shrugged but then lunged at her. She pulled the trigger, and the gun boomed. Hendrik stopped and looked down at his chest. A red blotch bloomed on his gray T-shirt, and it was growing fast. He looked at her with disbelief written all over his face. Then he sunk to his knees and fell face-first at her feet.

Harlow stared down at the dead man. Her gun hand was shaking. She'd just killed a man, but all she felt was relief. Thank God, she'd still had her gun with her. Danny, one of the other aid workers had gotten it for her when she expressed fear for her safety. She'd paid him and didn't ask any questions.

Taking a deep breath, she nudged him with her foot just to make sure he was dead and then quickly stepped over him. Her knees barely held her up. She walked over and leaned on the counter by her cell phone. She drew deep breaths, trying to calm the adrenaline still rushing through her system. She wanted to call Cain, but she didn't have his number. What was she supposed to do? It wasn't like she could dial 911. Why did no one hear the shot? It had sounded very loud to her. Her ears were still ringing.

She saw movement out of the corner of her eye and swung around, bringing her gun up. Doc was coming in the door with what looked like a cup of coffee in his hands. He was talking to Cain, who was directly behind him. When Doc came to an abrupt halt, Cain looked up to see the problem. In an instant, he took in the situation. Then he was across the room to her, taking the gun from her hand. "Are you okay? Did he hurt you?"

She shook her head. She couldn't manage speech at the

moment. She started to move away from the counter, but her knees gave out. Cain caught her and picked her up in his arms. He went to the opposite side of the room and put her on the only other bed. "Are you sure you're okay?"

She nodded more vigorously. "Y-yes. Just scared."

Cain stared as if assessing her. He glanced over at the guy on the floor. Doc was checking the man's pulse at his neck, but then he shook his head at Cain.

"Can you tell me what happened?" Cain asked. He stood beside the bed with his arms folded across his chest. His green eyes glittered with rage and something else.

Harlow looked up at him. She needed to feel his arms around her, but she knew by the pulse in his jaw that wasn't going to happen. She bit her lip and then drew in a deep breath. "I—" Her voice cracked. She cleared her throat and started again. "I was in the bed when I heard a sound. I looked up, and that man was coming around the corner." She spoke quietly and concisely, adding every detail she could remember.

The other members of the team flooded in then, as did Commanding Officer Burns. "What the hell happened here?" he demanded.

"Sir," Nick responded. "It appears that this man, who came from the other ship, tried to kill Ms. Moretti. He told her he was ordered to do so."

Officer Burns asked, "Why was she left unguarded? Why was this man left to wander around the ship?"

Harlow felt Cain tense beside her. He was standing at attention, but his pulse was pounding in his jaw. He was livid. She could feel it coming off him in waves.

Nick said, "Chief Petty Officer Axel Cantor was guarding her until Petty Officer Second Class Usher took over from him. I'm not sure what happened to Petty Officer Usher. He was supposed to be posted at the door. As to why the man was allowed to move around the ship, sir, that is outside of my purview. I have no knowledge of that."

Burns' face had changed as Nick spoke. It was a dull red now. "I want this mess cleaned up, and I want a report from you on this asap! I won't have any more incidents on my ship. Are we clear?"

"Yes, sir," they said in unison.

Burns stormed out. Nick turned to the others. "You heard him. Let's get this done."

Axe went over to Cain. "I'm so sorry, man. The kid came to replace me. I didn't think he'd leave his post." He reached over and touched Harlow's hand. It made her want to cry.

"Not your fault," Cain ground out. "If I find that little fu—"

"Cain!" Nick shook his head.

Cain clamped his lips together, but the pulse in his jaw ticked double-time.

Axe nodded. "I hear you, brother," he murmured to Cain before he went over to the dead man and helped a young yeoman turn him over. "Whoa. I know this guy."

"What?" Nick said.

"Wait." Axe squatted down next to him. "He looks like one of the guys from the Suez mess. Christo, I think his name was. He was dead in the hangar. Shot."

Nick came over and looked down at the dead man. "You're right. He looks just like him."

Harlow spoke up. "He said his name was Hendrik and that Christo was his brother."

Cain grunted. "More Silverstone."

"Yeah? Fuckin' crazy." Finn shook his head. "How many people do you think Vance had on that ship?"

Nick blew out a breath, rubbing his forehead hard with his fingers. "I don't know, but we need to interview every single one of them."

Harlow frowned. "What about…?" Her voice died when Cain gave her a quick shake of his head. She glanced around and realized the whole room was full of people who were listening to their conversation, even if it didn't look that way.

"Are you sure you're okay?" Cain asked again in a low voice.

She nodded. "I'm fine."

"Okay. Be ready to go. As soon as we have a way off this ship, we're out of here."

She looked up at him. "You're taking me with you?"

"Well, I'm sure as shit not leaving you here." Cain turned and walked over to Nick. He said something to his team leader, and Nick nodded.

She hid her smile behind her hand. She was going with them. Yes! She did not want to be left behind. Not when she was this close to getting Vance. Not when she could be close to Cain again. She wasn't passing that up for anything.

CHAPTER EIGHT

C ain yawned for the umpteenth time and rubbed his face. "The containers could be anywhere by now," he grumbled. He was still so pissed off about the attempt on Harlow's life that he could spit nails, but his body was shutting down. He needed sleep.

Nick leaned back in his chair across the table from Cain. "Yeah, and there's nothing here to identify them. The company listed as the owner of the one that went over the side is not listed on any other ships that left the Israeli port that day." He ran a hand through his hair.

"Let's call it a night. The captain has us bunking down with the other chiefs so we can just crash on board. Since none of the crew from the other ship is hurt, the captain is keeping us in the area until we can figure out what to do about the money. He had his guys scooping it out of the water. Some higher ups from DHS are coming out tomorrow. They want to see for themselves and discuss the feasibility of bringing up the cash if it's still down there. I gather they're worried word will spread about the money, so they want the Coast Guard to have a presence to deter anyone from coming looking for the money."

Elias walked into the small room and came to an immediate stop. "Whoa, this is tiny."

Cain nodded. It really was the size of a supply closet, and by the smell of it, it might actually have been one at one time. He grabbed the chair that was at the head of the table and slid onto it.

"What did you find out?" Nick asked.

"Nothing. Nada. Zip." Elias shook his head. "We talked to a lot of the people who worked on the ship. There was a big shake-up recently at the head office of the shipping company, and the new management moved everyone around. Half the ship is new, and we have no way to find out about their work history because Seascale Shipping is refusing to hand over the files."

Nick put his face in his hands. "Fuck."

"Yeah. I tried everything, but I got nowhere. We need a subpoena, and since the head office is in Norway, we need it there."

Nick dropped his hands. "Is Axe still with Harlow?"

Elias nodded. "He feels so guilty about leaving her earlier that he is determined to be with her the rest of the time we're here."

Jealousy burned through Cain's gut. He wanted to be with Harlow, but if he stayed in her room, it was only a matter of time before he had her in his arms. He just didn't have the strength to keep her at arm's length at the moment.

He'd thought he'd been getting stronger since the tragedy in Iraq. He'd been working on his physical and mental health for a while until he had felt strong enough to take on his father. But resisting Harlow when she was so vulnerable, that took a heart of steel, something he did not have when it came to her.

Nick nodded. "And Finn?"

"Here," Finn said as he walked into the room and stopped. He slipped sideways behind Nick's chair and then sat at the last chair on the far end of the table across from Elias.

"So does anyone have any bright ideas?" Nick asked.

Finn shrugged. "Maybe there weren't any more of Vance's men on the ship."

Elias snorted. "You don't really believe that do you?"

"No, but I am out of ideas on how to find them."

Cain sat staring at Nick. He knew how they could find the men. It was obvious. He was sure Nick had thought of it, but Nick wasn't saying anything. Knowing Nick, he was going to let Cain come to the same conclusion first. No doubt, he was worried if he suggested it, Cain would get mad. He was not wrong. Harlow had been through enough.

Cain swore. "In the morning, we get Harlow to take a look at all of the crew of the other ship. Since she had been following Vance for months, she will probably be able to recognize his people."

When Nick gave him a slight nod, Cain had the urge to break his nose, which was stupid. Nick was his teammate and leader and a good friend, but the mere suggestion of having Harlow anywhere near Vance's men just made him sick to his stomach.

"That's a great idea," Finn said. "Makes a shitload more sense than us getting a subpoena in Norway."

Nick nodded. "Yes, but we're gonna have to figure out the best way to do it. We don't want her exposed. She needs to be able to identify them from a distance or in a way she can see them, but they can't see her."

The room went quiet. Cain couldn't think. His brain had locked up at the thought of exposing Harlow to Vance's people. He was too damn tired to come up with anything that would work.

"There's some other stuff to discuss. Cain has a source working on things, but Mexico as a destination could mean cartel involvement. I reached out to Admiral Bertrand, and he said he'd get back to me as soon as he knows more, so let's sleep on it. We'll talk again in the morning." Nick stood up.

Cain followed suit, and they all filed out of the room. He needed sleep so he could clear out the cobwebs. This day had gone from bad to worse. He just couldn't deal with anything else at the moment.

Six hours later, they were all sitting around a table in the mess hall, eating shit on a shingle a.k.a. S.O.S. a.k.a. ground beef in a gravy over toast. It had always been one of Cain's favorites. He would have enjoyed it if he'd gotten more than four hours sleep. He couldn't settle even though he'd been exhausted. His brain just kept going back to Harlow being stuck in the container, all the other crazy risks she had taken, and then the attempt on her life. He should have been the one tracking Vance. Of course, he wouldn't have figured out it was Vance because he never would have gotten a look at the file in the first place.

Harlow had taken way too many risks, and it was sheer luck that she hadn't died. Guilt burned like acid in his gut. He really thought he'd gotten through to her. He should have known better. Instead, he'd left her out there on her own.

"Cain, you're pretty quiet. Any ideas?" Nick asked.

Cain glanced over at his team leader. He surmised that they were talking about Harlow, identifying any of Vance's crew remaining on board the ship. "I think the ship has sailed on Vance's men not being able to identify her." He swallowed. Those words had burned his tongue like scalding water but he knew they were true.

"Why do you think that?" Finn asked, then forked the last bite of his breakfast into his mouth.

"Because she's already infamous as the stowaway with the crew of both boats. She interacted with people on the other ship. They can point her out to anyone who asks. Hiding her face isn't going to help any. And we're gonna be all around her to keep her safe and we're not exactly subtle." On that point he was not willing to budge even a little. She needed to be protected. He would not leave her alone out there.

Nick cocked his head. "You've been thinking about this for a while."

Nothing else to do when he couldn't sleep last night.

"Do you have an idea on how you want to do this?" Nick asked.

Cain bit back a sigh. He didn't *want* to do this. "The best way is in the mess. If we get the captain or the XO to make sure every crew member from the other ship is in the mess, maybe they make some sort of announcement that everyone will be there to hear. We also have Harlow there. She can pick out anyone she recognizes. We'll place her at a back table so she can watch as people come in. Two of us will sit with her and the others can spread out around the room."

Nick's eyes narrowed for a second and then he nodded. "Okay, that works. Cain, why don't you go get Harlow and get her ready. Make sure she's willing to do this. There is risk involved."

"She's willing. Trust me," he growled. "She didn't go through everything to stop now, no matter how dangerous it might be." And that was the whole problem. What the hell was he going to do with her? Once they hit land again, she was going to leave and go right back after Vance unless he could find some way to stop her. Last night, he'd told her that she was coming with them.

That wasn't quite true. She was leaving the ship with them, yes, but after that, he would have to figure out a place to keep her safe. As of right now, he had no clue where that would be.

He got up from the table and cleared his tray. Then he made his way down to the medical bay. He walked in and found the place empty. "What the fuck?" he mumbled.

Where the hell could she be? She was supposed to be resting. He was gonna have to either stay with her all the time or handcuff her to the damn bed. Axe wasn't there either.

When there was a sound behind him, he whirled around to find Harlow walking into the room. She had on a pair of gray sweatpants that were rolled up because they were obviously way too big for her and a navy hoodie. Her auburn hair was damp and hung down over her shoulders in soft curls.

"Where the hell have you been?" he demanded.

She cocked an eyebrow at him. "Excuse me?"

"You're supposed to be resting, not wandering around the ship."

"I was taking a shower and getting some clean clothes to wear, not that it's any of your business. Besides, Axe was with me. He just left when he saw you in here."

She went to walk around him, but he moved to block her path. "Harlow," he ground out, "there are people on this ship who would harm you if they found you alone. Didn't you learn anything from last night?" For all the planning he'd done to keep her safe when IDing Vance's men, it was moot really. They knew who she was and that she was here. It didn't make sense to hide her away, but it made him feel a bit better anyway.

Harlow blinked, and then her eyes narrowed. "Is that your way of asking me to help you find Vance's men?" She shrugged. "Axe told me. It's fine. I'll do it."

Cain shook his head. She was entirely too casual about this. "You need to take this seriously."

She grinned suddenly, her blue eyes sparkling. "I do. So why don't you save me the lecture and tell me what the plan is to ID the men."

Cain wanted to throttle her and kiss her all at the same time. This woman would be the death of him. "Harlow," he growled.

She waved a hand at him. "Yes, it's serious and you need my help, so let's get moving. What's your plan?"

He closed his eyes and swore in his head. "Okay," he said as he opened his eyes and explained what they had decided on.

"Great," she said when he was finished. "When are we doing it?"

It drove him crazy that she wasn't concerned about her own safety. "Harlow, you've been through a lot, and this is dangerous. I—"

"I'm gonna stop you right there," she said, holding up her hand. "I don't really care what you think. I'm doing this because I was the one who tracked down Vance, and I am the one who is going to make sure he pays for killing my brother and the rest of the team. Now, you can stand there and lecture me all you want, but it won't change a damn thing, so why don't you save us both the agony."

He clamped his jaws together and nodded his head once. He didn't trust himself to open his mouth at that moment. He would say something stupid and hurtful—or he would kiss her senseless—so it was better to remain silent. Cain had found that, in life, staying silent meant fewer hassles. Of course, he was stuck with Harlow no matter what at this point, so there was no such thing as less hassle when it came to her.

"Is everything okay?" Nick asked as he entered the medical area.

"Fine," Cain grunted.

Nick raised his eyebrows, but Cain just ignored him. "She'll do it. We're good to go."

"Hi, Harlow," Nick said. "You're looking better this morning."

"Thanks. I'm feeling a bit better. Are we ready to do this?"

"Er, yes, we are. You know that this could be—"

"Dangerous? Yeah… Cain mentioned. It's fine. I'm game. I'm not stopping until Vance is behind bars."

Nick shot Cain a look that said Harlow was a little bit too exuberant about this. *Don't I fucking know it.* Cain just gave a small shrug. His gut tightened and sweat broke out between his shoulder blades. Having Harlow do this still didn't sit well with him, but he knew it was their only option.

Nick and Harlow started out of the room, and he fell in behind. "Put up your hood now," not that it would help any but no need for her gorgeous auburn hair to be on display. Miracle of miracles, she did so without an argument.

It took them a few minutes to get up to the mess hall.

"Ready?" Cain asked as they approached the mess.

"Uh-huh."

"We're gonna sit at the table in the back left of the room. You should be able to see everyone file in from there. Nick and I will stay with you. Axe, Finn and Elias will position themselves around the room. You let us know if you see anyone that you know is part of Vance's crew."

"Got it," she said as they walked through the doors into the empty room. She headed for the back table and claimed the corner seat so there was only a walkway and a wall behind her. Cain sat to her right at the end of the table. Nick sat on her left. They all had earbuds in except Harlow. Nick would tell the guys who to grab when the meeting was over, and Cain would watch for trouble.

The people started to file in. Cain sat silently by and kept watch for anything that looked remotely threatening. Axe came in with the first group. Elias and Finn would come in with the crew as well. Less obvious that way.

They'd asked Commander Burns to make sure everyone was searched in case there were other knives or guns that had been secreted away, but Cain didn't trust the man. There was something funny going on with why the Petty Officer assigned to Harlow had left his post. He rolled his shoulders to release the extreme tension cramping his muscles. He scanned the room once more, knowing he wouldn't relax until Harlow was off the ship.

"The guy on the far right wearing the gray hoodie. He's one of Vance's." Harlow kept scanning the growing crowd.

Nick relayed the information to Axe and the others. They had agreed beforehand not to do anything until they could get the men on their own. Calling them out now would only increase Harlow's risk factor and the risk level of everyone else with them.

"The guy in the jeans and the blue button-down shirt and the guy in the red baseball cap. That's it. That's all I recognize."

Nick again relayed the details over the radio to the others below, then said, "We'll grab them once Harlow is back down in the med bay."

The crowd had grown, and everyone jostled to get seats. The number of people entering petered out and then Commander Burns walked in. An ensign closed the doors. He gave Cain a nod to indicate the entire crew of the other ship was present.

Cain nodded back and scanned the room as Commander

Burns updated everyone on when they were going to be transferred to another ship and taken to shore. It was scheduled for tomorrow. After taking a few questions, Commander Burns thanked everyone for being patient and wished them all luck. Then he left the room.

Cain scanned the room as everyone filed out. A few people had come along behind their table. He tensed but didn't sense any true threat. Only a few stragglers were left when Harlow stood up. "So that's it then."

Cain was getting to his feet when he saw a flash out of the corner of his eye. Someone was coming along behind them. He moved on instinct and threw himself over Harlow. The attacker's knife sliced through his arm as he knocked Harlow to the ground.

There was a scuffle and Nick yelled, "Got him! Her! It's a woman!" He had her pinned to the wall.

Cain lifted his head and looked down at Harlow. "Are you okay?" He knew she wasn't hit because the knife had grazed his right arm, but he was worried about her head. He'd cradled her fall as much as he could, but she still had landed hard.

She looked up at him, and their gazes locked. Terror swam in the depths of her big blue eyes along with some other emotion. Something he knew was reflected in his own. She pressed up and kissed him hard on the mouth.

Damn her. But he kissed her back.

"The room is secure. We have all identified parties in custody. Is anyone hurt?" Axe's voice filled his ear.

Cain broke off the kiss and rolled off Harlow and pulled her to her feet. "Are you good?"

She nodded.

She looked shaken up, but she seemed fine otherwise. "We're good," Cain replied as he took the lead down the hallway with Harlow immediately behind him. Nick brought up the rear. Elias, Finn, and Axe had taken the woman along with the others they'd pulled out of the crowd down to a holding area.

Cain moved quickly through the ship and had her back in the medical area in minutes. Nick closed the door and locked it after they'd entered. "Sorry, Doc, we need the room."

Doc nodded and then squinted at Cain. "I'll just bandage his wound, and then I'll be on my way."

Cain brought Harlow over to the bed and helped her to sit on top of it. "Wound? What wound?" she demanded.

Nick looked over at Cain and frowned.

Cain shook his head. "It's just a graze."

"What?" Harlow demanded. Her face lost all color as she noticed the blood dripping down Cain's arm.

He put his hands on each of her shoulders. "It's a scratch. I'm fine. We got the woman that tried to stab you. You're safe." She nodded, but her face remained pale, and her bottom lip quivered. Cain turned. "Hey Doc, maybe you want to treat her first. She's awful pale."

Doc glanced at Cain's arm and then went over to Harlow. While he gave her a once-over, Cain watched his every move. "Try and take it easy, young lady." He glared at Nick and Cain. "I am entrusting her to your care for the next little while. Don't let her get too excited. She's been through a lot, and she does need rest."

They nodded.

"Now you." He glared at Cain.

"I don't need—"

Doc pointed at the hospital bed across the room. "Sit your ass down, cowboy."

Cain wanted to argue, but it was faster just to get it over with. "Fine," he grumbled and went and sat on the bed as instructed.

Doc came with his paraphernalia and started to clean the wound. "It's just a shallow slice."

"I know."

Doc leaned in and started to speak to Cain in a soft tone just above a whisper. "She's going to be fine, but she's more fragile than she thinks. She's been under pressure for a long time. I know you know what that's like. You've trained for it. She hasn't. When all this is over, you need to take her on a nice, long vacation somewhere warm so she can do nothing but lie in the sun and play in the waves. Do you hear me?"

"Yeah, but Doc, it's not like that. I can't—"

"Son, you can save your denials. I've been around the block quite a few times. When people look at each other the way you two do, it's a hell of a lot more than friendship."

Cain ground his teeth together in frustration. There was no point in explaining that he didn't not *want* to date Harlow; it was that he couldn't. Perry had warned him off that first day after he saw them together. Cain would not go back on that promise.

"There, all done. Take this antibiotic." Doc stood and handed him a pill. "You're good to go." He gathered his instruments and equipment and left the room. Nick locked the door.

As soon as Doc was gone, Cain jumped off the bed and went over to Nick. As he passed Harlow, he said, "I'm fine. This is nothing."

She narrowed her eyes at him but bit her lip, as if to hold back her thoughts. There was slightly more color in her cheeks, which was good, but there was also a determined look in her eye, which was all bad.

Cain decided to ignore it for now. More important matters were still pending. He asked Nick, "Any word on who the woman is? I should have seen her right away, but I missed her."

Nick snorted. "You saw her before me or Axe, even Elias and Finn. You reacted quickly, and we handled the situation. What's done is done. There's no blame to go around. Harlow is safe, and we're gonna make sure she stays that way."

Stupid. This was all his fault. Nick talked a good game, but it was Cain's job to keep an eye out for trouble, and he'd blown it. Harlow was so fucking distracting. And her kissing him on deck. Just plain crazy, yet so damn good. He wanted her so badly it hurt him physically. He swayed on his feet.

"You okay?" Nick asked.

"Yeah." Cain looked around and pulled over a stool. "Adrenaline crash."

Nick nodded.

Cain blew out a long breath. He needed to be away from Harlow. He was gonna have to ask to be reassigned to tasks that didn't involve being around her. It was stupid and embarrassing, but it was true. He just couldn't do his job the way he should when he was around her.

It was really the last thing he wanted, to be away from her, but the last thing he could ever deal with was if Harlow got injured or died because of him. That would be the end for him. He'd never get over that one. He'd let her brother and his teammates down back in Iraq. There was no way he'd let Perry down again by letting harm come to his sister.

"Cain, I want you to stay here with Harlow. I don't think she's in any danger, but I think we should be prepared. I don't trust Burns with this. That's twice he's screwed up as far as I can tell. He was supposed to have everyone searched and yet that woman still had a knife."

These might be the men that had a hand in killing his teammates. He wanted in. He needed to get away from Harlow. She was fogging up his brain. His need to keep her safe warred with his desire to take her to bed. Cain shook his head. "No, I want to be there when you question them."

Nick hesitated. "I'm not sure that's a good idea. You're too close to this."

"And you're not?" he shot back. "Vance is the reason you were injured."

"Fair point." Nick tapped his earbud. "Finn, report to medical."

"Roger that," Finn responded.

Ten minutes later, Cain and Nick were walking down the passageway to the makeshift interrogation room. "You want to tell me what's really going on?" Nick demanded.

Cain frowned. "What do you mean?"

"Between you and Harlow."

"Nothing is going on. She's the little sister of my team-mate. Off-limits."

Nick grunted. "He's dead."

"She's still off-limits."

They arrived at the door to the interrogation room with Axe and Elias standing outside. Axe said, "This is the woman that tried to stab Harlow. Burns has already been down here demanding answers like it's our fault."

"Yeah," Nick commented. "He seems to be on a mission."

Elias spoke up. "By the way, on the other ship's manifest, this is supposed to be Cara Delany, but I'm guessing that's not her real name. She was supposed to be a kitchen worker on the other ship, but none of the other kitchen staff recall her anywhere near the kitchen. I took her prints, and DHS is running them." He pointed to his earbud. "I'll tell you if we find anything."

Cain snorted. "Yeah. I'm sure all the IDs are fake. Let's see what she has to say." He put in his earbud, opened the door, and walked into the room.

Cara Delany, or whatever her name was, sat handcuffed to a chair on the other side of the table. She was wearing jeans and a blue button-down shirt. She had her dark hair pulled back in a ponytail and her brown eyes were snapping as she glared at them.

Nick and Cain sat down. Nick leaned back in his chair. "So, you work for Silverstone. What's Foley paying these days? Is it worth going to prison for?"

She just sat there with a smug smile on her face.

Cain offered, "We're searching the room you're staying in and going through your burner phone."

She blinked.

He nodded. "Yeah, we found that. It wasn't hard. What's gonna happen when we start calling the numbers? Vance is not gonna be pleased with you. And you know how he deals with people who become a liability." Cain smiled. "He cuts his losses." He wanted that to sink in. She was now a liability to two of the most ruthless men who walked the planet, Roman Vance and Asher Foley. "How do you think that's gonna work out for ya?"

In truth, he had no idea where her phone was, but they'd be looking for it asap once they finished this interview. It was just logic that she had to have one.

She continued to glare at them, but the smug smile was slipping.

Nick continued along the same thread. "I'm sure Foley and Vance told you they have lots of contacts in the government and you would skate on any charges, or they could get you out of the country quick-time. Here's the thing. We're the Coast Guard. Not the FBI or the DoD where Foley has all his friends. We're more selective about who our friends are.

"You are going to be our guest for quite some time. It will be a while before we hit land again. Your shipmates are all transferring to another ship tomorrow, which is going to take them to Miami. You and your fellow Silverstone employees are going to stay on board for more questioning. It could be a month or more before you hit dry land."

Axe's voice sounded in Cain's ear. "Her real name is Irene Benton. Former Army. Dishonorable discharge. She was caught stealing oxycodone out of the med center, but they didn't bother to charge her. Sounds fishy. Something odd about it. Maybe Foley pulled strings."

"So…" Cain picked up the conversation again. "You can stay here and be reasonably comfortable, or you can be miserable. It all depends on whether you choose to be our friend or not, Irene."

She jumped when he said her name.

"Did you think Foley and Vance could protect you just like they did when you were dishonorably discharged but not prosecuted?" He gave her a pitying smile. "You actually believe they can protect you."

Nick shook his head. "That is sad. Look around the room, Irene. The only one in here is you. Foley and Vance can't help you now. You can, however, help yourself. Where are the other two containers going?"

Irene swallowed but didn't say anything. Her defiant posture was now gone but she still wasn't convinced.

Nick continued. "You know, this money was for the cartel. They didn't get it. What do you think is going to happen now? Were you promised a piece of the pie? Now the pie is smaller by at least a third. The cartel is not going to put up with not being paid. They're coming for their money. Do you want to be in the way of that?"

Cain leaned forward. "Where are the other two containers going, Irene?"

She looked as if she would speak but remained silent.

They almost had her. Cain shifted gears. "You do know that you were never getting out of Mexico alive, don't you?" Cain asked. "Hendrik was supposed to kill all of you after delivery had taken place. Why protect the men who wanted you dead?"

She shook her head. "That's not true. Hendrik would never kill me. We were…" Her voice faded out.

"Hendrik is dead. He tried to kill the witness just like you did. It was his job to kill everyone once you were in Mexico. Foley doesn't want any witnesses. Think about it. Isn't that their usual method of operation? When was the last time they left a witness?"

Irene paled. The reality of her situation was starting to hit home.

Nick said in a quiet voice, "This is your chance, Irene. Get ahead of it. What do you know?"

Irene's chin quivered before she finally said, "Belize— that's all I know. The other one is going somewhere else. I think in the Caribbean, but I can't be sure. I was just supposed to deliver the money to Mexico and the Cortez cartel. That's it. Vance said he'd tell me where to be once the delivery was done."

Nick pushed just a bit more. "Is that what normally happens, Irene? Or do you usually know what the next assignment is?"

She started to respond and then just stared at him with her mouth hanging open. The penny had finally dropped. She fully realized that she was expendable to Foley. "Shit," she breathed.

"Irene," Cain said in a firm voice, "you're going to tell us everything you know about the current operation and any other operations that Foley and Vance have going. We're going to record everything, and when it comes time, we'll tell everyone you helped us out."

She nodded as she blinked back tears. The knowledge that she'd been had was settling in on her, and it stung. Cain knew what that felt like. He'd lived with his father's unfulfilled promises for years.

Cain and Nick stood up and left the room. Axe and Elias were waiting in the hallway. Axe opened his mouth to speak, but Cain shook his head. "Elias, go in there and watch her. I don't want anything to happen to her. We need to get everything we can from her."

Elias nodded and went into the room.

Cain gestured for Axe and Nick to follow him. They wound their way through the ship until they came out on deck. Cain took them to the side and then looked around to make sure they were alone. "Sorry for the cloak and dagger, but it occurred to me while we were sitting in there that Burns might be listening in."

Nick froze. "You think he's working for Foley?"

Cain shrugged. "Maybe not Foley, but I definitely think something is going on. Every time one of his crew is assigned a task to help us, something goes wrong and we're left holding the bag. At least, that's the feeling I'm getting."

Axe nodded. "I feel it, too. There's something funky going on here. The sooner we're off the *Jones,* the better."

"Okay, let me call Bertrand and see what we can find out about Belize. I'm also going to see if we can get these Silverstone people offloaded quick-time. I want them kept safe. Somewhere Foley can't get to them."

Cain leaned on the rail. "See where Gerhart and the *Walton* are. They helped us last time. We know we can trust him."

Nick smiled. "That's a brilliant idea." He pulled out another satellite phone and walked off to make the call.

Axe nudged Cain. "I'm really sorry about Harlow, man. I should have stayed with her."

"Bullshit. You did your job, Axe. You followed orders. The thing is, I think the kid who was at the door followed orders, too. Burns told him to leave Harlow alone. I just don't know why. There's something going on here that's bigger than us and Burns. We're all players in some game that we don't know the rules to, but you can bet your ass, I'm gonna find out."

CHAPTER NINE

Cain looked pale, and his mouth was in a tight line. Never a good thing. "What's wrong?" Harlow asked.

Cain focused on her. "Nothing. I think we're leaving soon." He glanced down at her clothing.

She put a hand to her hair; she knew she looked a mess. Her hair was wildly curly, she had on no makeup. The clothing she'd borrowed was miles too big for her. The sweats were okay because she could roll them up, but the hoodie was big enough to be a dress. She hated that she looked horrible, but she hated even more that she cared what she looked like in front of Cain. The worst part, though, was even though he had been stabbed, he still looked hot as hell in his uniform with his hair in that ponytail. How did men do this?

"So, where are we going?"

Cain stared at her but said nothing.

Frustration had her grinding her teeth. Cain could be so stubborn sometimes. He was immovable like a stone wall. It drove her mad.

But not as mad as having him close to her. He stirred her

into a frenzy of emotion just by being near her. She still couldn't believe that she'd kissed him in the mess hall, right in front of his team leader. It had been stupid, but it had been instinctive. He had been on top of her, and she'd been scared. She'd been in desperate need of his touch. The fact that he kissed her back for all of two seconds was a miracle. Now, if she could only get him to do that on a regular basis.

She let out a long sigh. It was dumb really. She shouldn't want Cain. He wouldn't be with her because of her brother. Even more than that, he hadn't helped her when she'd asked. He'd told her to stop what she was doing rather than help her to figure out what happened to her brother, his friend.

"So what happened with the woman?" she asked.

"She's telling us what she knows. It's not much, but I guess every little bit helps." Cain stared off into space again.

He was obviously distracted, and it was getting to her. "What is it? What are you worried about?"

"You."

She reared back. "Me? I thought you said I was safe now."

"Yes, but the Silverstone Group… They are…relentless." Cain rubbed his face with both hands. "There's just a lot going on, and I want to keep you out of the crossfire."

She frowned. "I can take care of myself, you know. I did it for months in Iraq."

"Yes, and look how that turned out. You almost died in a shipping container."

"It was *one* stupid mistake, and I'm fine." She crossed her arms over her chest.

"Harlow," Cain began in an almost pleading tone, "for once in your life, can you just stop and think? These people are no joke. Vance knows you exist now. It's not like before when you could hover in the background and not be noticed. He is actively seeking to have you killed. You got damn lucky with Hendrik because he underestimated you. Vance's people will not make that mistake again. They already recalibrated and had Irene Benson try to kill you. Nick and I bluffed her about what we knew, but she can only help so much. There are a lot of Silverstone operatives out there, and now you are on their Most Wanted list."

She glowered at him. "What would you have me to do? Pack up and go home?"

"You just don't get it. You can't go home. Not until this is over. Vance and his people will know where 'home' is, and they'll come hunting you. I've already asked Nick to get your parents moved somewhere secure. Until we get Vance, no one in your family is safe, especially you."

Nick came into the room. "Hi, Harlow. How are you feeling?"

Up until two minutes ago, she would have said "fine" or even "pissed off," but now she wasn't sure. "I'm okay," she mumbled.

But was she? No. She'd inadvertently put her parents in danger. She just didn't think Vance would bother with her. She was a small fry. But really, she just hadn't thought, period. That was the truth of the matter. Her pursuit for justice for her brother had all been an emotional response. Logic had fallen to the wayside, and now she was bitterly disappointed in herself.

In all the time she was digging to find out what really happened to her brother, it never occurred to her that she might be bringing trouble to her parents' door. She'd wrapped herself in a cloak of righteousness and thought she was the only one who was able to avenge her brother. She would do it for all of them! But, in the end, she was only doing it for herself. Because she wanted a new life. An exciting life that had meaning and now it was hurting her family. A hollow feeling filled her chest. She really did fuck this up big time.

"Harlow?" Nick said.

"Um, I wasn't paying attention. Sorry."

"I said we're going to leave the ship in the next day or so. I'm working on getting your parents moved somewhere safe. They, um, aren't too keen to go. Your father doesn't want to leave the farm. He says it's strawberry time, and they need to pick the berries or they'll rot. But we really need to move them. It doesn't have to be far, maybe just over the border into Pennsylvania. We can send people to check on the strawberries in New Jersey."

She sighed. "My father will be seriously pissed if his strawberries rot. He loves them." Berry picking time had always been her favorite while growing up in New Jersey. Ripe strawberries meant the beginning of summer.

"It might help if you called them," Nick suggested gently.

She glanced at Cain and then back at Nick. "I don't think that's a good idea. My parents will be really angry with me right now. Speaking to me will just give my father an excuse to dig his heels in. It's better if you tell him I can't be reached so he'll just have to listen to you."

Nick frowned.

"Trust me. My father will just lose his shit if I talk to him. It won't help matters."

"Okay, then." Nick let out a big sigh.

Exhaustion rocked Harlow. She felt like she could sleep for a week and still be tired. So much had happened. When she rubbed her face, she winced. Her bruise still hurt.

She cut into Cain's conversation with Nick. "Why did Hendrik help me on the other ship? I mean, he helped me into the lifeboat. Why did he do that if he was going to try to kill me later?"

Cain adjusted his uniform and leaned against the wall off

to her right. "Even if he recognized you then, he couldn't do anything because there were too many witnesses. You were just another crew member, and it was his job to get them off the ship. If he didn't help you, it would have raised flags with the other crew members."

"Still." Harlow shook her head. "He could have pushed me over the side or something."

Cain shrugged. "I don't think he had those orders yet. Remember, Daughtry thought you would be found dead when they opened the container. He probably didn't bother to say anything about you to Vance. It probably wasn't until they realized you were a stowaway, and the money was found that Daughtry told Vance about locking you in the container."

Nick, who was sitting on a stool on her left, rolled forward a bit. "Once he made the call and said you were here, then the order came down to kill you. Which reminds me. Has anyone found those cell phones yet?"

Cain shook his head. "Not yet. I'm guessing one of the people Harlow IDed knows where they are. Once they're questioned, hopefully we'll know more. Finn and Elias are working on that now. Axe is staying with Irene until she's finished writing down everything she knows."

Harlow asked, "How will you get them to flip? I mean, it's great that you guys have this woman who tried to kill me…" She paused at those last words, and a shiver went across her skin. A sense of her own mortality weighed heavily on her for a moment, then she cleared her throat and continued, "But what do you have on them that they're going to be willing to flip on Vance and Foley?"

Cain studied her for a second. "The original plan was to deliver the money to Mexico, and then once that was done, we think Hendrik was supposed to kill these other people who'd helped with the delivery. Vance can't have all these operatives running around the world, knowing about the money. Word would spread too quickly, and people would be after him, not the least of which would be the U.S. government and the army.

"Once we make them come to realize that...I'm pretty sure they'll give up what they know. Remember, these aren't the most loyal bunch. They signed on to do whatever to get paid a lot of money. I'm not sure loyalty is what keeps them quiet. Fear is probably a bigger motivator. Foley and Vance have a long reach."

Nick rolled his stool back and forth a bit. "This *is* the missing money, by the way. Admiral Bertrand told me that Vance's commanding officer when he left the army was none other than Asher Foley, who also happens to own and run Silverstone. They were stationed in Iraq at the right time. Foley was part of the crew that helped bring the money to Iraq in the first place." He looked over at Cain. "And he confirmed that Vance was also in Iraq when your team was hit. It looks like they were trying to get the money out, but the SEAL team you were training with was causing them all kinds of problems. He confirmed Harlow's information.

"DHS is working with Treasury and the rest of the alphabet soup in Washington to prove that Foley stole the money and to track him. Bertrand wants us to stay on the money trail. He's not sure who else is going to be sent but he indicated he wants us to take point no matter what."

Cain raised his eyebrows. "We're to keep going even if we're ordered to stand down by some other department?"

Nick smirked. "Yeah. There's got to be some serious shit going down in Washington right about now. Bertrand just wants us to keep our heads down and find the money."

Harlow's heart constricted painfully upon hearing those words. She had known it in her soul as soon as she read the report, but it wasn't explicitly written out that Vance was responsible. She'd wanted to kill him, but after she shot and killed Hendrik, she'd lost the sense of vengeance she'd held so tightly to her chest over the last year.

She'd been kidding herself all along that she wanted to bring down the whole of Silverstone, when really she was just being a coward. Vance had killed her brother and his teammates. There'd been opportunities when she'd been close enough to him that she could have taken a shot, but she hadn't. She'd let her brother down.

Blinking back tears, she glanced over at Cain. His pulse thrummed in his jaw. His green eyes glittered. A flutter started in her belly but moved downward. He was always sexy as hell when he was angry. She swallowed hard. She knew, in part, she was to blame for some of that anger.

"He also caused your injury, Nick," Cain said. "There's a lot Roman Vance has to answer for, but we have to find him first."

Nick tapped his fist on his thigh. "Agreed. The one place he won't be is in Mexico. The cartel must be pissed they aren't getting paid."

"How did Foley and Vance get involved with the cartel?" Cain asked. "I mean, I just don't see their worlds intersecting unless Foley got into drug dealing, which just seems like a hugely stupid move."

"I asked Bertrand about that. Apparently, about fifteen years ago, when Foley and Vance left the army, Foley set up Silverstone, but he wasn't making any inroads with the Washington crowd. At least not enough. Then, one day, Congressman David Lamston was kidnapped down in Mexico City."

Cain scratched his chin. "I vaguely remember this. He was supposed to be on vacation or something, and the cartel grabbed him right from his hotel. They killed two of the security detail assigned to him."

"Yeah," Nick agreed. "They stuffed him in the trunk of a car and drove off with him. Foley rescued the Congressman from the cartel and brought him safely back Stateside. That brought him and Silverstone all kinds of great press. He was in after that. It made him.

"Lamston went on to be on several important committees, including the one that deals with military contractors. When he went back into private life, Lamston joined one of the top celebrity law firms out in LA. He uses Silverstone for any clients that need extra security."

"What's the rest of the story," Cain asked. "I feel like there's more to this."

Nick grinned. "Bertrand certainly thinks so. He always thought it was just too neat the way Foley rescued Lamston. It just didn't ring true, and once he met Foley, that was it. He thinks the man is lower than a snake's belly—quote, unquote. When I called and told him about Vance, he did some digging. He'd heard rumors that Foley knew some people involved with the Mexican cartels, which had come in handy on occasion for people in Washington.

"Turns out Asher Foley went to high school in Arizona with a kid named Jesus Espinoza. Espinoza is the number two in the Cortez cartel in Mexico, the same cartel that kidnapped Lamston all those years ago, and Espinoza was identified by a hotel worker as one of the kidnappers. The worker disappeared after that."

Harlow reached for the tea Cain had brought her, but it was cold, so she set it back down. "I'm sorry. I'm a bit fuzzy. Are you saying that Lamston's kidnapping was a hoax perpetrated by Foley and Espinoza so Foley would get good publicity?"

"Yep." Nick nodded. "Bertrand thinks Lamston was also in on it. His move out to LA was no accident. He'd always wanted to be famous."

Cain narrowed his eyes. "Bertrand thinks this money that was supposed to end up in Mexico was payment for Espinoza's help. Long time to wait."

Nick shrugged. "I'm guessing the guys were friends, and Foley made the deal, thinking it wouldn't take him too long to get the money out of Iraq if he had the right contacts. But with the war dragging on longer than anyone anticipated, it was just harder than he thought. Too many people paying close attention to what was going on. Finally, when everyone's focus is on Russia, it was his moment to get the money out but he still has to pay Espinoza his share."

Cain pushed off the wall. "It's a good theory, Tag, but we have zero proof, and at this point, it doesn't really matter since the money is gone. Foley is good buddies with Ted Caveller, head of the FBI, and we all know what a stand-up guy he is." Cain snorted. "Asshole." He glanced at Harlow. "Sorry. He was…involved in something that didn't put him in the best light."

"Not to mention Foley's close with the Department of Defense and all his old Army buddies." Nick shook his head. "Bertrand wants us to move very carefully on this. We have no proof except Harlow's eyewitness account at this point. We need to track down those other two containers."

Harlow shivered. She was the only proof that Vance and the Silverstone guys had dug up the money. No wonder they wanted her dead. Foley wouldn't want her around to link his people to this, and she could link him directly. That put a huge bull's-eye on her back. It was too bad she hadn't taken pictures when they'd dug up the pallets, but she might have pictures from another visit. She thought he'd come at least once before to Iraq.

Cain was staring at her. "I can see you're thinking of something," he grumbled. "And that worries me."

She licked her suddenly dry lips. Cain had the power to

make her nervous just with a look. Not that he would hurt her; she'd never felt safer with anyone. What made her so nervous? She didn't really know. She only knew that her belly tightened, and a tingling sensation started in her lady parts. Her sexual attraction to the man was off the scale. "I…I was just thinking, or rather wondering, if I had pictures of him with Vance and the others. I took a lot of pictures when I could. I never really thought much about Foley. Just concentrated on Vance, but maybe I have pictures of him doing something…" But doing what? Nothing that could help them now. "Forget it."

"No," Cain said. "Where are the pictures?"

"Back in Iraq at my place."

Cain shifted his gaze to Nick. "We need someone to pick up those pictures."

Nick nodded. "Did you get any shots of Vance and his men digging up the money?"

"No. I didn't bring my Nikon, and I was too far away to use my cell camera." Disappointment rocked her. It would be so much better if she had pictures. "Sorry."

A phone sounded. Cain pulled a satellite phone out of his pocket. "I gotta take this, but we need to discuss where we're going to put Harlow to keep her safe." He strode across the room and disappeared from view.

"Wait." Harlow frowned. "What the hell is he talking about? I'm going with you guys. He said I could go with you."

"No." Nick shook his head. "I'm sure he said he wasn't leaving you here."

Her stomach burned, and she closed her hands into fists. "You can't shut me out of this. I am the reason we got this far."

Nick turned to her. "You are our only witness. You need to be kept safe. That means you need to stay somewhere that we can have you guarded twenty-four-seven until we resolve this mess."

She shook her head. "No. No way. *I* was the one who tracked down Vance." She pointed at her chest. "*I* was the one that tracked the containers. You aren't kicking me out of this now. No fucking way."

If they thought she was going to sit in a room somewhere, waiting for them to go out and get Vance, they had another fucking think coming. She might not be a trained operator, but she knew a thing or two, Perry had made sure she did. They weren't keeping her from this. She owed her brother. She owed Perry. There was no way she was sitting this one out. She loved her brother too much to give up now.

CHAPTER TEN

"Maddox," he said into the phone as he opened the door to the outside. He moved down the deck to find a spot that he wouldn't be overheard.

"Cain." His father's voice still held the bitterness it always did when he said his son's chosen name.

"What did you find out?"

His father sighed. Did the old man really expect small talk? Cain took a beat. He had to calm down. Ever since the attacker took a run at Harlow, he'd been coming off the walls. Then when Benson had thrown her knife, he'd really come unglued. The idea of someone hurting her was making him crazy. And speaking to his father merely exacerbated his issues when he needed to focus.

"I found out the destinations of your two ships." His father's voice was clipped, but he also sounded older. Tired.

Cain glanced around him as he stood next to the railing. "Okay, where are they going and have they reached land yet?"

"Not sure if they have docked as yet, but they are headed for Belize and the Caymans."

Confirmation on the Belize thing. Cain's gut unknotted just a bit. His father had come through. Again.

His father continued. "I do know that the money has not been deposited in any banks yet. I'm told they are still getting the paperwork together to make it all look legitimate."

Cain thought for a moment. "Do you know what ports in these countries the containers are supposed to arrive in?"

There was a pause from his father. The sound of muffled voices came down the line. Then his father was back. "I do not know. I do have the numbers for the containers and the ship names. You will have to track them down from there. I have already emailed this information to you."

That was doable. "Okay, is there anything else?"

"No." His father's voice had turned cold again. "You owe me. We will speak when you are back." He hung up.

Cain's shoulders slumped. He didn't want to dwell on how much he owed his father at this point. It was going to be ugly when his dad asked for payback. He was sure of it. He put the phone in his pocket and then ran his hands over his face. How had everything turned to shit so fast? One minute he was having a reasonably nice dinner with his father, and the next his father's people were trying to force him into a car.

Then there was Harlow. Jesus, she was his kryptonite. From the moment he'd laid eyes on her, she'd owned every part of him. But bro-code meant he couldn't have her. Just seeing her again was like opening an old wound. The pain of being near her and not being able to have her was intense. He wanted to grab her and take her far away. Then spend the next month in bed with her making her every desire come true. But that wasn't going to happen. And now she'd put herself in the middle of this mess. How the hell was he going to keep her safe and still do his job?

Cain stretched out his arms. The uniform he'd put on

after his shower was a bit tight. It made him feel like a caged animal. He was frustrated and tired, but more than anything else… Scared. Even back in Iraq when the IED went off, he'd been scared, but not like this. The thought of something happening to Harlow was too much.

How the hell was he supposed to leave Harlow behind? How could he trust someone else to keep her safe? But if he stayed, he was leaving his team in the lurch, and there was no way he would do that. Not ever.

He had wanted to hug her so badly after she'd shot Hendrik. She looked so terrified sitting on the bed, but he knew if he'd wrapped his arms around her, then he probably wasn't going to let go. Ever.

And then she'd kissed him on the deck when he'd tackled her so she didn't get stabbed. Talk about bad timing. Who the fuck kisses someone when people are trying to kill them? But if it was so bad, why did he kiss her back? *Because he'd kiss her any opportunity he got.* Jesus Christ, he was a mess.

And then there was his father. What the fuck was he supposed to do about that? He was going to have to tell the team where his information was coming from. When they discovered that his father was the head of one of the largest mafia families in the world, what would they think? Hell, he didn't even know what to think himself. That was another reason he couldn't be with Harlow. He wasn't bringing her into the mess that was his family. She didn't need to be connected to the mafia in any way, shape, or form. He'd fought against it every day of his life and it had been hell at times. Harlow definitely did not need to be part of that struggle.

He rubbed his face with his hands once again and then took out his phone and forwarded the email to Nick. Then he sent a quick text to Nick to ask them all to meet him in the office. He didn't want to talk about this in front of

Harlow and asked Nick to make sure Doc remained with her. He was sure he could trust the doctor to let them know if he was ordered to leave by Commander Burns or any of his crew.

He made his way down to the supply-closet-sized conference room they were using. The others were already there, sitting around the tiny table. Finn had paper in front of him and was already making some origami animal. Cain entered and shut the door after himself, then leaned against it.

"So, what did you find out?" Nick asked.

"One ship is on the way to Belize and the other is going to the Cayman Islands. So, confirmation there of what Irene Benson said."

Elias piped up, "Confirmed by two of the Silverstone guys."

Cain nodded. "My understanding is they haven't docked yet, but my source wasn't sure. I already emailed you the name of the ships and the numbers on the containers. We should be able to track the ships and see exactly where they are."

Elias leaned back in his chair. "That's good. These guys didn't have details. How sure of your source are you?"

That was a damn good question. How much did he trust his father? "The information is good. My source…tends to be correct, if not always one-hundred percent reliable."

"What the hell does that mean?" Nick demanded.

Cain sighed to himself. "It means I'm sure this information is good."

"I think we're going to need a little bit more than that this time, Cain." Nick crossed his arms over his chest. "You've been dancing around something for a while now. It's time to spill."

This was it. This was the moment when he had to come clean. He knew he'd forgive his teammates just about anything and, by rights, they would probably forgive him, too, but there was always that niggling doubt. None of them had mobsters for fathers.

Cain straightened up, crossed his arms over his chest, and took a deep breath. "My source is my father. The man himself isn't one-hundred percent reliable, but his information is always correct."

The room was silent.

Finally, Elias spoke up, "I didn't think you had any family. You've never mentioned your father before."

Cain hesitated. "It's complicated. I have a father and two half-sisters, and I guess a stepmother if you go in for that kind of thing."

"And how exactly would your father get this information?" Nick asked.

"My father has a lot of contacts in some...dubious places. He can usually find out all sorts of things without too much difficulty."

Axe snorted. "I'm sorry, man, but what the hell is going on? Who is your father? Why are you dancing around this?"

Cain ground his teeth. This was harder than he'd thought. These men, they were his real family. He hadn't thought he'd ever find a place to fit in again after losing Perry and the other team. If they turned on him because of his biological family, it would be a hard thing to get over, not that he would blame them.

"My father is Salvatore Ricci."

Finn looked up quickly.

"Okay," Nick said, "Who is Salvatore Ricci? You say that like we should know him."

Finn finished his latest origami animal and glanced up. "Salvatore Ricci is the head of the Bianchi mob family. It's one of the largest organized crime families in the world."

Cain nodded. "My mother was his mistress. She died

giving birth to my twin brother. My father was… distraught, so he sent me off to live with her family."

"Cain," Nick said. "The son that killed his brother in the Bible. Did you pick the name?"

"It seemed fitting." He'd always felt his father had blamed him for his brother and mother's deaths. Picking Cain as a name was a way to acknowledge that, and if he were being truthful, a way to piss off his father. It was a "fuck you" to the old man. And *I know what you're thinking, and you can't hurt me with it*. But that wasn't strictly true because Cain had always felt that his father didn't approve of him no matter what he did. And that hurt.

"Wait. If Cain isn't your real name, what is?" Elias demanded.

"Cain is the name I choose to go by. Maddox is the name of my mother's family. But the name on my birth certificate is Giancarlo Ricci."

Finn grabbed another sheet of paper and started folding. "Since you have two half-*sisters,* you realize this makes you the heir apparent of one of the largest crime families in the world."

Cain frowned. "My father and I have a hands-off policy. I stay out of his life, and he stays out of mine."

"But you just asked him for help, and I'm thinking it wasn't the first time." Nick shot him a knowing look.

"That's…true, I guess. We *did* have a hands-off policy. I guess I've violated it a bit lately." He ran a hand over the back of his neck. "A lot lately. Hell, I even moved into the apartment he offered. I was…struggling a bit after Iraq and…I just couldn't seem to care so much. My father likes things done his way. He offered the apartment, and I didn't have the energy to fight with him about it."

"So that's why we haven't ever been to your place." Axe grinned. "Which apartment is it? The building is amazing.

We were thinking you had some sort of one-room thing, and you didn't want us to see it because it was small."

Cain smiled sheepishly. "It's the penthouse."

"Shit," Axe said and shook his head.

"But I was packing to move out when you called, Tag. I'm actually all packed and ready to go. The place came furnished." He shrugged. "Like I said, I didn't have the energy to fight my father. But now I plan on staying in a hotel for a bit until I find a place to live."

"Those men in your parking garage, who were they?" Elias asked.

Nick's glare swung from Elias to Cain. "What men?"

Cain grimaced. "They were part of my father's security team. He wanted to see me, but I declined. We had a fight, and he didn't like that I walked out."

"Walked out of where?" Tag asked. "Maybe start at the beginning."

Cain sighed. "I had dinner with my father just before we left, but we got into an argument. I think because I'm feeling better these days, and I decided to be done with…things. He didn't like it. He got mad when I walked out. His people arrived to *escort* me to his location so we could finish our… discussion. Elias helped me dissuade them from trying to force the issue."

Tag's eyes narrowed. "Is this going to be an ongoing problem?"

Cain shook his head. "We'll meet when I'm back in Miami, and that will be that. I expect he'll disown me. Not a huge loss."

"Except now you owe him," Nick pointed out.

Cain nodded. "Except now I owe him." He shrugged. "He knows I won't work with him. I'm not the heir apparent. There are plenty of other guys in the family that can take over if my father ever decides to retire, or if he dies. It's not on me."

Nick made a non-committal sound. "I guess there's not much we can do about any of it at the moment. We'll take your father at his word since it backs up what the others say. The ships are headed for Belize and the Caymans. We'll use the ship names and container numbers he provided. Let me call Bertrand and fill him in. We'll catch up again after I speak to him."

Cain nodded. "Look guys, I'm…sorry I didn't tell you sooner. It's not something I pay much attention to, to be honest. I see my father once or twice a year. He's very removed from my life, but I still should have told you."

"Yes, you should have." Nick agreed. "But there are worse things. Don't worry about it. It hasn't affected your work, and I don't expect it will. We're a team. You always put us first. No one cares who your father is, *Giancarlo*," he said with a ghost of a smile before he nudged Cain out of the way and left the room.

Axe snorted with laughter. "That's right, G. It's all good."

Wonderful. Just fucking wonderful. He shook his head. "Feel free to forget that name."

"Oh, no chance of that," Axe snickered.

"No chance whatsoever," Elias agreed.

"I'm going down to check on Harlow." Cain started out the door and then stopped. "I…just want to say…thanks. You all…" He wanted to tell them how much they all meant to him, but he'd never been good at sharing his thoughts or his emotions. He preferred to remain silent most of the time. It kept him from getting into trouble as a kid, and even more so as an adult.

"We rock. We know. You don't have to tell us." Finn grinned.

Elias hooted. "Yes, we are incredibly open-minded,

awesome individuals who you will buy very expensive steak dinners for at one of the finest restaurants in Miami when we get back."

"And I want really expensive wine to go with it," Finn added. "And maybe our girlfriends should come, too."

Cain had to laugh. "Deal. And…thanks." He left the room with a much lighter step than when he'd entered. A hundred-pound weight had lifted off each shoulder. He could breathe again. Cain had never been much on sharing, but that secret had cost him all his life. He was glad his friends knew.

He walked into the medical office and went around the corner. The bed was empty. He whirled around. "Hey, Doc. Where's Harlow?"

"She's fine. She went up on deck to get some fresh air. It's been a rough couple of weeks for her." He assessed Cain. "Go easy on her. If you have to tell her bad news, do it gently."

"Will do." Cain left the room and headed topside. His gut knotted. *She was fine.* Everyone who would have been a threat to her was dead or in custody. She was perfectly safe up on the deck by herself. Knowing that and believing it were two different things. Especially given the team's suspicions about Burn's involvement. He quickened his pace. The urge to get to her side and see for himself that she was okay rode him hard.

When he walked out the door to the deck, Harlow was nowhere to be seen. His heart rate ticked up a notch. He moved toward the bow and crossed to the other side of the ship. Harlow was close to the bow, leaning on the railing.

He let out a long breath and moved immediately to her side. "Are you alright?"

She turned to look at him, and there were tears running down her cheeks. "I'm fine." She started to wipe away the tears with the back of her hand. "Just a little over-emotional, as Perry would've said."

Cain gripped the railing with his left hand. He could not pull her in for a hug. He'd hugged her once before, and it had led to a kiss. A kiss that was burned into his memory. But he repeated to himself: *She was off-limits. Perry's sister.* Plus, he was a mafia Don's son. She did not need that in her life.

He cleared his throat. "Perry was wrong. I have never seen you over-emotional." He had no idea where that had come from, but it was true. He'd loved Perry like a brother, but the man had no clue when it came to women, including his sister. When Harlow smiled, it was like the sun had come out. Cain's gut relaxed.

"Thanks," she said. "I loved my brother, but he wasn't very good at dealing with anyone who was crying."

A small sob escaped her throat and Cain instantly folded her into his arms. He had no defense against Harlow's tears. She wrapped her arms around his waist and they stood like that for several minutes. Finally, when he felt her sobs subside, he released her. He felt the loss immediately.

"So"—Harlow wiped her face as she leaned against the rail again—"what brings you up here? I imagine you all must be busy dealing with…things."

"Partially, but it's not our ship, so we don't have regular duties, and Burns is keeping a close eye on what we're doing. We wouldn't be here at all if money hadn't been floating on the surface of the water. As to the dead guy and the rest of the Silverstone group, we're working on a way to deal with them."

"Will you get in trouble because I shot Hendrik?" She tucked her auburn hair behind her ear so it didn't blow across her face. Her blue eyes were watery and sad.

He cleared his throat again. He was having a hard time

focusing on the conversation. She looked so beautiful leaning there that it took his breath away. "Um, we'll have to see how that plays out. Don't worry about it." He raised his hand to touch her and then dropped it again. He wasn't sure he could make it through a second contact without kissing her. "You had no choice. It was him or you. Perry would be proud of how you handled the situation. Please don't beat yourself up about doing the right thing. You are allowed to protect yourself."

She bit her lip and nodded. The need to kiss away the sting she had to be feeling on her lips was almost crippling. He wasn't sure he'd offered her any solace but if he touched her now, he'd haul her into his arms and kiss her until they were both breathless and that wouldn't help things.

He cleared his throat. "Honestly, being on this team, answering directly to Admiral Bertrand, gives us a bit of leeway that otherwise might not be available to us. No one ties us up in too much red tape. Well, not usually." He still had a bad feeling about Burns. Something was going on there, and it wasn't good.

She nodded. "Makes sense. Why tie the hands of the men that are doing the hard work?" She released a shuddering breath and blinked hard. Another lone tear slipped over the edge of her lower lashes. "So, any news on the two other ships?"

Cain didn't want to lie to her, nor did he want to fight with her. He bit the inside of his cheek. "Yes, we know where they're going. We're tracking the containers now. We don't think they've hit port yet, but we'll find out shortly."

She straightened and squared her shoulders. "So when do we leave?" She had that look in her eye, and her jaw was set. This was going to turn ugly in no time.

He prevaricated, "I don't know. We need more details before any decisions are made."

"I'm coming with you," she stated.

Cain shook his head. "That's not my call. As I said, you won't stay here, but the admiral will have the final say on that one."

She narrowed her eyes but didn't say anything. However, he could read her mind and knew he'd just bought himself a momentary reprieve. The reality was that she was correct. She was the only one who could readily identify the Silverstone guys quickly. If they didn't take her, they'd have to find a list of Silverstone employees another way, and doing that without alerting Asher Foley seemed fucking unlikely. He was just too damn well connected.

She gave him another smile and then shivered a bit. She was still wearing the sweatpants but had taken off the hoodie and was wearing a medium blue T-shirt that hugged her curves. "I think I'll head back down. I'm getting hungry and a bit cold." She rubbed her arms. "I know it's the start of summer, but it's still a bit nippy out here. The sunshine is nice, though."

"The wind on the ocean is often cooler than it is on land. And, yeah, it's nice to be in the sun." He glanced at his watch. Was it really only one p.m.? "I can bring you some food if you like."

"That would be nice." Harlow left the rail and started walking back toward the door. Cain followed.

He opened the door for her. As she went to step through, the ship rolled and she started to fall. Cain instinctively wrapped his arms around her to steady her. She ended up crushed against his chest. He looked down into her eyes. Big mistake. The desire he'd been fighting since he'd first seen her was reflected in her big blue eyes. It made his heart lurch. He started to lower his head. He wanted to claim her lips.

"Maddox!"

Cain startled and gripped Harlow tighter. He whipped

his head around and saw Commander Burns striding down the corridor toward them. He let go of Harlow, careful to make sure she had her footing, and then stood at attention. "Sir."

"With me." The XO strode out to the deck, and Cain fell in behind. *Saved by the yell? It was better this way,* he tried to tell himself, but his body didn't agree. His cock was still semi-hard, and he was having a hard time getting the scent of Harlow's hair out of his mind. He wanted that woman like nothing else on earth. It was enough to drive him over the edge.

"Maddox, are you listening to me?"

"Yes, sir. As I said in my report, Ms. Moretti had no choice in the matter. The man, Hendrik, attacked her with a knife. She fired to prevent him from harming her. It was clearly a case of self-defense."

Commander Burns stopped and stared at him. The XO had made it clear he wasn't thrilled they were on board. He thought they were unnecessary. Now that a man was dead and another Silverstone person had gotten a chance to stab Harlow, he was looking for someone to blame. If he could plant the blame on the team, then it would be better for him. The thing was, he was the one who had stepped in and said his people would handle things. Nick had argued with him, but Burns was the XO of the *Jones.* Team RECON was just visiting.

"Why was Ms. Moretti left unattended?"

"You would have to ask whoever was posted at the door, sir. We were told that the crew of the *Jones* would keep her secure, sir." He tried to be as diplomatic as possible, but it wasn't his thing. He didn't play politics. It was something his father had always harassed Cain about, his indifference to the happenings around him, but he didn't want to bring this guy's wrath down on the team if he could avoid it. Plus, he was pissed that it was this man's fault Harlow had to shoot Hendrik in the first place.

"When are you leaving my ship?" the XO demanded.

Cain chose his words carefully. "We are verifying some information at the moment. As soon as we have confirmation, we'll be on our way."

"Verify it quickly then. I want your team gone asap. Take Ms. Moretti with you. Drop her on the mainland. She needs to be off the ship. Too much disruption. CGIS is flying in, and I do not want more distractions."

Message received. He wanted to control the narrative with the Coast Guard Investigative Service guys. If the RECON team was gone, then the XO could blame them. He couldn't do that if they were still on board and could be questioned.

"Dismissed." Burns turned and strode off to the bridge.

Cain turned and went back inside. Harlow wasn't there waiting for him, so he made his way down to the office. Harlow's lunch would have to wait. Nick and the others were around the table.

"We've got a problem," he said as he entered and closed the door behind him. "Burns, the XO, wants us off here asap."

"Yeah"—Nick nodded—"I know. I just got off the phone with Bertrand. Burns is already trying to blame us for what happened on board. He sent a preliminary report, which is all lies. So Bertrand wants a report from us now. The guys were just giving me details. I'm gonna need the same from you."

Cain nodded. "CGIS is on the way, and Burns wants us out of here before they arrive, including Harlow. He said to dump her on the mainland when we go."

"Shit. He wants us out of the way so he can throw us under the bus." Finn shook his head. "Fucking unfair."

"Yeah," Axe agreed. "And because he's an XO and we're nowhere close to that rank, it's not going to go well for us."

"Bertrand will have our backs," Elias stated.

"Agreed." Nick opened the laptop in front of him. "But he's going to need our reports to back up his claims. Apparently, Burns had a lot of friends in D.C. Bertrand is more worried than he's letting on."

"Shit," Cain growled.

Nick continued. "Bertrand has a call scheduled with the head of the Belize military. Hopefully, they'll work with us to get the container before it's offloaded and Foley manages to hide it again."

Cain said nothing. He knew the money was headed for a bank, and once it was there, it would be gone for good. Transferred into a million accounts across the world. Then Perry and the rest of the team would have died in vain. No matter what happened, he was going to make sure Roman Vance paid.

CHAPTER ELEVEN

Harlow sat up and swung her legs over the side of the bed. She was starving, and Cain hadn't shown up yet with any lunch. It was after two p.m. She slid off the bed and went around the corner. Doc was sitting at his desk but turned to face her after hearing her approach.

"I'm starving," she said with a smile. "Can I get you anything from the mess hall?"

"No, I'm good, thanks, and you can't get me anything anyway. You aren't a crew member so I'm not supposed to let you wander around the ship."

She frowned. "But you let me up on deck a while ago."

Doc grimaced. "Yes, and I got my knuckles soundly smacked for it. I'm afraid you have to stay in here. I will be happy to get you some lunch."

She sighed but gave Doc a smile. It wasn't fair to be angry at him. "That would be great, thanks."

He got up and left the room. Harlow looked over at his computer, but it was locked. She didn't want to get the EMT in any more trouble than he already was, but she was so tempted to look for his password so she could get online. Sitting on the bed doing nothing was brutal.

She paced around the room. It was the damn XO guy who had yelled at Cain. She had watched their discussion from just inside the doorway. Burns had been pissed and not remotely trying to hide it. Cain, on the other hand, had been as cool as a cucumber.

He looked so damn fine in his uniform, and she loved his undercut. One day, she was going to see him with his hair down. Her breasts tingled just thinking about it. She wanted Cain so bad she could taste it. She'd been sure he was going to kiss her when she'd fallen into him earlier. Then Burns had shown up and ruined the moment. *Dammit!* Harlow had been fantasizing about Cain for so long it was second nature, but today she knew he'd been close to kissing her.

She went over and sat back down on the bed. He had a hang-up that she was Perry's little sister, or at least that's what he said. Could it be more? Maybe. But she knew for sure that he liked her. His desire had been reflected in his eyes.

On the other hand, it made more sense to stay the hell away from Cain at the moment. He was more likely to leave her behind out of loyalty to her dead brother. Nick, on the other hand, would be logical. She would appeal to him. They needed her to identify more of Silverstone's men.

But more importantly, they needed her to be safe. They could send her pictures of Vance's men, and she could identify them that way. She was the only thing they had to link Vance to the money. They needed her, and now her family, to be kept secure or their case against her brother's killer would go away.

She knew she should stay behind somewhere they could protect her. It was logical, but she just couldn't bring herself to accept it. She'd worked long and hard to get the goods on Vance. Yes, she'd screwed up and ended up in the container, but she'd gotten herself out again. Being left behind would be devastating.

She thought about her parents, and guilt washed over her. After everything they'd been through, she was dragging them through even more shit. It really was her fault. She just couldn't let it go. But Perry didn't deserve to die, and she just couldn't make peace with it. She needed closure and getting Vance would do that for her. It was selfish, but it was true.

It was also true that she was...happy for the first time in a long time. Being on the trail of Vance and his men had made her feel like she was actually accomplishing something. Maybe happy wasn't the right word. Maybe productive was better. She just finally felt like she was doing something worthwhile. She hated that it was costing her family though. That made her heart hurt.

If she were being totally honest, she didn't want to lose touch with Cain again either. He was probably right to avoid her. They weren't a good match. She was too impulsive, and he was too controlled. He would drive her nuts all the time, but she'd sure like an opportunity to take him to bed and get that itch out of her system. He was the road not taken, and she really wanted to go down that path. She let out a long sigh.

"Penny for your thoughts," Cain drawled as he leaned against the wall across from her bed.

Her head shot up. She'd been so deep in thought she didn't hear him come in. Heat crept up her neck and into her cheeks. She wasn't about to tell him she was thinking about bedding him. His ego was large enough. "I...errr...I was thinking about Perry and my folks. I'm dragging Mom and Dad through the awful pain of losing Perry all over again. Pretty selfish of me."

Cain pushed away the wall and came over to the bed. "It's done now. We're here. Don't second guess yourself. You did what you had to do for you. There's nothing wrong with that. Just… Uh, in case there is collateral damage, Harlow"—his voice went soft—"just be careful from now on, okay? I worry about you."

Her gaze locked with his, making her pulse skyrocket. She licked her lips. "Uh, what about my lunch?"

"I met Doc on the way up. He's bringing it. Sorry, I got caught up in something."

"Good news? You seem happier somehow. More relaxed."

He smiled lazily. "In a manner of speaking. How about you? How are you feeling?"

She felt the weight of his stare as though it was the weight of his body on hers. *Snap out of it, Harlow.* Didn't matter how much she wished it; he'd resist. He was scrutinizing her and she felt as though he could see into her soul. "I'm…okay," she said in a quiet voice.

But it wasn't really true, she realized suddenly. She wasn't okay. She wanted the whole mess to be over, to be finished. For the first time since the beginning of her investigation, she wanted to be done with this phase of her life so she could go back to cleaning teeth and hanging out with friends. Homesickness washed over her. Her eyes prickled.

"Harlow"—Cain's voice broke into her thoughts—"you're going to be fine. I promise."

She nodded and brushed a tear away with the back of her hand. She usually wasn't much of a crier. It had to be the exhaustion. She tried to smile.

Cain crossed his arms over his chest. The pulse in his jaw was jumping. What had set him off this time? She blinked. "Are you okay?" She wiped the other cheek with the back of her hand again.

The pulse in his jaw ticked faster.

What was wrong with him?

His green eyes glittered and took in her every move.

She reached out and touched his arm.

"Fuck it," he mumbled as he reached down and put a hand behind her neck.

He tilted her head and claimed her lips in a fierce kiss that rocked her to the core. When she opened her mouth, Cain's tongue swept in, tasting and dancing with hers. She put her hands on his chest and felt his muscles contract under her touch. She deepened the kiss. She'd wanted this for so long. Her breasts were tingling, and she had just started to slide her arms around his neck when she heard the familiar crash of the food cart.

Cain jumped away and crossed his arms over his chest again. Harlow's head reeled. *Did that just happen?* One minute she was kissing the man of her fantasies, and the next he was halfway across the room looking bored.

"I've got lunch," Doc said as he rounded the corner. His eyes narrowed at her appearance, and she felt the heat in her cheeks once more. Then Doc glanced at Cain, who returned his look calmly.

How the fuck could he kiss her like that and be so calm? She was all kinds of wonky. "Um, great," she croaked. "What is it this time?"

Doc stopped the cart beside her bed. "Voila!" He lifted the cover off the dish. "A cheeseburger and fries."

"Doc, I love you!" She clapped her hands. Her stomach growled right on cue.

"I aim to please." He grinned at her as he moved the food to the tray that went across her bed. "And for dessert, everybody's favorite, chocolate lava cake."

"This is awesome, Doc. Keep feeding me like this, and I may never leave."

Doc laughed. "Glad to have the company. Anyway, enjoy. I'll be back in a bit to check on you." He shot Cain another glance as he rounded the corner.

"Looks good," Cain said.

"You want to join me?" she offered.

Way more than a bite of her cheeseburger was on the menu, and Cain knew it. His eyes darkened, and the pulse in his jaw started to jump.

"That will have to wait," Nick said as he came around the corner. "Cain, I need you to review everything I wrote before I send it off to Bertrand. He agreed with our proposal on offloading the prisoners, and that's going to happen later today. I just want to make it's sure ship-shape before I send the official report."

Cain frowned but nodded. "I'll go do it now." He turned and left the room without a backward glance.

Harlow's heart thumped hard. Cain's kiss had been extraordinary. More than she'd imagined. More than she'd bargained for, to be truthful.

"Harlow," Nick said.

She turned to focus on him. "Do you mind if I eat while we talk? I'm starving."

"No problem, but I want a fry."

"Deal." She smiled at him and handed him a fry as he sat down on the stool and rolled it closer. "So why did you want Cain out of the way? What do you need to tell me?" When Nick cocked his head, Harlow laughed. "I'm not just another pretty face, you know."

"I see that." Nick smiled and stole another fry. "So, I spoke with Bertrand. He agrees that you need protection."

"Okay," she mumbled through a mouthful of cheese-burger. This wasn't news to her.

"The thing is, we also need you with us to identify Vance's people. We only have a vague idea of who some of these people are. You have followed him for months. You have the knowledge. Bertrand and I talked about pictures and video, and that would have worked if the ships hadn't docked yet, but they have. We cannot capture every resident's picture and run it by you. You need to be there."

She swallowed. "I already told you guys I'm seeing this through. I'm game. Let's do this."

"Harlow…" Nick's tone changed. "There's something I need to tell you first." He put a hand on her arm.

She stopped chewing. The burger sat heavy in her stomach. "What?" came out as barely a whisper.

"Your folks are fine, but Vance already made a run at them. We had a team there and managed to get them out in time, but they are pretty shaken up. I think you need to speak to them, and you all need to decide together how you want to proceed."

"Are you fucking crazy?" Cain demanded as he stormed around the corner. "She needs to be in protective custody just like her parents. There is no option here. She is *not* coming with us. No fucking way. I will *not* tell her parents I got another one of their children killed. I won't do it."

"Chief Petty Officer Maddox!" Nick glared at him. "You're supposed to be reviewing files."

"What? You think I'm an idiot? I figured you were up to something. She's not coming with us, Tag. It's too fucking dangerous."

Nick stood up. "It's not up to you, Cain. It's up to Harlow and her folks. Stand down!"

"I will not stand down. There is no fucking way I'll allow her to be put in any more danger than she's already in. Just no."

"It's not your call, Maddox." The clear warning made Nick's voice gruff and forbidding.

"No, it's mine." Harlow's voice was calm, which was odd because her insides were a mess. She was lost and untethered from reality, at least that's what she felt like.

Cain was livid. It was in every line of his body, but it

wasn't because he cared about her. It was because he didn't want to be accountable for her death. He didn't want to be the one to break the news to her parents. When he'd told her not to pursue finding out about Perry's death, she'd thought it was because he was genuinely worried about her. The phone calls they'd shared, the sorrow over Perry, she'd thought they'd connected on a deeper level. Even though it had annoyed her that Cain wouldn't help her, the fact that he cared about her had also kept her going on some very long nights.

All this time, she'd thought he cared about her. Like she cared about him. Lust was one thing, but they had a connection. Or so she thought. Turns out lust was just lust. Cain obviously didn't want the responsibility for her. Well, he wouldn't have it.

"I'll speak with my parents and let you know my decision. Please leave. I would like to finish my lunch in peace."

"Harlow," Cain ground out. "You—"

"Stop," Nick said and put his hand on Cain's chest. "That's an order. Get your ass back to the conference room and read the files."

Cain opened his mouth again, but Nick held his ground. Cain swore, then turned on his heel and strode out.

Nick shook his head. "Sorry about that." He pulled out the satellite phone and put it on the tray next to her lunch. "Here's the number where you can reach your folks." He laid a piece of paper beside it. "Good luck." He smiled and then left the room.

Harlow stared down at her lunch. She'd lost her appetite, but Doc had told her earlier she should make sure she kept eating full meals for a while yet. And eating was one way she could hold off calling her parents. She didn't know what to say to them. She'd put them through hell because she'd only been thinking about herself, and now their lives were in danger. Her eyes misted over, and she sniffed. She'd never get through the call if she started crying now.

She finally pushed the empty tray away and stood up. She needed to be on her feet for this call. Grabbing the phone, she headed up to the deck. Fuck Burns. She needed to be outside for this.

Five minutes later, she was standing on deck. The wind had picked up and she shivered. The smell of the salt was stronger now and hit her in the back of the throat. The sounds of the waves hitting the hull over and over again calmed her raw nerves. She dialed the number. When a male voice on the other end answered, she explained who she was. A minute later, her mother's voice was on the line.

"Mom? Are you okay?" Just hearing her mother's cheery tone made the pent-up anxiety release its grip on her throat and breathing became a bit easier.

"Oh, Harlow, honey. We're fine. How are you doing?"

"I'm okay, Mom."

"Let me put you on speaker."

There were some muffled sounds, and then her father's voice came over the line. "Harlow, sweetheart, are you okay?" His voice was gruff.

Her eyes immediately filled with tears. She gulped hard. "Yes, Dad, I'm fine." She took a breath. "I'm so sorry I caused all this. I didn't mean to put you and Mom through anything else. You've had to deal with enough sh—crap."

"Oh, honey," her mother said. "We're okay. These men are taking good care of us. We just had a bit of a fright, that's all. The nice man said that you had uncovered some… What did he call them, Howard?"

"Bad actors."

"Yes, some bad actors, and you are instrumental in bringing them to justice."

Harlow snorted. "I don't know about that, but I did find out some stuff."

"Is this about Perry? Did you find out what happened?" her father asked.

"Yes, Dad. This is about Perry. I found out what happened. I found out who killed him, Dad." Her chin trembled, and she stifled a sob.

"Oh, honey." Her father's voice cracked, and he sobbed right along with her.

She finally got herself under control again and said, "I'm sorry I went to Iraq and got you involved in this mess, but I'm not sorry I found out who killed Perry. I just needed to know. For me. I know now how selfish it was, and I hope you two will forgive me."

"There is nothing to forgive, honey," her mother said. "You did what you thought was right. You did right by your brother. We can't fault you for that."

"Your mother is right. It's us who owes you an apology. We should have been more supportive. I just… I couldn't take the thought of losing you, too, Little Bit."

She almost broke down again when her father used her childhood nickname. "Still, now, you both are in danger. I should have been more careful."

Her father laughed. "Well, yeah, but, honey, careful is just not your style."

Ain't that the truth?

Her father continued. "Look, they're telling us that you can still help out, but it will be dangerous. What's going on?"

She took a deep breath and explained the situation in broad strokes. She didn't want to say anything too detailed in case someone was listening in. "So they told me to talk to you so we can make the decision together."

"Honey," her mother said, "I want you here safe with us,

but I know you would never forgive yourself if you don't see this through."

"That's right, Little Bit. We want you safe, but you have to do this for yourself and your brother. We know that. Please... Just be as safe as possible. We're so proud of you, honey." Her father's voice broke again.

"I love you, Mom. I love you, Dad."

"We love you too, honey," said her mother.

Harlow clicked off the call and started wiping tears off her cheeks.

"Here." A handkerchief appeared over her shoulder.

She turned to find Cain right behind her. "Thanks." She wiped her tears, but he only grunted in response.

"I know you aren't happy that I'm going, but you know you need my help on this. You don't want to lose Vance any more than I do."

He stood there glaring at her, arms crossed, jaw working.

She handed back the handkerchief. *Who carried one of those anymore?* "So suck it up, buttercup," she said with a grin. Then she passed him by and, without a backward glance, went back inside and down to the medical bay. Since Perry died, Harlow could count on one hand how many times she felt okay. But now, she felt a lightness she hadn't felt in a very long time. She had her parents' blessing. She was free to really hunt Vance this time, and she could not wait.

CHAPTER TWELVE

The helicopter came down with a soft bump. In his peripheral vision, Cain registered Harlow waking up. He was still livid that she was with them. She needed to be somewhere safe. On the other hand, he wouldn't be able to fully focus if he didn't know she was safe, and the only place he knew for sure she was well protected was by his side. *Goddammit.*

She pulled her backpack from under the seat and then straightened. She ran her hands over her face as if to wake herself up.

Cain stepped out of the helicopter and then reached back and grabbed Harlow around the waist, plucking her up and placing her on the ground. "Keep up," he growled and walked ahead.

"A please would be nice." Harlow's voice held a hint of pissed off.

She was right. It didn't hurt to be polite, regardless of how fucked up the situation was. He stopped, pivoted, and added, "Please."

Her smirk was tight. *Fuck it*. He strode away from her.

"Don't worry. He isn't always an asshole. He'll get over it," Axe said. "But he is right about keeping up. You're gonna have to be able to haul ass if we tell you."

Good, at least Axe was reinforcing his directions. Cain had his jaw clamped together so hard it ached. He needed to get his head in the game, not listen to Axe and Harlow. It was twilight and the sun was setting fast. There were a few clouds around but nothing significant. He was thankful for that. The idea of getting rained on did not appeal. The sound of the insects buzzing around was momentarily drowned out by an incoming airplane. He strode faster across the tarmac and caught up to Nick. "Did we hear anything yet?"

"Bertrand said the Belize military would take us to the container. That's all I know." He looked up and saw a bunch of vehicles approaching. "This looks like our ride now."

The military trucks pulled up and stopped. A tall, bald man with a weathered face emerged. "Major Artan Cal," the man said in a strong Spanish accent as he walked toward them, hand outstretched.

"Master Chief Nick Taggert." Nick shook his hand and introduced the rest of the team. He ignored Harlow completely, which made Cain happy. No need to spread her name around even if this guy was a friendly.

The major spent the next few minutes filling them in.

"When are we going?" Cain asked.

"As soon as it's dark," Cal responded. "We're not waiting until late. No point. They won't be moving the money at night. It's supposed to go to a bank in Chetumal the day after tomorrow. I have people watching it, so we will have good intel before we enter."

"Sounds good." Nick glanced at his watch and then looked at the sky. "It's almost dark now. Do you want to go over the layout so we're ready to roll?"

The major nodded. He walked over to the truck he'd gotten out of and grabbed a map and a file. He carried them to the front and rolled it out on the hood. The guys gathered around. Cain made sure Harlow was always in his peripheral vision. She was standing just off to his left.

"The container is in this area. They have camouflaged it by covering it with brush, but there are a couple of roads leading right up to it. We're good to go in." He opened the file and pulled out pictures. "I have had my guys on it since this morning. It looks like there are just four guys watching it. There are two more in town, hassling the banker to work faster."

They spent the next twenty minutes going over details that Cain only half listened to. It was a simple entry, if what Cal said was true. Cain's gut was telling him something was off. He glanced over at Harlow. Their eyes locked. She didn't like it either. When she gave a slight shake of her head, he lifted his chin. It wasn't just bad military strategy, there was a feeling of negative energy in the air that lit Cain's nerve endings. Cain wasn't usually a believer in all that new age stuff but he'd learned to trust his instincts. Apparently, so had Harlow.

"So, we go in about twenty minutes. If you need to use the facilities or get some water"—the major pointed toward the building behind them—"help yourself."

"Thanks," Nick said and stepped away from the truck. They went back and stood next to the Coast Guard helicopter they'd come in on.

"I don't like it," Cain said in a hushed tone. "My gut says it's off."

Nick said, "Agreed."

Harlow came to stand beside Cain. "There's no way in hell Vance would only have a half dozen guys on this after losing a container. He sent five to go with the one to Mexico, and he was willing to kill most of them. There's just no way he wouldn't send more with the money he is keeping, especially since the other container went overboard."

"Good point." Nick gave her an assessing look. "Where did you learn about military strategy?"

"Perry spent hours reading about it and then would make me sit and listen when we were kids. Even as teenagers he would tell me all kinds of stories about what he read. Then once he joined the military, he made me learn survival skills and how to shoot a gun."

Nick nodded approvingly. "Smart man, your brother."

Cain grunted. "Back to the point. The whole thing feels like a setup, but the thing is, I don't think it's Cal. He seems legit."

Axe cleared his throat. "That was my read as well. I think Cal is working with the information he has and giving it to us straight. I just don't think he's operating on the right intel."

Elias said, "So what do we do about it?"

"We keep our eyes open and do our best to be on top of whatever situation arises," Cain stated.

Nick gestured for the team to make a tighter circle around him. When they all stepped in, heads bowed, he said, "Stay loose and ready. Cain, you are responsible for Harlow. I want her in your sights at all times."

Cain ground his teeth. He'd already decided that was his end goal, but still wasn't confident that was the best idea. He gave Nick a thumb's up.

After Nick finished giving out orders, they donned their tactical gear, including Harlow. They had vests, belts, and helmets with lights. Three of them had night-vision goggles. Cain chose to go without the night goggles and rely on his instincts instead. They had saved him more times than he could count. But there was something else that was bothering him and so he went over to Nick. "Look, I don't know that me looking after Harlow is a good idea."

"Cain"—Nick finished checking his handgun and holstered it—"you and I both know you aren't going to let her out of your sight regardless. If I assign her to you, at least you'll be doing your damn job. This isn't an ideal situation, and your attention is already divided between what's going on and her. You need to focus and get through this. We can argue about it later."

Cain had to concede that Nick had a point. His attention *was* divided, and it annoyed the shit out of him. "Fine," he agreed against his better judgment and strode over to Harlow who was leaning on the helo.

He spoke in soft tones so the others wouldn't hear. "I'm not happy about anything right now, especially being assigned to protect you. But it's my job, so I need you to listen to me and follow every direction to a tee. None of us like this setup, and I have to be alert to help my team. Do. Not. Do. Anything. Stupid."

"Huh! Axe said you'd get over being an asshole. Guess he was wrong." She glared at him.

Good. Having her believe he was scum was preferable to her coming on to him when he seemed to be weak and defenseless against her charms. Still, the label stung. "I am not an asshole. I'm a highly trained Coast Guard operative and so I'll repeat; don't do anything stupid."

She opened her mouth to argue when Major Cal whistled the team over to him. "Fine," she said through clenched teeth.

They walked across the tarmac and got into the two vehicles behind Major Cal's. Nick and Cain were in the first one with Harlow and the others in the one behind. Twenty minutes later, they stopped on a dirt track. The radio crackled to life. "We go on foot from here. The other team is walking in from the other side."

Everyone piled out, and Cain stood next to Harlow. "Stay close." It was dark, but the moon provided enough light to see down the dirt track. It was a road of sorts but not something that was heavily traveled. The jungle was in a battle to reclaim the space and it seemed like it was winning.

They moved in silence. To her credit, Harlow stayed close. They walked for about ten minutes and then came to a stop. The container was just ahead around a bend. The men broke off and headed into the trees. Cain nodded to Harlow and pointed for her to follow. After another five minutes of walking, Cain squatted down and motioned for Harlow to do the same. He could just make out the container through the trees. The buzz of insects was more intense now. The smell of the jungle filled his nose. His heart rate ticked up just a bit. *Calm down*. He inhaled for four seconds and held his breath, then released the air through pursed lips. Like a sniper holding his breath just as he squeezed the trigger. Worked like a charm.

Calm again, he glanced over at Harlow and then leaned in close. "Make sure you stay low. If shooting starts, hit the ground." Okay, maybe the breathing trick wasn't so successful. His heart still thudded against his ribs. Normally, an operation like this wouldn't bother him in the slightest, but with Harlow, he felt like he was standing out in the open with no tactical gear and a target on his chest.

"I will." She laid a hand on his arm. "Cain, I can take care of myself. Concentrate on helping the team. I'll stay out of the way."

He gave her a nod and studied the view in front of him. It was all well and good for her to say, but he was operating with one hand tied behind his back.

Cain's teammates were crouched down in line with him, spread out over about fifty feet with ten feet between them. Axe was on the near end next to the road and Nick was on the far end. Cain and Harlow were in the middle behind the container. Cal's team was grouped off to the left, by Axe and his second team was coming in towards the shipping container from the front. The major had given them each a radio, but Cain used his earbud with his RECON teammates instead. "Where the fuck are the guards?"

Elias's voice sounded in his ear. "I was about to ask the same question."

"This is all wrong," Nick responded. He must have picked up the radio because Cain heard him ask Cal where the men guarding the container were.

"My people say they are all around front."

"How many?" Nick asked.

"Four," was the response.

"I think—"

The sound of gunfire filled the air. Cain shoved Harlow down so she was flat on the forest floor as he swung his gun up. "Stay down," he hissed as he scanned the area.

"Major." Nick's voice came across the radio. "What the hell is going on?"

"It's okay. My men have taken down the guards. You can come out."

Cain hit his earbud. "I don't like this."

"This is some FUBAR shit right here," Axe seconded.

Major Cal and his squad stood up and were headed toward the container. Cain glanced over at Harlow. She was up on her feet now, squatting beside him. "Should we go?" she asked.

Cain shook his head. "This just isn't right."

When Nick stood up, so did Axe and Elias next to him. Harlow straightened as well.

Cain reached over to grab her and yelled, "No!" But it was too late. The explosion blew her backward a good ten feet. Cain was flung backward as well, his ears ringing. It took him a moment, but he got to his hands and knees and crawled over to Harlow, covering her body with his as debris fell from the sky.

"Harlow!" he yelled. "Harlow!" Her eyelids fluttered, but she didn't open them. *Goddammit.* His chest hurt. He couldn't seem to breathe. *Please don't let her be dead.*

Nick and the rest of the team were immediately beside them. Burning money fell from the sky. Cain brushed a burning ten-dollar bill off his leg.

"Cal, what the fuck just happened?" Nick roared.

There was a long pause. "They rigged the container to blow when my man opened the door. We've called for medical. Two of my men are seriously injured. Are your men okay?"

Nick looked down at Harlow. "Is she okay, Cain?"

Cain's heart had stopped beating the moment Harlow had stood up. He had known deep in his heart it was wrong. When he saw her thrown backward, he just stopped breathing.

"Harlow," Cain growled, "open your eyes." She couldn't be hurt. She just couldn't be dead. *Dear God, do not let her be dead.* "Harlow, honey please open your eyes," Cain pleaded.

Her eyelids flickered, and this time they opened. "Cain," she murmured. "What happened?"

"Are you okay? Does anything hurt?"

She blinked. "My head hurts a little, but I'm okay."

Cain rolled off Harlow and squatted next to her. He checked her over, but nothing seemed broken. He helped her to her feet slowly.

"Cal, my people are fine," Nick said into the radio.

"Understood."

Sirens shattered the quiet and lights strobed as the men stamped out the burning money. Cain didn't want to take his eyes off Harlow, but Axe stepped up. "Why don't I take her over to the ambulance and get her checked out?"

"I'll take her," Cain said and grabbed her arm.

"Cain, I need you here," Nick said. "You're our resident explosives expert. Axe can take her."

Cain wanted to argue, but he understood. He had to put the team first. Harlow had to come second in this case.

"Don't worry, man," Axe said. "I've got her. I won't leave her side."

Cain nodded once and watched them walk out of the woods until they were gone from view.

Nick touched his shoulder. "Take a minute."

"What?" Cain snarled.

"Cain, you need to take a minute and just breathe. I get it. We all do. But you need to get yourself together. Take a minute. Then meet me over at the container." He disappeared in the opposite direction through the trees.

Cain stood there for a second, but then bent double, resting his hands on his knees. He thought he might throw up. Jesus Christ, he'd almost died, watching her get blown up. He swallowed hard. He couldn't do that again. Not ever. He wouldn't recover. He took a few deep breaths and straightened. His hands trembled with the residual adrenaline powering through his body, and his knees were wobbly.

Nick was right. He had to focus. Cain didn't know how Nick or Axe or Finn had survived this. It was just too fucking much to have the woman he…cared about next to him in battle. It was just all kinds of wrong. He let out a long breath and moved out of the trees. He would have to talk to Nick. He could not go through something like that ever again.

He moved over to what was left of the metal shipping container. The doors had been blown off, and part of the roof was peeled back, making the box look like an opening to hell. The acrid smell of scorched paper filled his senses. His ears were still ringing slightly but the crackle of a nearby fire poked at his senses, and he turned to look. Cal's men were stamping out a small fire in some grass. Cain stepped closer to the destroyed shipping container. It looked like there might have been three pallets but it was hard to tell. There were a few smoldering piles of money but not enough to really identify how much had been in the container.

Nick came to a stop next to him and Cain said, "This was a setup." He kept his voice low since Cal's men were all around the place. "That's not money burning in there, or at least not all of it is money."

"Agreed." Nick glanced around. "I don't think Cal and his men were in on it."

"No, it was a total shock to him. The question is…was it Vance and his people or someone else?"

Nick whipped around and looked at him. "What? Who else?" Then realization dawned on his face. "Shit."

"Yeah," Cain ground out.

He ventured closer to the still smoldering container, the heat of the explosion warming his face. The door mechanism had been rigged to blow as soon as the guy grabbed the door. He squatted down and looked at part of the wall. Then he stood and went farther into the container. He stared at the burn marks and shook his head.

He came back out and stood next to Nick. "This wasn't the work of Vance's people. Definitely not the same group that tried to sink the *Oceanus Explorer* a while back. Whoever rigged this really knew their shit. This was done by ex-military or a highly trained bombmaker."

Nick nodded. "Good to know."

Cain clamped his jaw together. His gut tightened. He was pretty sure he knew who set this up. Not the bomb maker but who was in charge and it was his worst fucking nightmare in more ways than one. "So where do we go from here?"

"The Caymans. It's our last shot."

"You think we still have a chance?"

Nick shrugged. "Let's hope."

"You think he'll be there in person?" Cain asked.

"Yeah. Vance only has one container left. He's gonna want to be there in person to make sure it all goes his way. And I want to be there to make sure it doesn't."

"Me, too. We'll get the fucker one way or another."

Nick nodded his agreement. "Now back to business. Get everyone together, and I'll tell Major Cal we're leaving. There's nothing more we can do here."

Cain nodded. "Nick, I can't be around Harlow." There. He'd said it.

Nick studied him for a minute. "It's hard to see someone you…care about…in trouble."

"No. For me, it's impossible. I can't function. I've…lost too many people. Having her close…overloads my system. I shut down. I can't function as part of the team if I shut down. I do not want to leave any of you hanging. That would…kill me. Eat me up." He looked around the clearing. "You all are my family—my chosen family. I don't want to do anything to jeopardize that."

"Understood. I'll have one of the others stay with her if it's possible."

Relief flooded him, along with another emotion he refused to name. He bowed his head. He needed to rein himself in, get his emotions back under control. When he was a child and his father did not come to see one of his games or to a school event, he would tell himself to become like a snowman. Cold inside and out. As he got older, he thought of it as becoming Mr. Freeze. If he frosted out his heart, then no one could hurt him.

Perry and the team's deaths had hit him hard, and he retreated back into his cold world. It was how he survived, but Nick and Elias and the others had brought him out of it again. Being part of this team had allowed him to deal with the loss of his old team. Allowed him to become human again, but he was still teetering on the edge. He'd just gotten his feet under him solidly, and then Harlow had turned up.

He started walking back to the others. Harlow could push him over that edge. It was better if he built a fucking igloo around himself than let her back in. He just didn't have the strength to lose anyone else.

"What's it look like?" Elias asked as he arrived at the group. They were all there, Harlow included. She looked pale, but she was on her feet so she must be okay. His gut loosened a little. He would normally ask, but it was just better for him if he didn't. *Mr. Freeze.* "Professional. Clean."

"You think it was one of Vance's guys?" Axe asked.

Cain shrugged. "Possibly." He didn't elaborate, and Nick didn't add anything either, which he appreciated.

"Now what?" Finn asked.

"The Caymans," Nick replied. "I already told the major we're leaving. He's declaring this a victory. Vance doesn't get his money, and they took down a few of his guys. He's happy to have us go so he can take credit. One of his men will take us back to the helicopter. I'll call Bertrand once we're in flight and figure out how we approach the last container."

A young soldier came to stand beside the group. Nick nodded to him and pointed to the vehicle. The guy nodded and went around to the driver's side.

"Let's roll," Nick said to the rest of the team.

They all climbed into one truck. Cain made sure to grab shotgun. The more distance between him and Harlow, the better. Now it was time to focus on Vance. That piece of scum had to go, and Cain was looking forward to being the man who made it happen.

CHAPTER THIRTEEN

Harlow's brain seemed to be slamming against her skull, but she refused to give in to the pain. She had to keep up with this team. If she held them back from getting Vance, she'd never forgive herself. She let a breath out slowly. The helicopter ride to Grand Cayman had almost done her in. All that noise was agonizing. She had taken a couple of ibuprofen she had in her backpack, but she needed more. At least now they were on the way to some hotel. She could have a shower and maybe a nap.

She glanced at Cain in the driver's seat of the SUV they'd rented. Not once had he asked her how she was doing. Hell, he hadn't even glanced in her direction. He was ghosting her, and they weren't even online. It wasn't her fault she stood up. Nick and the others had already gotten to their feet, so it seemed okay. Admittedly, he'd told her to do exactly as he said, and she hadn't waited, but how was she to know the damn container would blow up?

"You okay?"

She opened her eyes to find Nick staring at her. He was

sitting beside her in the second row. "Um, just a bit of a headache."

"That might last a while. Are you sure you want to continue with us? I can have some guardsmen take you back to your parents."

He spoke in a quiet voice, which she greatly appreciated. She whispered back, "But then I can't help you, and now that you're down to one container, you need all the help you can get."

Nick acknowledged her words with a nod. "But it's not worth your life. Do you understand that? There is nothing that's happening here that is worth losing a life over. We don't get Vance today, there's always tomorrow. We'll get there. It's truly not worth dying over."

She nodded. "I know, but I have to do this."

"Okay, but if you change your mind, let me know."

They pulled up to the hotel, and Cain went in to get them all checked in. The rest of them waited for Cain to come out with the room keys.

"Where do we start looking for Vance?" she asked Nick as she leaned against the SUV.

"Damn good question. Once we get in and get settled, we're gonna have to form a game plan."

"If I can offer a suggestion…" she said as the others gathered around her. "If we don't know where Vance and his people are, then we should start with what we do know."

"Which is?" Elias asked.

"The bank where they're going to deposit the money." Cain's voice came from behind the group.

She nodded and then regretted it. Less nodding was better with her aching head. "He's right. We have to find the bank and then the banker. There's gotta be someone we can ask who would know which banker is crooked."

Nick cocked his head. "I like the way you're thinking." He paused for a minute. "I might be able to make a call. Let's get in and get sorted. Then we'll work the problem some more."

They all started moving at once, gathering their gear. Harlow stood there. She was still wearing the sweats and a hoodie she was given on the ship. She'd given back the borrowed tactical gear. A new wardrobe was in order for sure. The motel was built in a U shape with two floors and a walkway around the outside. The building was painted a faded turquoise with white trim around the windows and doors.

She followed the guys up the stairs to the second level. Cain stopped a few doors down and pointed to the door in front of him. "One." Then he pointed to the next two doors. "Two. Three."

Nick grabbed the key from Cain. "You and I will be in here. Harlow, you're in the next one. You three in the last. Have them bring up a rollaway bed for one of you."

"Already done," Cain said.

"Good. Harlow, we'll be on either side of you, so if you need anything, just yell. We'll keep an eye on you so you'll be safe. Go in and rest. When you get up, we'll take you shopping. I would imagine you would like some decent clothes."

She gave Nick a quick smile. "Yeah, that would be nice."

Cain offered her the key. She met his gaze, but it was cold. His eyes were flat. They sparkled when he was happy and glittered in a different way when he was angry. She'd never seen them flat before. She shivered as she opened her door and entered the room.

It was much nicer than she anticipated. There were two queen beds with floral spreads in bold colors. The walls were off-white, and the furniture was all dark wood. The floor was a pale tile.

She went into the bathroom and used the facilities, then

came out and lay down on the bed. The EMT had told her to wake up every couple of hours to make sure she was fine. If she became lightheaded or started puking, she needed to go to the hospital. So far, so good. She was tired, and her head hurt, but she was alive and still in the game. That's all she could ask for at the moment.

———

Harlow opened her eyes and sniffed. Pizza. No doubt. She glanced at her watch. It was after dinner time, and she was ravenous. She was also desperate for a shower. She got slowly to her feet in case she felt dizzy, but all seemed good. Her headache had receded to a light, dull thumping. Almost an echo of what it was.

She went over and knocked on the inside door. Axe opened it with a grin. "I told you that she'd wake up from the smell. No one can sleep through pizza."

Harlow smiled and walked into the other room. The guys were lounging in the chairs and on the beds, eating pizza. She immediately looked for Cain. He was sitting on top of the desk with his slice. When he looked up, their gazes locked for a moment, but he quickly looked away.

So much for him being in a better mood. *Whatever*. Life was too short. She was going to do this and then be on her way and never have to see Cain Maddox again. Determined to ignore Cain, she grabbed a slice of pizza and said, "So, what's the plan?"

Nick laughed. "Straight to the point. I like it. We were just discussing it. I've already made some calls. We have to wait and see what turns up. Hopefully, we can figure out which bank and then which banker. In the meantime, I think it's time to get you some clothes. Once you've eaten, we can go get you some new things to wear."

"That sounds great, thanks." She took a large bite of pizza.

A half hour later, Nick, Cain, and Harlow left the hotel. She had the immediate impression that Cain didn't want to be there. He said something she missed.

"Axe is making some calls to his network of people to see if he can find anything out about Vance that might help us, and Elias is getting us the toiletries and foodstuffs we need."

Cain said nothing but his lips were in a thin line.

Nick turned toward her from the passenger seat. "There's a high-end shopping mall not far from here."

"Sure." High-end shopping mall? Shit. Harlow had pretty much drained her savings while she was looking for her brother's killer, so she couldn't really afford nice clothes. The Aid worker job in Iraq did not pay well and she'd pretty much blown through the savings she had from her dental hygienist job. She glanced at the backpack in her lap. She could pull out a bundle of money and use that but somehow, she didn't think Cain and the rest of the team would like that.

She sighed. The hell with it. She'd splurge a bit. After everything she'd been through in the last year since Perry had died, she deserved to treat herself a bit.

They pulled into the parking area. It was an outdoor mall with canopies and outdoor seating everywhere. Nick hadn't been kidding about it being high-end. Fendi, Hermès, Louis Vuitton… Upscale was one thing; this was off the charts.

Harlow sent Nick a worried look. "Er, this might be a bit too upscale for my wallet."

"Don't worry. There're some regular stores in there as well, or so it says on the website. I think we just parked on the expensive side."

"Okay, let's give it a shot." Harlow stuffed her hair into the navy ball cap Nick had given her. It wasn't much in the way of a disguise, but she didn't really anticipate running into any of Vance's people here anyway. Nick had on a pair of jeans and a blue T-shirt along with a black ball cap. Cain wore faded jeans and a white T-shirt with another navy ball cap. They looked like tourists if you didn't look too closely.

They navigated the open-air walkways past the high-end shops. Harlow looked in the windows of all the stores without really seeing anything. Her mind was stuck on Cain and his lack of communication. His attitude crawled like ants under her skin.

Finally, they came to some more moderately priced stores. The guys let her go into the underwear store on her own but kept watch from outside. She smiled to herself at the thought of making Cain stand in the middle of a bunch of bras and underwear while she made her choices.

She found some cute lacy sets in blue and black, as well as more serviceable stuff. In the next store, she selected some shorts that looked super cute on her and a few shirts to go with them. She added a pair of sandals and decent running shoes to her cache and then grabbed two pair of jeans as well as a sweater. Better to be prepared. It was all a big splurge for her. but she couldn't wear the sweatpants forever.

They were heading back to the car when she asked, "Do you mind if we make one more stop?" She tilted her head toward the shop to her left. It sold sundresses and bathing suits. She reasoned she might need both if they were going to be here for any length of time.

Nick hesitated but nodded. Cain just stared at the ground, totally disconnected.

Harlow ignored him and went inside. She picked out a couple of dresses and bathing suits and quickly tried them on. The cornflower blue dress clung to her curves and made her eyes sparkle. It was perfect. She glanced at the price. It was more than she should pay, but she looked fabulous in it.

She definitely wanted to wear it in front of Cain. She grinned. Let him see what he was missing. The white dress with big colorful flowers all over it also looked great. The bikinis fit as well. She decided to take everything.

Ten minutes later, she was leaving the store when she almost walked directly into one of Vance's men. He was passing the shop, right in front of her as she was fiddling with her bags. When she let out a small, involuntary squeak, he turned and looked directly at her. She did an about-face and fled back into the store. Her heart slammed against her rib cage. She kept moving until she could duck behind a clothing rack.

She immediately squatted and tried to catch her breath. She was almost hyperventilating. Leaning out slightly, she tried to locate the man, but he wasn't anywhere in her line of vision. It was then that she realized her phone was going off in her pocket. She'd taken her earbuds out when she was trying on the clothes. She quickly put them back in and answered.

"What the fuck? Are you alright?" Cain's voice boomed in her ear.

"I saw one of Vance's men. I almost walked right into him!"

"Where is he? What does he look like?" Nick demanded.

Harlow stood up cautiously. A woman at the next rack was looking at her like she was an alien. *Great*. She needed to avoid attracting attention. "I don't see him."

"Shit. Come to the front of the store," Nick said. "But do it slowly. Let me know if you see him."

She did as she was told and moved cautiously toward the front door then out into the walkway and looked toward her left. That was the direction he'd gone. "I don't see—Wait there he is. Right next to the large potted palm. The tall, thin guy in jeans and a loose white button-down."

Nick grunted, "Got him." He walked by Harlow and moved down the walkway toward the man. She had started to follow when someone grabbed her arm. She whirled around to find Cain standing next to her.

"What are you doing?" he demanded.

"I thought..." She glanced after Nick.

Cain shook his head. "You thought following a man that could recognize you as a threat was a good idea?"

When he put it that way... "It was instinctive, okay? I've been following people for months. I didn't think."

"No. You didn't." He bit off whatever else he was going to say and kept his hand on her arm as he marched them the opposite direction down the walkway and into the parking lot. He had them back in the SUV in minutes. He helped her into the back seat. "Safer," was all he said. Then he paused and said, "Harlow, I really need you to be...careful. I can't handle losing anyone else." He looked like he was going to say more but then he closed the door and went around and got in behind the steering wheel. He started the vehicle and left it idling.

Harlow wanted to argue with him, but even *she* recognized it wasn't the right moment. At least he'd stopped yelling at her. In fact, it looked like he was in pain. Maybe he did care? Cain was in constant communication with Nick through his earbud as they tracked the man. Then Cain called him on his cell.

Nick's voice filled the inside of the vehicle. "He's climbing into a white Mercedes convertible."

"Understood," Cain responded. He roared around the corner of the mall and down through a fire lane. He took the next corner way too fast and then immediately slammed on the brakes.

"Are you trying to kill me?" she demanded as she rubbed her neck. Cain ignored her and slowed down next to Nick.

The SUV hadn't come to a complete stop before Nick jumped in, and they were on their way again, following behind a white Mercedes that Nick identified as the one Vance's man got into.

"Did you get a good look at him?" Cain asked.

Nick shook his head. "He never turned around."

Harlow frowned. "What was he doing at the mall?"

Cain shrugged. "Most likely it was a meet."

"Agree," Nick grunted. "But not sure who. It could be the banker. Some sort of pre-meeting before they show up at the bank with the money."

"It might also be someone else. Someone that can help them move the money."

Harlow snorted. "It could also be that he met with Santa to discuss what to get his kid for Christmas, or maybe he just needed underwear. It's pointless to guess. If I learned anything following Vance, it was to never speculate on what the hell he was doing. It rarely made sense. We don't have all the pieces of the puzzle. Guessing will just lead us down the wrong road."

Nick turned and looked at her over his shoulder, eyebrows raised.

She sighed. "Trust me on this one. Whatever Kapoor was doing in the mall, it won't be what you think."

"Kapoor?" Nick asked.

"Yeah, that's what Vance called him. I think it's his last name, but I don't know his first."

Nick turned back around in his seat as they cruised down the street. They were close to the ocean now. The houses had given way to hotels, and as they progressed down the street, the hotels gave way to resorts. Then the resorts were farther and farther apart. The hedges and flowers separating the street from the properties were getting larger and more colorful.

"These places must cost a fortune to stay at," Harlow commented as they passed one with a massive gate and security.

The Mercedes signal light flashed and then the driver steered left onto the driveway of a very upscale resort. The gate was iron bars, and there was a guard at the booth. The hedge that preserved the privacy of the place had to be about fifteen or twenty feet high. There were brightly colored flowers in large pots lining the driveway leading to the security booth.

"The Jasmine Door's Turquoise Dream," Harlow read. "What kind of a name is that?"

"A very expensive one," Nick supplied.

They drove slowly past the Merc at the guardhouse, and Harlow craned her neck to see past the gates, but it was nearly impossible.

"Fucking hell," Nick growled. "Did you see who that was?"

Cain nodded. "Un-fucking-believable. Axe is gonna go ape shit when he hears this."

Harlow frowned. "I don't get it. What do you mean? Does Axe know Kapoor?"

"Yeah, he knows Kapoor. We all do, except when we met him his name wasn't Kapoor. It was Patel, Rohan Patel." Nick shook his head. "Head back to the hotel. We need to fill the others in on this and plan our next step.

Harlow asked, "How do you guys know him?"

Cain's pulse jumped in his jaw. "It's a long story, but he was on a ship with Axe, and he did some not-so-nice things."

"Sounds like Kapoor," Harlow agreed. "He always appears like the nice, polite one on the surface, but he's deadly as hell."

"How do you know?" Cain demanded.

She sighed. Did she tell them the truth? They would

think she was crazier than they anticipated. On the other hand, what did it matter? Cain was already keeping his distance. "Because I befriended his...girlfriend, for lack of a better word. She told me all about him."

Cain shot her an astonished look in the rear-view mirror and damn near rear-ended the car ahead of him. He swore up a storm before glaring at her again. "Do you want to explain that?"

"Not really."

Nick turned to stare at her. "I think perhaps you'd better."

She let out a long breath. "When I first got to Iraq, I was looking for a way in. I thought it made sense to be on the inside of the group so Vance would trust me, and then I could get close enough to find out the truth. All I had was a name in a file and some rumors. So, I followed them around for a month or so, just identifying all the people in his world. Kapoor...er, Patel, whoever... and a couple of the others have women they visit when they're in the country. I thought if I got to know the girls, then maybe it would be a way in."

"Are you saying you were thinking of...dating Vance or his men?" Cain's voice was like ice.

Sharing this had been a bad idea. Shit. "It was a... thought. So I met and hung out with these women a bit. I did their teeth and helped them out a couple of times with small things like watching their kids or helping to get rid of a drunk guy or two. They started talking to me."

Nick cleared his throat. "Just to clarify, these women were prostitutes, and Vance and his men visited them on a semi-regular basis?"

"Er, yes, I guess you could say that. They were women who were desperate and needed money to survive. Vance and a couple of his top guys had a special relationship with a few of the women. Kapoor was one of them. His...woman was

Petra. I'm not sure where she was actually from or how she ended up in Iraq because she wasn't a local.

"Anyway, after I'd hung out with her and the others for a couple of months, she got drunk and told me all about him. She was terrified of him. Apparently, he was a killer for hire, essentially within the Silverstone Group. If you wanted someone offed, Kapoor was your man. Or, depending on the assignment, if you needed someone to do whatever was necessary for success, then Kapoor was the man to send. She'd overheard him on the phone a couple of times, and he told her if she ever mentioned anything to anyone, he'd slit her throat."

Nick studied her. "You speak of her in the past tense. What happened?"

She shrugged. "I don't know. I think I told you that I worked as an aid worker doing dental work. I would follow Vance as often as I could. My bosses let me have a lot of leeway to travel around and see different groups of people because they don't have much in the way of dental professionals, but sometimes I had to go to a specific place or spend a few weeks with a specific group of people. It was frustrating because I was always afraid Vance would be gone when I got back. Sometimes, he was, but he always came back to Iraq. Now I know why. He didn't want to be far from the money.

"Anyway, I'd been away for about three weeks. When I got back, the women were gone, and the place was boarded up. I asked around a bit, but no one would talk about it. Finally, one woman who had a stall at the market took pity on me and explained that the women had all up and vanished in the middle of the night. No one had seen them since, and everyone was too afraid to ask questions."

"You think Patel had something to do with it?" Nick asked.

"It wouldn't surprise me. On the other hand, they all

wanted out and were doing their best to put aside some money so they could start again somewhere else. Maybe they took off on their own. All the kids were gone, too. There was nothing left in the building, but that could have been people clearing it out once they realized the women were gone." Her stomach rolled. She hadn't spoken out loud about this, and she didn't want to. It hurt. She'd liked Petra and the others. "I like to think they made it out." She swallowed hard. "I know that's naïve, but thinking the worst didn't, and still doesn't, help me any." She blinked away some tears that were threatening to fall. "Anyway, let's just put Vance and his people away. It's the best we can do to help Petra and the rest."

Nick said nothing but turned back in his seat. She caught Cain's gaze in the mirror. His eyes glittered and the pulse in his jaw jumped. His knuckles were white on the wheel. He was pissed. Well, that made two of them. Life sucked. She'd seen it and experienced it the hard way. Maybe she'd done things she wasn't exactly proud of, but in the end, getting the man that had her brother killed was worth it. It had to be.

They pulled into the parking lot of their hotel and got out. She went to her room with all of her purchases and sat down on the bed. What had seemed like so much fun that morning had turned into something that seemed so frivolous and stupid. They were here to get Vance and his men. She'd spent way too much money on things that wouldn't help her in the long run.

There was a weight on her shoulders that she just couldn't shift. It had been there since the day she found out her brother had died. Sometimes, she thought it would always be there, no matter what, but then there were moments, just quick flashes that happened ever so briefly when she could breathe again. It was then that she thought maybe, just maybe, she could get all this sorted and the weight would disappear.

There was a knock on the connecting room door. She went over and opened it.

"Why don't you come in here? We're planning on how to deal with the latest developments." Nick gave her a grim smile.

At least he was including her. She looked around the room. The guys were pretty much sprawled everywhere except for Axe. He was pacing, his hands opening and closing. He was struggling to calm down. She knew what that felt like. Maybe, someday, she'd get the whole story.

"So...ideas?" Nick asked.

"I guess we follow them," Elias suggested.

Finn took a swig from his water bottle. "When they leave the resort, yes, we need to follow them, but how many are there at the resort? We're gonna need more vehicles."

"We need eyes in the resort," Cain said from his spot on the desk.

"What resort is it?" Finn asked.

"The Jasmine Door's Emerald or was it Turquoise something or other," she replied.

Finn perked up. "It's a Jasmine Door?"

Nick ran a hand over his face. "Why is that important?"

"Well, because Tory"—he turned to Harlow—"my girlfriend, is close with the owner's girlfriend, Spencer Gordon. She worked at DHS as well. That's where they met. Anyway, Jameson Drake owns the resort. He did Tory a favor, and we stayed in the Jasmine Door in D.C. I can call her and ask her to reach out to him to get us in."

"Even if we get in, what are we gonna do?" Axe demanded. "Patel or Kapoor, whatever his name is, will recognize us, and so will Vance. He's seen all of us. Hell, he even shot Cain in the leg."

Harlow whirled around and stared at Cain. She closed her hands into fists as her heart raced and adrenaline surged in her veins. He hadn't mentioned that. No one had. She looked at his legs and then back up at his face. Why hadn't he mentioned it? He didn't limp, so maybe he wasn't in pain. Elias limped on occasion. She'd asked, and he said he'd been shot in the leg, but there had been complications with the gunshot wound, bad enough that he still had a hard time with it. Maybe Cain's wasn't so bad?

Nick nodded. "Yeah, it's a problem. The only one he may not recognize is Harlow."

"What?" she and Cain both barked at the same time.

"Think about it. She followed them around for ages, but no one noticed. They know she was in the container and that she can tie Vance to it, so they want her dead, but they didn't physically see her, only those on the first container ship. I'm sure they have a picture, but how good is it? It's not like they're thinking she'll be here stalking them. Logically, she should be anywhere *but* here. And she would be if we didn't need her to identify Vance's guys."

"You want to put Harlow in a resort with these guys?" Cain ground out. "That's insane."

"Yeah, it is, but Nick's right," Axe said. "Harlow is probably the least recognizable of us, except for maybe you, Cain.

"How do you figure that?" Finn asked.

Axe pointed at Cain. "If he wears his hair down and puts on a pair of board shorts, he'll be just another guy on vacation. Harlow needs to be there for us to identify all of Vance's people so we can follow them all and find the money. If she dyes her hair and throws on a bathing suit, she's just another sunbather by the pool."

Axe stopped pacing and leaned against the back of the door. "These guys are looking for threats. That's what they've been trained to do. Hell, it's what we do, too. Harlow already proved that she can blend in enough so they don't find her a threat. We just need Cain to tone it down and they'll pass as another rich American couple on holiday. No threat. No need to pay attention. Vance's people will go about their business, and we'll nail them."

"No." Cain shook his head. "It's too big of a risk."

"You're right, Cain. It is a big risk," Nick agreed. "But we're running out of time. Seriously. If we don't get a line on the money soon, it will be gone for good. Vance and Foley will get away with it. With everything."

"Tag—"

"I'll do it," Harlow said, interrupting Cain's next protest. "I didn't come this far to stop now. It's always been risky. I want them to pay for what they did to my brother. I'll do it." She crossed her arms over her chest and glared defiantly at Cain. She'd do it with or without him, but she'd feel a hell of a lot better about it if she could do it with him.

"Fucking hell!" Cain muttered, but he nodded once.

Nick turned to Finn. "Call Tory and get us into the resort. See if she can think of another way to get more of us in without tipping off Vance."

"What about in the security office?" Axe suggested.

Cain shook his head. The pulse in his jaw throbbed. "No, if it was us, what's the first thing you'd do?"

Axe nodded. "Bribe someone in security to let me know if anything odd is going on."

"Elias," Nick said, "go to the mall and get Cain some clothes. Harlow, we need you to dye your hair. I'm sure there are a million hair places on this island."

"Yes, but dying my hair will take hours and no one is going to do it without an appointment. Maybe Finn's girl-friend could get me into a salon at the resort?"

"Good idea." Nick pointed at Finn, who was already on the phone. He nodded. Nick turned back to her. "Go grab a shower and get organized. We're gonna move as quickly as possible on this. I don't like that we had to leave from watching the resort as it is."

Harlow turned and walked back into her room, closing the door behind her. She leaned against it for a minute and closed her eyes. She was taking a huge risk jumping from the frying pan into the fire, and she wasn't just talking about Vance and his men. Spending time alone with Cain was going to be hard as hell because no matter how much that man was an asshole, she still wanted him. Bad.

CHAPTER FOURTEEN

Cain sat at the dry side of the swim-up bar in a pair of red board shorts and sunglasses. His long hair hung down over his face. He took a sip of his beer. The bar had a good vantage point of the whole pool stretched out in front of him. Patel and two others were in lounge chairs at the far end of the pool. The more they drank, the more they ogled women strolling by.

He did not want to be here. This was not good. Not only did he feel exposed, but he was at a distinct disadvantage. He couldn't carry a gun in his swim trunks, which was entirely the point. He obviously posed no threat to Patel, or so he wanted them to believe.

The problem was, he wasn't sure he could keep Harlow safe. He didn't like being out in the open like this. It made his skin crawl. Worse, it made him jumpy, and being jumpy would get them spotted, which would get them both killed.

He took another sip of his beer and attempted to relax. He could do this. Finn and Elias were working as waiters, so at least there were more of them on the property. They would do their best to keep an eye on things but stay far enough away that they wouldn't come in direct contact with Patel and the rest of Vance's people just in case they were recognized. It wasn't going to be easy.

Cain glanced at his watch. Harlow was supposed to be finished with her hair a half hour ago. He started to go check on her when Elias walked by and said she was fine, just in the room, changing. She'd be down in a minute. Finn would keep an eye on the hallway until she came down. He had just taken another sip of his beer when someone tapped him on the shoulder. He turned and almost choked.

Harlow stood next to him in a blue string bikini that was the exact color of her eyes. Her auburn hair was gone, and in its place were long blond waves. "Hey babe," she said and planted a kiss on his mouth. He instinctively reached out and grabbed her waist. She straightened and gave him a wink. "Did you get us some chairs by chance?"

He stared at her dumbfounded. She looked sensational in the bikini. Her curves were lush, and her waist fit neatly into his hands. She'd completely knocked him off-kilter. How the hell was he supposed to manage when she looked like this?

He tried to say something, but she'd left him speechless. He liked the blond, but not as much as the red. He missed the red. Her hair color didn't matter to him, but she was attracting a lot of attention. The bikini fit her perfectly and showed off her curves to their full advantage. His first instinct was to cover her up and then pound on any male that looked in her direction.

When he still didn't say anything, she prompted him, "Why don't you order me a cocktail and then we can go sit by the pool?"

He couldn't stop staring at her. Worse, all he could think about was taking her to bed. He'd been so determined to keep her at a distance, but all he really wanted to do was pull her close.

As if she could read his mind, she moved into his arms, wrapped her arms around his neck, and leaned over his shoulder to order a drink. Her breasts pressed against his chest, and his brain shorted out. Then she leaned back and smiled at him. "Babe, maybe we should get some food, too?"

He blinked.

She leaned in and whispered, "Are you okay?"

"Er, yeah." He gave himself a mental shake. "Fine. Yeah. Food." *Great.* She'd reduced him to speaking in single syllable words.

"Cool."

She smiled at him, but there was uncertainty in her eyes. He needed to get his shit together. "Food," he said abruptly. "Let's order here and then take it over to the chairs." He put his hands back on her waist.

"Sounds great." She gave him another smile but didn't move back. She still had her arms around his neck, and she was holding herself so close to him that the heat from her body was swelling a situation south of his waist. He needed her to back up, or there was gonna be a major issue.

"Harlow," he growled in a low voice, "what are you doing?"

She chuckled. "Nothing, babe. Just so happy to be on vacation." She leaned in and kissed him again, rubbing her breasts on his chest.

Jesus Christ. If she didn't stop soon, he'd be hard as a rock. "Harlow," he growled again, "stop it. You're in over your head."

She leaned in and kissed his cheek and then murmured, "Prove it."

"Your drink," the bartender said.

Cain jolted off his stool and turned around. He grabbed the drink and his beer and moved away from the bar.

"I thought we were going to order some food," she said as she came alongside him.

"We were, but you can't seem to behave. Don't push your luck, *babe*. You might have second thoughts once we're alone together," he ground out as they made their way over to two lounge chairs that he'd set up earlier. He put the drinks down on the table in between the chairs and took the one on the right. He checked that his gun was still in the beach bag between the chairs and then laid back and stretched out on the lounger.

She sat down on the left with her feet on the ground facing him. She dropped her voice and murmured, "You can't keep calling me by my name. It's not common enough. Call me Vanessa."

He blinked. How the fuck was he supposed to remember to call her Vanessa when he couldn't remember his own name at the moment? His equilibrium was completely off-kilter. "Fine."

There was a sudden shadow, and Cain looked up to find Finn standing over them dressed as wait staff. "Would you like to see a menu?" he asked and handed Cain the laminated cardboard along with a couple of earbuds.

"Thanks."

Then Finn disappeared.

Cain quickly put his earbud in as he tucked the hair behind his ear. He reached over and placed his hand on Harlow's leg. Her earbud was underneath it. She reached up and covered his hand with hers in a seemingly romantic gesture that stole breath from his lungs. He removed his hand quickly and sat back into the lounge chair.

She looked slightly perplexed. "How am I supposed to put this in without being obvious?"

He took a deep breath and sat up to face her again. "What would you like for lunch, *babe*?" He placed his hand over hers again and took the earbud back. Two could play this game. He leaned over and kissed her along her jaw line while he inserted the earbud in her ear. *Damn, he wanted to put something else inside her.* He gave himself a mental shake. "What would you like to eat?" he asked dropping his hand to cup her shoulder.

She blinked and stared at him blankly. Glad he wasn't the only one who was affected by their closeness. He made sure his sunglasses were in place and laid back in his chair.

"Now that you two are all cozy, what the hell do you see?" Nick asked.

What? Where was Nick? He wasn't supposed to be onsite. A flash of guilt hit Cain in the chest. He'd been so distracted by Harlow in that bikini that he'd forgotten why they were there. He glanced over to where Patel and the other two had been sitting. When he saw they were still there, relief flooded through him.

"The three are still seated in the same chairs by the pool. They're drinking and ogling women."

"I got pictures of the other two men, Tag. I've already emailed them to you," Finn added.

"Good," Nick replied. "Harlow, do you recognize them?"

Harlow stretched out on the chair and glanced at the men. Then she tilted her face up to the sun. "No. The blond guy, I've never seen before. The dark-haired one with all the tattoos looks vaguely familiar, but I would need to go through my pictures to place him. Vance had a lot of people coming and going in Iraq."

Cain asked, "Tag, are you here?" Maybe it wasn't too late. Maybe he could leave Finn and Elias with Harlow. But the thought of leaving her here made his stomach drop. That wasn't going to work.

"Yeah, but only for a few minutes. I wanted to drop off the earbuds. I have a call in a bit. With any luck, I'll have the name of the banker. Then we can move on him and see what's what."

"Okay." Cain took a sip of his beer.

Harlow spoke quietly. "FYI, they can drink a lot and still be cold-stone sober," Harlow murmured. "Don't let them fool you."

Cain gave her a nod. "It's odd. They don't seem worried at all. Do you think the money is already deposited, Nick?"

"I have no idea. We're all flying blind. Like I said, if my source comes through, then we can figure it out for sure."

Shit. Cain hated being in the dark.

"Nah." Harlow shook her head slightly. "If the money was already deposited, they wouldn't be here. They'd be off *really* celebrating. This? This is just for show. I've seen it a million times. They're putting up a front while watching everyone. They are waiting."

Cain glanced at Vance's men. *Damn.* Harlow was right. From this angle, he could see that the two men with Patel were both armed. Handguns under their T-shirts. Patel was shirtless, but Cain thought he'd seen a glint of metal in the towel in the chair next to him. Knife most likely. And they were wired. The sun reflected off the wire of the dark-haired guy's earbud.

Cain had been so caught up in Harlow that he was dropping the ball. It had to stop. He was putting the team in danger. He'd told Nick this wasn't a good idea, but there wasn't another option, so he just had to do better. The team was counting on them.

Cain flicked his hair back with his hand. "She's right. They're being watchful."

"They've only had two beers each," Finn added.

"Okay. Harlow, have you noticed any other of Vance's men?" Nick asked.

Cain glanced over at her, and she bit her lip. She'd been so busy playing with him, she'd forgotten what they were there for as well. It had to stop. He would keep them both on track, even if it meant being an asshole. He could do asshole. It was just the loving boyfriend routine that was tripping him up.

"Not yet," she mumbled, "but I'll keep looking."

"Would you like something from the menu?" the server asked. She was short with dark hair pulled back in a bun and a sunny smile.

Cain cleared his throat and picked up the menu Finn had left. But Harlow was already ordering. She picked all his favorites before she ordered him another beer and her another cocktail. Not that she'd touched the first one. But as soon as the waitress left, she took care of that and downed a rather large swallow.

"Okay, guys. Keep me updated," Nick said and then went silent.

Harlow took another sip of her drink and then they both laid down in their lounge chairs. Cain studied the people poolside, trying to figure out if anyone else worked for Vance or if anyone was paying attention to Patel and his crew. Nothing stood out to him.

The server came back with their food. The nachos smelled great, and his stomach rumbled. It was late afternoon, but he hadn't eaten since breakfast.

Harlow reached for a conch fritter and popped it in her mouth. "Yum." She smiled.

He turned away. Her smile always hit him in the middle of the chest. Now, her in that bikini was hitting him below the waist.

They ate in companionable silence until the couple next

to them inquired about the food, and they chatted for a while. Peter and Danika were their names, and they were here on vacation. He had to do some work during the day, but it was a small sacrifice. He was in banking. She was in real estate.

They introduced themselves as John and Vanessa. He worked in IT, and she worked for a non-profit. Those were their cover stories. The couple eventually wandered off, and they went back to lounging in the sun.

But not long after, Harlow swung her legs over the side of the chair. "Care to go for a swim before we head upstairs?"

He shook his head. "I'll watch from here."

She nodded and then dug in her bag and put her hair up with a tie she'd pulled out. She got up from the chair and made her way to the stairs that were closer to the bar. The water was heated so she went right into the pool. She lowered herself to her shoulders and stayed that way.

Cain immediately realized his error in judgment. Now he had to watch two fronts, Harlow and Patel. He should have joined her in the pool. Then they could watch Vance's men together. The problem was that Harlow in that bikini, all wet and rubbing against him, was not conducive to paying attention to anything except his hard-on. He let out a sigh and continued to watch from his chair.

Harlow chatted with another couple. At that moment, Patel got up and started walking around the pool. Cain and Harlow were in the second row of chairs from the poolside, so even if Patel walked by, he wasn't all that close. But if he went into the pool, he would come within feet of Harlow. It was one thing to be across the pool from the guy. It was another to be directly in his path. What if he recognized her? Cain's heart hammered against his ribs. He started to get up.

"Stay where you are," Elias directed. "If you get up now, it will be obvious. The other guys are watching."

Fuck. Cain tried to appear relaxed, but adrenaline filled his veins, and his heart rate was a fucking speeding train. From behind his sunglasses, he glanced at the other two men. Elias was right. They were more alert. They'd both straightened and made sure their hands were empty. The energy they were giving off said they *were* watching. *Shit.* If Patel hurt Harlow, Cain would kill him right here, right now. He didn't want to say anything that would alarm her so she made a mistake. She might have made it through Iraq, but she was an amateur. The first thing amateurs did when they were told not to look was to turn around and look.

Patel was still walking around the pool. Maybe he was going to the restroom or something. He came to the stairs that Harlow had used to enter the pool and started down them. Harlow was talking to someone else and had her back to the stairs.

"Harlow," Cain said, "Patel is coming into the pool."

She started to turn.

"No, don't look." But it was too late. Harlow had turned and was now facing Patel.

Elias said, "Don't move, Cain. Patel's buddies are surveying the place with a lot of interest."

Cain checked the two men again. The blond was leaning forward with his hand at his side. Better for grabbing his gun in a hurry. The dark-haired man was still leaning back but had his arm behind him. They *were* nervous. Did that mean they knew who Harlow was?

Finn appeared just down from Cain in a bar staff uniform. He started walking along the edge of the pool toward the stairs. "If Patel tries anything, I've got him."

Patel finished entering the pool and moved toward the bar area where Harlow was currently standing. She said a quick goodbye to the people she'd been chatting with and turned toward the stairs again. They were going to pass one another.

Cain's heart stopped beating. His lungs ceased functioning.

"Nice bikini," Patel said in a British accent, his voice loud in Cain's earbud. When he turned his head to look directly at Harlow, Cain got a shot of his profile.

"Thanks." Harlow gave him a tight smile.

"So…what do you do to keep in such good shape?" Patel gave her an appreciative glance and then a lazy grin.

Cain wanted to strangle the guy. *Fucking hell.* It took everything he had not to hop up and deck the asshole.

Harlow smiled back at Patel and said, "I have a ton of hot sex with my boyfriend. Keeps me limber."

Patel's eyebrows went up, and then he threw his head back and laughed. Harlow continued out of the pool. She came back to the chair and grabbed her towel. Cain sat up. He was speechless. Her comeback was…perfect.

The sound of laughter filled Cain's ear. "Girl, you are good," Elias said with a chuckle.

"Remind me never to take you on," Finn agreed. He continued around the pool and disappeared.

"Thanks." She smiled at Cain and winked. Then she took a closer look at him. "Are you okay?" she asked as she toweled off. She leaned down and kissed him, giving him an amazing view of her breasts.

"I'm fine," he croaked. "You?"

"Fine, babe." In a lower voice she added, "It was a little hairy there for a moment, but he was just testing the waters to see if I was interested."

Cain clamped his jaw shut. He wasn't sure about that. The way Patel's people had reacted, he might have been testing the waters in a different way. Maybe they were checking to see how Harlow would react. This assignment was going to kill him one way or another. He didn't know who he wanted to throttle more, her or him. "I think we should go to the room. It's late, and there aren't many people left at the pool. It will be obvious if we don't move soon."

"Agreed," Finn said. "I'll keep an eye on them for now. You two have a dinner reservation at the hotel restaurant at eight. So do Patel and his buddies."

"Good to know." As Cain stood, Harlow also stood at the same time. When she stumbled, he caught her and held her against him. Their gazes locked, and her eyes widened slightly. He knew that his eyes reflected both his lust for her but also his rage at Patel and the whole situation. He took a step back and reached down to grab her wrap. He held it up for her. Their fingers brushed as she took it and his anger at Patel and their entire fucking situation morphed into an entirely different emotion—desire. Harlow tied the sheer wrap around her waist. She piled everything else in her bag and then fell into step with him. He was very aware of her all the way to the room.

He opened the door and ushered her inside. Tory had come through in a big way, or maybe Drake had. They had a suite that overlooked the turquoise water in the bay. It was stunning. They entered the living room with its pale tile floor and off-white furniture. The walls were white with pictures of the local area, tropical trees, and sandy beaches.

Off to the right was the bedroom and attached bath. "Taking the earbuds out, guys. Need showers. Call if you need us," Cain said.

"Will do," Elias said.

Finn responded with, "Roger that."

Cain took out his earbud and stuck out his hand for hers. Harlow smiled and dropped it in his palm. "Alone at last."

She was trying to kill him. "Right," he grunted. "Do you want to shower first, or do you want me to go first?"

"I'll go first if you don't mind." She turned and walked into the bedroom.

He couldn't help but watch the sway of her hips as she went. Once he heard the door close, he collapsed on the couch and sunk his head into his hands. This was fucking torture. He ran a hand through his hair and then pulled it back off his face with a hair tie.

His cell rang. He pulled it out of his pocket. Elias. He hit the green button. "What's up? Everything okay?"

"I was about to ask you the same question."

"What do you mean?"

"Seriously? Cain, you're a mess, man. Are you sure you can do this?"

Cain closed his eyes and swore up a blue streak in his head. "No," he finally managed to croak.

"Shit," Elias grunted. "I know you got it bad, bro, and I know how much it sucks working with Harlow. Believe me, I understand completely, but you gotta put it in its place. You're putting her at risk if you don't."

"I know," he mumbled. "I'm trying to get myself right but…I'm… struggling."

"Cain, you had my back more times than I can count, man. You are ice in any situation. Always on it. This… I don't know what to tell you. You gotta find a way to put it away. Block it off. None of us want Vance to go free, but you got more skin in the game than anyone. Use that. Use your anger. Whatever it takes, but you gotta get there, bro."

"Yeah. You're right. I know it."

Elias snorted. "You're Giancarlo Ricci after all. No woman can come close to that badassery." Elias hung up.

"Fuck," Cain spat and then started to laugh. Elias had a point. He *was* Giancarlo Ricci, and if he learned anything from his father, it was how to remain calm and deal in any situation. He could do this. No, he *would* do this. He didn't have a choice.

Twenty minutes later, Harlow came out of the shower in nothing but a towel. He glanced at her. He was tempted to throw her up against the wall and bang her brains out. Maybe it would get it out of his system. Instead, he nodded at her and went into the bathroom. Cool was better.

But ice was best.

CHAPTER FIFTEEN

arlow stood in front of the mirror. The dress looked divine on her, if she did say so herself. The blue was the perfect shade to match her eyes. It was a halter dress, so it brought attention to her curves before it flared at her waist. And the shoes were a perfect match. Cream colored strappy sandals. She checked her makeup and added a bit more lipstick.

She glanced in the mirror again. It was going to take her a while to get used to the blond. It was an altogether different look. Perry would have made fun of her for sure.

Perry. Her heart crumbled. What the hell was she doing? She was here to catch Perry's killer. That was her job. Instead, she was fantasizing about Cain. She closed her eyes and said a quiet apology to her brother. She'd let her desire for Cain cloud her judgment. Flirting with him all afternoon had been stupid.

It was his fault, though. He'd taken one look at her in that bikini, and his green eyes had glittered with pure, unadulterated lust. It was a heady thing to know a man like Cain wanted her. Like really *wanted her*. She'd seen it in his eyes, felt it in his touch when he put his hands on her waist. He'd *reacted* to her. About fucking time, too. She'd been reacting to him since the first time she'd seen him. Every part of her body went all hot and tingly when he did nothing more than walk into the room.

She stared at her reflection and then closed her eyes. It was time to grow up. To be an adult again. Today by the pool had been fun, but she'd been so distracted trying to get Cain's attention, she'd made a big mistake and ended up coming face-to-face with Kapoor. Not only that, but she'd had to interact with him! Even if she wasn't a professional like Cain and his team, she was intelligent. She'd signed up for this and knew better.

Hauling in a steadying breath, she opened her eyes. She scowled at herself in the mirror. *No more.* She would get her mind back in the game like she'd done the whole time she'd followed Vance. Faltering now wasn't an option, not when she was so close.

She leaned forward and touched a tissue to each eye, making sure she hadn't smudged her makeup. Then she straightened and put her shoulders back. It was time to get Vance, Kapoor, the whole lot of them. Once and for all.

She opened the bathroom door and walked out. Cain wasn't in the bedroom. She went into the living area and looked around. Cain was out on the balcony. He must have heard her because he turned and came in.

Her heart fluttered like a hummingbird. His dark wavy hair was hanging down by his jawline. It looked thick and shiny. She longed to sink her fingers into it. His green eyes were cool and assessing. The black button-down shirt he wore just made his eyes stand out all the more. He had on black dress pants as well, which hugged his butt. She'd noticed immediately when he was on the balcony with his back to her. He had an amazing ass.

She let out a breath. "You look good."

"You, too. Ready to go?"

She nodded once. He handed her the earbud, and she worked it in. She was determined to be cool and professional. It looked like he had made the decision to be the same.

A slight hollow feeling yawned in her chest. *No.* She wasn't going to be disappointed. He was right to be professional. This was business. This was for Perry.

They went down in the elevator and crossed the lobby to the restaurant. The waiter took them to a table on a balcony that overlooked the water. They were in the middle of the row of tables that were lined up along the glass railing. She knew instantly Cain was uncomfortable. His back wasn't to any wall, and he couldn't see the whole room from where he was sitting.

He also had his shirt tucked in, so no gun, but that was the plan they'd made at the beginning. He had to appear as innocuous as possible if they were going to get her close enough to identify all the players without drawing attention to themselves.

Still, she knew he was struggling with it. She wasn't happy either. If he had a gun, she wouldn't feel quite so vulnerable. She caught his eye and offered him a supportive smile. He winked and gave her a quick smile in return.

The waiter came over and brought bread for the table and took their drink orders. Harlow leaned back and took in the view of the water. It was beautiful here. Maybe someday when this was all over, she could come back. But probably not. Although paradise, she would always associate this place with Perry and his killers.

She turned and casually scanned the room. Almost immediately she stiffened. Her stomach hit the ground. "The man at the end of the bar, wearing the blue polo shirt. He's one of Vance's. Hugo. That's what they call him."

"Roger that," Finn responded through the earbud, startling her. She'd forgotten the team was monitoring their every syllable.

Harlow took a minute to readjust. She'd followed Hugo a great many times when Vance wasn't around. It was scary seeing these men again in this setting. What if they noticed her? She should have worn something less...what? Less revealing? Mousier? She gave herself a mental shake. It didn't matter now, but again, so much disappointment in herself. She just wanted to look good for Cain, and that had been a fierce motivator and how her decisions had rolled yesterday.

She tucked that away for now and resumed her sweep of the room. She was on the clock now. As a man came around the bar from the restrooms, she stopped again. "The man wearing the white button-down and khakis who just sat down by himself at the table against the wall. Jonas. Don't know if it's a first or last name."

Cain leaned forward. "These two men, are they close to Vance, part of his inner circle?"

"Um, not really. They were more errand boys as far as I could tell. Kapoor is on the inside. And there was this other guy that Vance seemed close to." She opened her mouth to continue but stopped. It was like she'd summoned him from Hell by just thinking about him.

"What? What is it?" Cain demanded.

"Vance just walked in with Kapoor." They were being led across the restaurant and out on to the balcony. The waiter set them down immediately behind Cain.

"What the fuck, Finn?" Cain growled in a low voice. "I thought you arranged it so we wouldn't be next to them?"

"I did. Let me check and see what's going on."

Elias asked, "Harlow, who is the other guy you were talking about?"

She hesitated. It was stupid, but she'd just said Vance's

name and he appeared. She was afraid to say the name. "James Daughtry," she murmured finally. She quickly looked around, but he wasn't there.

Cain's eyes narrowed. "What do you know about him?"

"Too much," she murmured. She picked up her glass and took a sip of her water. "If Kapoor is a stone-cold killer, then Daughtry is the opposite. He likes to torture before he kills, or at least that's what Petra said." And she had no doubt it was true. He'd said as much when he had her trapped in the container. "He likes to be cruel. One of Petra's friends has the scars to prove it." She'd told Harlow that she'd been well paid for her misery, but there was no way the money was worth the pain and suffering Harlow saw in that woman's eyes. Harlow was lucky to have escaped his wrath.

"What is it?" Cain asked. "What aren't you saying?"

She met his gaze. "Daughtry was the man who caught me in the container. He…he held me down…and…attempted to get my clothes off…" Her voice broke, and she swallowed. When Cain interlaced his fingers with hers, his touch infused her with the strength to continue. "Vance called him, so he had to stop. That's when he shut me in the container. I was very lucky."

A pulse jumped in Cain's jaw. Harlow knew he was in a cold rage, but there was nothing she could do about it. Maybe she shouldn't have said anything.

"I am so sorry you had to go through that. If I could change it, I would." He kept his fingers laced with hers. "All I can promise you is he'll pay for that."

Warmth spread through Harlow's chest. She swallowed hard and nodded. Cain's words were good, but his touch was even better. She felt safe sitting here with him. As if nothing in the world could touch her.

A moment later, Elias asked, "Okay, anyone else?"

Harlow tore her gaze away from Cain and looked around

the room. "The two men from the pool today just walked in. They're seated with Jonas."

Elias cut in, "The guy with the brown hair is David Mosley, and the blond is Karl Bowen. Both are former Army Rangers."

Suddenly, several of the wait staff came over to the tables behind Harlow and Cain and started moving them.

"Finn?" Cain demanded.

"Sorry. Some large party is coming in to celebrate a birthday. They're regulars so they get special treatment. Nothing I can do."

Harlow stared over Cain's shoulder at Vance's back. "Maybe we should move."

Finn cursed then said, "Sorry, Harlow, the place is full. They won't let you. You're gonna have to sweat it out."

Harlow met Cain's gaze. This was not ideal. She was a little too close for comfort. Even with blond hair, there was a good chance any of them might recognize her. It was one thing to sit across a pool from them. It was an altogether different matter to sit right next to them for hours.

When Harlow started to fidget with her cutlery, Cain leaned over and took her hands in his. "You are fine. I won't let anything happen to you. You've identified the players. The rest is up to us."

Their server approached the table and asked, "Do you know what you would like for dinner?"

Harlow blinked and then picked up the menu. They both ordered the special, some fish done in a sauce with vegetables. Harlow wasn't remotely hungry anymore. She glanced around the room as she reached for her water. Her hand jerked and knocked her glass, but Cain caught the water before it spilled. He questioned her with his eyes.

"Sorry. Just a little bit jumpy."

"Does anyone else find it a bit odd that Vance is sitting on the terrace?" Finn asked.

"Yes," Cain murmured. "He should be in there with Jonas and the others, his back to the wall and able to see the whole restaurant. God knows, that's where I'd be if I had a choice."

"Do you think he's made us and this is some sort of ploy to bring us out of the woodwork?" Harlow asked.

"I don't see how," Finn commented. "Just because he's outside doesn't change anything. We're not going to talk to him."

"It's a meet," Cain stated.

"What?" she asked.

"He's sitting there so someone can keep an eye on him. In a bit, he'll get up and go meet someone. They'll be watching to see if Patel leaves with him. I'm willing to bet they told him to come alone."

Harlow frowned. "But the others are in the restaurant."

"Yes, but only we know that." Cain cast a deceptively idle glance around the terrace. "If I were a banker about to embark on this kind of deal, I'd want to meet in private, but I'd want some assurances that Vance wasn't going to kill me after this was all over. Once the money is invested, then Vance and Foley can move it all over the world. This banker becomes just another loose end. I think this is a negotiation or renegotiation meeting."

"That makes sense," Elias agreed. "So do a billion other scenarios, such as he just likes to sit outside, but I think you're on the right track. The banker heard about the other shipments on the news. Cal has been milking what happened in Belize for all it's worth. He's been telling the world he single-handedly foiled an international money laundering ring. Now the banker's getting cold feet."

Harlow toyed with her fork. "Will we follow him when

he leaves the table?"

Cain shook his head. "*We'll* follow him. *You'll* go up to the room. This is way too close for comfort as it is."

She wanted to scream and lash out at him. Where did he get off telling her what she could and couldn't do? She'd gotten here on her own. She could handle herself. Her mind flashed back to Daughtry and the scene in the container. *Well, mostly.*

She and Cain sat quietly, making small talk and pretending to be a couple while they waited for their dinner. Harlow's nerves were shot. She wanted to be out of there. Cain seemed to sense it. He took her hand and rubbed his thumb on her palm.

Vance snarled something all of a sudden, but all she caught was "Asshole—major trouble—Foley."

She glanced at Cain, but he shook his head.

When Kapoor stood from the table, she glanced up. Their eyes met, and he smiled at her. She gave him a nod and went back staring at Cain like he was the love of her life.

Cain frowned.

"Kapoor just made eye contact."

"Shit," he mumbled and continued to stroke her palm with his thumb.

"Vance keeps looking out at the water. Do you think he could be watching for something?" she asked. Anything to keep her mind off what his caress was doing to her insides.

Cain froze. "Elias, check the boats. Vance is sitting so someone can see him from the water."

"Shit," Elias said. "I'll call Nick and Axe."

Harlow squeezed Cain's thumb. "I'm not following."

"We need people in boats. If the meet is on the water, we want to at least be able to see who he meets with. He could get into a tender and go out to any boat offshore. We need to be able to follow him."

The waiter arrived with their food, and Harlow was grateful for the interruption. She needed a moment to get her equilibrium back. Cain was killing her. The worst part was he was so caught up in what was going on, he wasn't remotely affected. She needed to be the same way but just couldn't seem to manage it.

Dinner went by slowly. It was a hard battle to fight. Staying focused while Cain stroked her arm or her palm or stared into her eyes was damn near impossible. She only caught snatches of Vance's conversation but nothing that was helpful.

Cain for his part played the attentive boyfriend to a tee. Every time he flicked his hair back, she had to rein in her libido. Her lady bits tingled when he stroked her arm. Forget looking into his eyes. They sparkled at her like emeralds. Pure torture.

"Are you okay?" He looked concerned.

"I'm sorry, what?" Harlow blinked. He'd been speaking, and she'd been fantasizing.

"I said would you like dessert?"

"Oh, God no." It came out as a groan. and Cain cocked an eyebrow at her. She offered him a half-hearted smile. "I'm full."

The waiter went off to get the bill. "I'm going to the ladies' room," she declared as she stood up.

Cain shot her a look that said *sit your ass* down, but it was too late; she was on her feet. She walked around the large table in front of them, keeping her eyes off Vance's table. She did not want to make eye contact with Kapoor again.

Elias caught her eye as she walked by the bar. "Harlow, I don't think this is a great idea."

She ignored him as she moved across the restaurant and down the hallway on the right to the bathrooms. All fine for him to say. He wasn't the one who'd faced the onslaught of

Cain's fake affection all night. She needed a few minutes of peace.

They were going to make her go to the room shortly, but she wanted to prepare an argument as to why she should be allowed to stay with them. To do that, she needed a few minutes to herself. And she really had to pee.

Once she entered the bathroom, she realized she had an issue. If she peed, they'd hear her. Okay, that just wasn't gonna work for her. Call it stage fright or whatever, but she was not peeing with them listening. She went into a stall and pulled the earbud out of her ear. She set it on the top of the toilet paper roll cover.

How the hell was she going to convince Cain that she was still an asset? She'd identified all the players, at least all the ones that had shown up so far. Maybe that was her angle. There could be more. *You need me to see who meets with Vance just in case there are more Silverstone guys in the woodwork.* It might work.

She finished up in the bathroom and then washed her hands. Tossing the damp toweling into the trash, she exited to the hallway, where she came face-to-face with Roman Vance. "Shit." She put her hand on her chest. "Um, sorry. You startled me."

He glared down at her, and his eyes narrowed slightly. Then he growled, "I'm on my way," and moved around her.

She leaned back against the wall and drew in a deep breath. Why the hell hadn't the guys warned her? Oh. Shit. Her earbud. She went back into the bathroom and retrieved the piece.

"Jesus Christ. Does anyone have eyes on her?" Cain growled.

"I'm fine," she said. She left the bathroom and stepped out into the hallway.

She heard a voice. "I'm coming. Don't lose him." Then

the sound of footsteps. "What?" The footsteps stopped. Adrenaline shot through her veins and sweat broke out on her back. She'd know that voice anywhere. Daughtry.

She turned left and went down the hall away from the restaurant and Daughtry. Coming face-to-face would be a death sentence. "Um guys, slight issue."

"What do you mean, he's not where he's supposed to be?" Daughtry's voice was closer.

She wanted to turn and look but knew it was a bad idea. There were no more doors on the hallway except for the one at the end. She had no choice but to move as quickly as possible through the door and hope she wasn't walking head-long into Vance.

"Harlow, what issue? Where are you?" Cain's voice was icy and controlled.

She burst through the door at the end of the hallway and found herself on a path behind the hotel. There were air conditioning units on her left. The path was gravel. It was obviously some sort of work area. There was a massive thick hedge on the right. The sound of the waves was fairly loud so it must be the beach on the other side of the hedge.

"Harlow?" Cain's voice rose on the question.

"In a minute." She couldn't think and talk. She ran behind one of the massive mechanical units and squatted down. She heard the door open again.

"Vance. Finally. Stay where you are. I have a new earbud. I'm coming to you." Daughtry went down the path. She listened until the crunch of the gravel disappeared. She straightened slowly.

The door burst open again, and she whirled around.

"Jesus Christ, Harlow," Cain thundered. "What the fuck are you doing?"

"Calm down and lower your voice," she snarled back. "I forgot my earbud in the bathroom so I had to go back for it.

When I came out again, Daughtry was coming down the hallway. I headed out here. I had no other option."

"You could have—"

"You can lecture me later. We have to move. Vance's earbud was shot so Daughtry is bringing him a new one. We have to move if we're going to follow them."

"We," he said, pointing back and forth between the two of them, "aren't going anywhere. You are going back to the room, and I will follow Daughtry."

"Great. What does he look like?" she demanded. "Finn, Elias, do you guys know? Do you have eyes on Vance?" There was silence in her earbud. "I'll take that as a no." She went and stood toe to toe with Cain. "I'm going to be a part of this because I need to be. For my brother and for myself. We can stand here and waste time arguing, or we can follow Daughtry to Vance and see who he's meeting."

The pulse in Cain's jaw was in overdrive. His green eyes went flat. He was livid. Well, so was she, so get over it. She turned and started down the path in the direction Vance and Daughtry had gone.

Cain caught up to her in two strides and grabbed her arm. "You are going to do exactly as I say. Jesus, you are killing me. Please, please, *please* stop taking chances. I can't take much more of this."

She nodded but didn't break stride. She was afraid if she looked at him, she might give in and go to the room. She needed to do this, but damn, Cain had been so supportive at dinner that he was making it hellishly hard for her to keep going. They came to fork in the path. Actually, it was more like a four-way stop. "Damn."

"Finn," Cain said. "We're at the end of the building on the path by the AC units. There are three different options. Where does each path go?"

"The one to the right goes to the beach. The one straight

goes to the tiki bar further down the beach. The one to the left of that goes to the pool and around to the front of the hotel."

"Beach, it is," Cain said and then grabbed her hand and tugged her out onto the sand.

When she stumbled, she stopped to take off her shoes. High heels weren't good in sand. "How do you know he's on the beach?"

"I don't, but he'd not likely be at the pool or back in the hotel. The tiki bar is down there." Cain pointed down the beach. "We can see it from here. This is the best option now." He turned to look her in the eye. "What does Daughtry look like?"

She hesitated.

"Harlow," he said in a warning tone.

"He's tall. Maybe an inch or so taller than you. He's got dark hair and eyes. He's wearing a white button-down with brown cargo pants. I didn't notice the shoes. He has a beard as well."

"Scanning now," Axe said.

Axe? Did that mean Nick was there, too? Great, she was going to get lectured from all sides for not staying at the table where it was safe.

"Daughtry's at the tiki bar having a beer, but his eyes are on the beach by the pier. Vance must be down that way."

"Copy that." Cain linked his arm through hers, and they proceeded to stroll down the beach. The sun had set, and now the moon was up. The tiki torches lit up the bar area, but the beach was pretty much in the dark other than the moonglow.

"I don't see him," she murmured.

Cain remained silent. He glanced at her, his gaze was unreadable.

"Your one o'clock," Nick said.

Harlow stared out at the water, desperately wanting to look but knowing she'd get yelled at if she did. Finally, she turned and glanced where they were talking about. She didn't see anything at first and then suddenly she did. Among the shadows. It was a couple kissing.

Cain's voice was clipped. "It's not him."

They were level with the tiki bar now, so Harlow turned to look in that direction. She scanned the people, frowned, then looked again. "Daughtry isn't at the tiki bar."

"What?" Cain turned and studied the crowd. They slowed their walk down to a snail's pace. "Yes. He's over in the back corner table."

She looked again. Squinting to be sure, she shook her head. "That's not Daughtry. He looks similar, but that's not him."

A string of curses lit up her earbud. "Axe, keep looking," Cain demanded.

"On it."

Harlow looked down the beach. It was hard to see anything now. She looked up at the pier. It wasn't very long, but it was well lit. There was a couple at the end, throwing things into the water. Probably some sort of food to attract the fish. There was another couple on the bench about halfway down. That was it.

Then she spied the man. She said, "Daughtry is at the end of the pier. Does that mean that Vance is out on the water somewhere?"

Cain picked up the pace slightly. "Maybe."

A stone wall ran along the edge of a walkway and then it turned right and disappeared under the pier. The rest of the structure was on stilts. Cain seemed to be guiding them toward the stone wall.

"Someone has to check beyond the pier," Axe said. "I can't see anything from my vantage point on this boat."

"I can't see it either," Nick confirmed. I'm back by the hotel."

Cain moved them into the shadows. "Stay here," he said.

"Wait, where are you going?" she demanded, grabbing his arm.

He glanced down at her hand. "Over the other side of the pier. The beach doesn't stop here. It curves around and turns rocky. Axe and Nick are on this side. So are Elias and Finn. Someone has to go over there and check it out." He started to move again.

"Why can't Axe move the boat," she whispered.

"Because I'm just…borrowing the boat," Axe responded.

She frowned. "Borrowing?" It clicked. Axe was on board someone's boat without their knowledge. He had picked one of the empty boats anchored in the bay and was using it as a vantage point.

"I get it. Well, then why can't I go with you?" She hated that she couldn't see his face clearly. They were in the shadows, and he had his back to the moon.

He purposefully looked down at her feet and then at the shoes in her hand. "The other side is mostly rocks. There's only a bit of sand. You won't be able to do it in bare feet or those shoes." He softened his tone, "I need to be able to move quickly and respond if anything happens. I can't do that if you are with me. I need you to stay here where it's safe and the guys can help if you run into trouble. Okay?"

She didn't like it, but she nodded.

He removed her hand off his arm and slid away in the shadows. She crossed her arms over her chest and rubbed her arms. Seeing Daughtry had really spooked her.

"Harlow, stand still if possible," Nick ordered. "Moving attracts attention. We're watching you. You're fine. We'll let you know if there's any trouble."

"Fine," she muttered but stopped moving. The night

would have been beautiful if she wasn't spending it on the beach, looking for a killer. The moon came out from behind the clouds and lit up the beach. She shrank back farther into the shadows.

There was a sound off to her left. Then she heard it again, and this time it was louder. It was coming from under the pier.

"Daughtry," a familiar voice growled. The sound had been the soft ringing of a cell phone. "I'm under the pier."

Harlow's whole body froze. Daughtry was right around the corner from her. She wanted to move, to run, but she couldn't make her body respond.

"He's late. He left his place on time. Morrison confirmed it."

Harlow's heart slammed against her rib cage. Her palms were slick with sweat. What should she do? She shrank back against the rock until it was digging into her back.

"Morrison lost him." There was silence and then, "Yeah, I know. I'll take care of him later. What do you want to do now?"

Daughtry's voice got louder. He came out from underneath the pier, moving in her direction. He turned and looked out at the end of the pier. "Yeah, I can see you."

Vance was up on the pier? But they hadn't seen him, and the pier was mostly well-lit. Were the shadows big enough to hide someone? She didn't think so. Where could he be then? There'd only been two couples on the pier—those at the end, feeding the fish, and the couple on the bench. Wait, the ones on the bench… She'd assumed it was a couple because it looked like a big lump, two people snuggling up, but it could just as easily have been a man hunched over with a blanket over his shoulders.

Should she say something? Did the others know what was going on? Would they tell her if they did?

Daughtry moved a couple of steps closer to her, but she remained motionless. "I can see you from here. I'm in the shadows at the end of the pier. Kapoor is watching from the path. You're covered."

Harlow was convinced the guys couldn't see Daughtry. No one was speaking to her, so they must be watching other areas. She tried to move slightly to her right to put some distance between her and Daughtry, but her dress was caught on the rocks. If he turned, he'd see her for sure and he'd recognize her. She knew it in her bones.

He knew she was alive. Vance had tried to have his people kill her on the ship. It wasn't too much of a stretch that she could be here.

But it was more than that. Daughtry would know her because he'd been close to her, felt her up, tried to rape her. She made an involuntary sound deep in her throat and then froze again. Did he hear it?

"Harlow, don't move. Don't make a sound." Cain's voice was soft in her ear. "I know it's hard, but you have to remain totally still. If you can relax, that's even better."

Relax? Relax! Was he out of his mind?

"He will sense you if you get too scared."

Too scared? Of course she was scared. What else would she be? She tried to breathe as quietly as possible, but she was sure Daughtry could hear her heart thudding.

There was a sound up above. Footsteps. Someone was walking along the pier.

"He's here," Daughtry said, "making his way to the bench."

Keep the meeting brief, she pleaded silently, but it felt like forever since she'd been standing there. She started to shiver.

"Do you have a clear shot?" Daughtry had dropped his voice, but it still carried on the offshore breeze.

Were they going to take someone out? Why? It couldn't be the banker then. That wouldn't make sense.

"We have a clear shot. Give the signal if you want us to put a bull's-eye on his chest."

Harlow's teeth began to chatter. She tried to relax, but it wasn't working. Daughtry was bound to discover her if she stayed much longer. She looked around frantically for a way out. She attempted once again to slide across the rock, but her dress was still caught.

Daughtry's voice sounded. "Light him up."

Harlow tensed and waited for the gunshots, but nothing came. There was only the sound of the breeze rustling the leaves. And the faint sound of voices. She cocked her head, but she couldn't quite make out what they were saying.

"Harlow, hang in there." It was Nick's voice this time.

She was hanging on, but just barely. Adrenaline washed through her making her twitchy. She was standing in an awkward position, and her body was starting to ache. She took in a deep breath and tried to quiet her chattering teeth.

Daughtry said, "He got the message. I'll meet him at the end of the pier and give him the burner cell."

At the end of the pier. That meant he was going to walk around the corner where she stood. Her throat closed over. She couldn't breathe. Panic clawed its way up her chest. There was no way out. If she moved, he'd see her for sure. He'd have to know she'd overheard his conversation.

"He's coming now," Daughtry said.

Icy fingers clutched her heart. This was it. She was about to be discovered. She heard movement. Daughtry was coming her way. A hand touched her arm, and then she was whirled around, falling into Cain's arms. He immediately locked her in his embrace and kissed her hard on the mouth.

CHAPTER SIXTEEN

C ain was aware that Daughtry had rounded the corner and let out a string of curses, but he pretended to be so wrapped up in kissing Harlow that he was oblivious. He had one hand buried in her hair and the other wrapped tightly around her waist, holding her against him. He was afraid if he eased up the pressure at all, she'd say something that would give them away.

Daughtry walked by and made his way up to the pier. Cain vaguely heard voices, but then nothing.

"You're clear," Elias announced.

Cain released her. She stumbled, and he grabbed her arm to steady her. "You okay?"

Harlow didn't say anything, just nodded.

He gave her a long look. She was not okay but there wasn't a damn thing he could do about it at the moment. He needed to get her back to the hotel asap. "Let's go." He grabbed her hand and then turned and started down the beach.

"Nice save, Cain," Nick said. "Axe, did you get a good picture of the guy?"

"Yeah, I got him. I'll go back to our hotel and get started on finding out who he is."

"Good. I'm right behind you."

Finn asked, "Did anyone see where the sniper was?"

Axe responded. "On a boat not far from me. But I'm not sure what that was all about."

"Vance wanted to show the guy that he was easily dealt with," Cain suggested, still leading Harlow up the beach, almost afraid to let go of her hand. He'd come this close… *Stop it right the fuck now. Focus!* "If it is the banker, Vance might want to show that the deal needed to go through, or it would be assured destruction."

Cain was aware that Harlow was shivering. He didn't trust himself to put his arm around her. She'd been so fucking stubborn and demanded she be out there with them, and then she got caught unaware and there hadn't been a fucking thing he could do about it. In truth, it was his fault not hers. He should have checked under the pier. She was only a damn dental hygienist. What the hell did she know about any of this shit? Perry had taught her some skills but in some ways that just made her more vulnerable. She knew just enough to be a danger to herself.

The time she had been trapped by Daughtry were the longest minutes of Cain's life. He'd needed a few minutes away from her to get his brain back in the game. She'd looked so fucking hot over dinner, and then the whole bathroom incident… His nerves were shot. She was his weakness.

All he wanted to do now was get back to the hotel and get her off this fucking island. They didn't need her anymore, and he needed her to be out of his world. She was like a fucking meteor scorching everything in her path, namely him.

They were back at the walkway where they'd started. He

kept walking, but Harlow stopped and tugged her hand from his. He halted and raised his eyebrows at her.

"My shoes," was all she said. She crouched down and struggled to put her shoes back on. She was cold and numb by the looks of things. It took longer than it should have, but she finally was ready to go again.

He took her hand and walked on the path to the front of the hotel this time. They went into the lobby and up in the elevator. Cain checked the strand of hair he'd left in the door to make sure no one had been in their room, pleased to find it intact. The keycard reader buzzed, and he shoved the handle down pushing inward. He tugged Harlow in behind him.

"Is there anything you need from us tonight, Tag?" Cain asked.

"No. We're gonna find out who this guy is, and then we can make a plan in the morning. We'll call if there's any trouble."

"Roger that." Cain reached up and pulled out his earbud.

Harlow did the same and handed it to him. "I know you're upset about tonight but—"

"There are no buts, Harlow. You could have gotten yourself killed." He wanted to yell at her but he was just so damn tired and overwhelmed by her. "You just need to stop," he said in a quiet voice. "You need to just stop!"

"No." Her voice was calm, but her eyes were shooting sparks at him. "I will not stop. I *will* see this through to the end. For Perry."

"The end almost happened tonight." Fighting waves of nausea from that reality, he walked over to the sliding glass doors. "You came face-to-face with Vance, and you almost came face-to-face with Daughtry, a man who tried to rape you. What the fuck more do you need before you realize this isn't a game?"

"You're right," she admitted, but her tone was still firm. "It's not a game. It's *my* fucking life, and I'm aware of who Vance and Daughtry are. I was there. I know what they've done, so don't lecture me about it. You need to just accept that I'm part of the team now. I may not be as proficient at things like the rest of you, but I'm here and I'm staying. I'm going to nail these bastards with or without your help. Now, I'm going to take a shower." She moved quickly and disappeared into the bathroom.

Cain collapsed on the couch and put his head in his hands. What the fuck was he going to do with her? He knew what he'd like to do, and it involved a bed and a lack of clothing. He leaned back and pushed his hair out of his eyes. What he really needed was for her to be safe. He couldn't function at one hundred percent as long as she was in danger. His fear that she would get hurt or worse was eating him up inside. He needed her gone. He was going to put her on a plane tomorrow even if it meant he had to drag her to the airport kicking and screaming.

Twenty minutes later, Harlow came out of the bathroom wearing a towel. Again. Cain glanced up at her and ground his teeth. It was pure fucking torture. She must know what she did to him. Her hair was piled high on her head. The scent of citrus wafted over to him from all freshly scrubbed skin. She was pale, though, and there were dark circles under her eyes. She needed rest and relaxation.

"Where are you going to sleep?" she asked.

"On the couch."

She walked over to him. "Do you have something I can sleep in? I didn't think about that part."

He stood, and their gazes locked. Cain tore his eyes away and moved around her to enter the bedroom. He dug in his bag and brought out a T-shirt. "Here." When he turned around, she was right behind him.

"Thanks." She took the T-shirt and threw it on the bed but held on to his hand. She turned it palm up and then ran her thumb back and forth over it.

He clamped his jaws together. He needed to move away from her. She was driving him crazy on purpose. He'd done the same thing to her hand during dinner. It had been petty, but he wanted her to feel as frustrated as he did. Now it was just damned dangerous.

"Harlow." His voice was gravelly to his own ears. Damn this woman and the effect she had on him.

"What? Turnabout is fair play." She looked up at him through her lashes.

"Harlow," he whispered, "you can't keep playing like this. We're here to do a job and get out. You keep pushing my buttons, and you're not gonna like what happens."

She stepped closer to him until they were mere inches apart and cocked her head. "Who says? Who says I won't like it?"

He ground his teeth. She was Perry's sister, therefore *verboten* but more importantly, the outstanding business with his father could put anyone in his life in danger. He could not sleep with her. He just had to remember they were here for a reason. *But she's going home tomorrow.* He would make her leave. She would be out of his world. Forever. *Just one night left.*

She reached up and dragged a nail across his chest. "Haven't you ever wondered what it would be like? You and me together?"

He stared at her. Wondered? Jesus. He'd fantasized about that very question night after night. "It can't happen."

"Yes, it can."

"No, Harlow." He grabbed her hand and held it. "It can't."

She moved forward and kissed him hard on the mouth. He backed up. "Harlow, I'm warning you. This isn't a game."

"No, it's not. It's two people who have major chemistry. There's nothing wrong with it. Perry is dead. He was your friend, but he's gone. As long as you don't mistreat me, then you have nothing to feel guilty about."

If she only knew. Mistreat her? God, he wanted to protect her and make sure no one would ever mistreat her. But he was not the man for her. She needed a man who was gentle, could care for her the way she wanted. She needed a man who didn't have anger issues and wasn't gone all the time on assignment. She especially didn't need him, the bastard son of the head of the Bianchi crime family. She didn't need to be linked to the mob. That would not bring anything good into her life.

"Harlow," he growled. "I cannot have sex with you."

She glared at him. "Fine then"—she twisted around—"but you're missing out."

He knew it to his core. He wanted her so bad his soul ached. "I'm gonna take a shower. Don't go anywhere. I won't be long."

He went into the bathroom and got undressed. He cranked the shower on cold. It was likely the only thing that could keep his libido in check, and he even had doubts about that. The water hit him full on the chest like icicles stinging his skin. It took his breath away but didn't do much to lessen the hardness below his waist. Gritting his teeth, he quickly washed his hair and body and then got out. He toweled himself off and realized that in his rush, he hadn't brought any clothing into the bathroom with him. He wrapped a towel around his waist and opened the door.

Harlow was standing in the bedroom, his T-shirt skimming the tops of her thighs. She whirled around when he walked into the room. His gaze was riveted on her curves.

She was so beautiful. Her breasts were full and high, and he knew from earlier in the day that the curve of her hip fit perfectly in his hand. He had the urge to touch and taste her everywhere. She stood there staring at him, looking sexy as hell in *his* T-shirt.

"Harlow." It came out as a growl, but it was really a plea. She needed to move away. Cover up. Do anything but stand there looking so fucking hot. When she bit her lip, he damn near came. He made a sound deep in his throat, which seemed to spur her on because she was across the room and in his arms in an instant.

She kissed his mouth, but he stayed rigid. This was a bad idea. But when she broke the kiss and stared up at him with desire and affection in her eyes, his heart expanded and the walls around it crumbled.

He walked her backward until she was up against the wall and then planted a hand on either side of her head. "Are you sure you want to go down this road? Because once you're in, you're in all the way. It's a line we shouldn't cross."

Fuck it. He was tired of being the strong one who said no. He wanted her so fucking bad his balls were blue. He wanted to bury himself so deep inside her that she couldn't ever let him go.

For a moment, she only stared at him. And this time, he couldn't read the emotion that resided there. "You need to say it, Harlow. You need to tell me what you want."

"I want you inside me, Cain. I want you so much it hurts. I want to spend the rest of the night fucking your brains out, and then I want to do it all over again tomorrow."

He captured her mouth in a searing kiss, forcing her lips open with his tongue. She let him in, and it was fucking heaven. Their tongues danced as she wrapped her arms around his neck. He grabbed her hips and pulled her closer. Then he slid his hands down to grab her ass. It fit perfectly in his hands, and he tugged her closer still. She let out a moan as she dropped her hands to his chest and then to the towel at his waist. She pulled at it until it dropped to the floor.

She brought one leg up and wrapped it around his hip. Her hot core was on his cock and, goddamn, if he didn't just about lose it. Then she started thrusting her pelvis against him.

"Harlow," he pleaded, "stop it or I'm gonna come before we get started."

"But I want you inside me, now. Fucking now!" she demanded.

He pushed her leg down and then tugged on her thong until it hit the floor. Then he pulled the T-shirt off over her head. He let his hands roam over her curves. God, she was perfection. He dropped his mouth to her right nipple and then to the left. She grabbed his hair with both hands and pulled his head back so she could capture his mouth in a fierce kiss.

He picked her up and dropped her on the bed so she fell back and then he lowered himself down on top of her. He went back to sucking her nipples as he moved his hand over her hip.

"I want you now, Cain."

The sound of his name on her lips made adrenaline rush through his veins, tightening his muscles, hardening his cock to the point of pain. She was his and only his. He sucked her nipple and then rolled it between his teeth. She gasped and then let out a low groan. He grazed his fingers across her belly and then went lower. When he moved his fingers over her center, her breath caught. When he moved down so his mouth hovered over her core, her breath sped up, her magnificent chest heaving.

"Cain," she moaned. She watched him as he lowered his head to taste her. She was wet and ready for him.

He'd dreamed about this for so long; since the day he'd first seen her in that damn bar. And yet reality was superior to anything he'd fantasized.

He licked her slowly, the sweet, salty taste of her coating his tongue, and then swirled through her folds in small circles. She fisted the sheets and made small panting sounds. He slid one finger inside her and then another, moving in a slow rhythm as he glanced up at her. Her head was thrown back, her back arched, her feet on his shoulders, opening her wide. A fierce wave of possession crashed over him. No man would ever touch her like this besides him. She was his. Forever.

He put another finger inside her and sped up the rhythm, her hips matching his pace. He captured her with his tongue, and she fisted his hair, holding him against her. Her hips were bucking wildly, and she called out his name as she came.

CHAPTER SEVENTEEN

Harlow couldn't get over the solid strength of Cain's muscles. She'd never been with a man that was so cut. She ran her hands all over the taut ridges of muscle as he kissed and sucked on her neck and throat. He was something to behold when he was dressed, but naked? Naked, he was something else entirely. His body was as chiseled as a statue of a god carved out of stone. Not an ounce of fat anywhere, which might have been damned annoying if he wasn't so fucking hot.

She straddled him, buried her hands in his hair, and kissed him hard. Then she deepened the kiss and started to move her hips. God, this felt so fucking good. She loved his long hair. It made her tingle every time she put her hands in it.

He broke off the kiss. His eyes were emerald green and filled with lust for her. They glittered as he put his hands on her hips. He groaned when she started sucking his nipples, running them between her teeth. He was so damn intoxicating. She loved the fact that he was hard for her. He wanted *her*.

She moved down and dropped kisses over the flat planes of his stomach and then moved farther south until her mouth hovered over his cock. She licked the very tip with her tongue and then made small circles. First one way, then the other. Slowly, she drew more and more of him into her mouth, sucking while twisting her tongue.

Cain groaned her name, his rough voice sending tingles of pleasure through her. His hips started to move, and she matched the rhythm with her tongue.

"No. This will be too quick. I want to be inside you."

Harlow smiled and rose up. She was about to climb on top of him again when he flipped her over and pinned her to the bed. His eyes darkened as he looked down at her breasts. She reached for his cock. She wanted to feel him move inside her. Their gazes locked as he entered her. It was so damn hot. She was vibrating with need for him.

He started moving slowly, but she pumped her hips faster. She needed more. "Faster. Harder. Cain, I can't wait any longer. I've been waiting so fucking long for this." He groaned. Then she locked her legs behind his ass and guided him deep inside her. "Fuck me hard," she demanded. He drilled into her, and she arched beneath his straining body. "God, yes!"

"Say my name," he commanded.

"God, Cain." She bit her lip and urged him on. She'd wanted him for so long and now it was even better than she'd dreamed. She let out a moan and fisted the sheets as she arched underneath him. "Cain," she called out again as she crashed over the edge into oblivion.

Two strokes later, he was right there with her. He collapsed beside her on the bed, out of breath. "Jesus, Harlow. You are going to be the death of me."

"Only if we can go like this." She smiled lazily at him. "That was amazing."

He nodded his agreement and then pulled her in close. He tucked his arm under her head for a pillow and lay the other hand on the curve of her waist.

She closed her eyes and soaked in the moment. Sheer bliss. Amazing sex with the man she'd been dreaming about for ages and a chance to get her brother's killer. It was all coming together. She opened her eyes and placed a hand on Cain's abs. He had *the* best body and, God, did he know how to use it. She propped herself up on an elbow and ran her gaze over the length of him. "How long do you need before round two?"

The sun was shining in the windows when she opened her eyes. She stretched out languidly and smiled to herself. She hadn't gotten much sleep but, oh, man, was it worth it. Her lady bits were getting tingly just thinking about it.

She lay her hand on Cain's side of the bed, but it was cold. She rose on her elbow and listened. There was no sound in the room. She sat up and cocked her head. No. Nothing. She was alone. Where the hell had Cain gone? He'd left her alone. What did that mean? Was she not in danger? Well, she wouldn't be unless Vance's people knew where she was. Maybe he went down to get them breakfast. Ooh, pancakes and bacon with a side of hash browns. That would be heaven. With Cain for dessert.

The door of the suite opened, and a second later, Cain strode around the corner. He looked better than fine in a forest green T-shirt and tan cargo pants, but she could only think about ways to get him out of those clothes and back into the bed.

His dark hair was damp, and he flicked it out of his face.

"Get dressed. Your flight leaves in two hours. I have to get you to the airport."

"Wha-what? What do you mean?"

"I thought I was pretty clear." He stood there with his hands on his hips. "Your flight leaves in two hours. You need to get moving."

She stared at him. "What flight? I'm not leaving."

"Yes, you are." His gaze was unblinking. His eyes were the green of the cold Arctic sea. "Get dressed."

"No." She hopped up out of bed and stood there naked. She didn't care. She wasn't going home.

Cain's eyes raked over her body before moving back to her face. Heat crept up her neck, but she wouldn't give him the satisfaction of covering up.

"Yes, you are. Your job was to help us locate Vance by identifying his men. You've done that. We know who they are and where they are. You can go home now."

Icy fingers gripped her heart. She struggled to catch her breath. "Morrison," she blurted. "You don't know what he looks like. He's still out there."

"Morrison is dead. They found his body this morning, floating off a wharf at another big hotel. They're calling it an accidental drowning. You have to go."

"But I want to stay. I need to be here to see it through. I have to help catch Vance. He *killed* Perry." She took a step forward.

He crossed his arms over his chest and the closed off movement stung her like a man-of-war. There was a finality in his tone when he spoke. "You've done that. Against all odds, you were the one that figured it all out. We wouldn't be here if it weren't for you, but now you have to go. Last night proved it's way too dangerous. Harlow, you need to go be with your parents. I promise I'll keep you updated."

She shook her head. "I'll stay in the shadows. I'll listen to everything you say."

His face turned hard. "It's too late for that. Daughtry is here. If he sees you, it's not just you that's in trouble. All our covers will be blown. They already know we're coming for them. If they see you, they'll know we're here." He glanced at his watch. "You've got twenty minutes." He turned and strode out the door again.

Tears started streaming down her face. A sob escaped her chest. How could he do this? How could he kick her out like this? He knew how much it meant to her to be here. She needed this. She'd thought after last night they'd be...what? A couple? Maybe not, but at least that he'd want her nearby. Instead, he was pushing her as fast, and as far, away as possible. Perry had warned her off him, said that Cain was a great guy, but not the guy for her. Apparently, he'd been right. What an ass she was, thinking he'd gone for breakfast to surprise her, but instead he surprised her with a ticket home. How could she have been so wrong?

She went to the bathroom and turned on the shower, climbing in before the spray was even hot. She needed to scrub the smell of him off her skin. He'd betrayed her. She thought she could trust him, but he'd broken that trust. She'd wanted him so badly, and she'd thought he felt the same.

And he did feel it, too. She knew it. Hell, he'd proven it, four times to be exact.

A single thought slammed her like a freight train, and she leaned against the wall for support. All this time she'd been telling herself she wanted him, lusted after him, but the reality was she was in love with him. She'd had sex with him, thinking there was a connection between them that was more than just physical.

But hadn't he warned her? He told her there was no going back. He made her say she wanted him out loud. She thought it was some sort of come-on, but he really wanted her to say it so when this moment happened, she would know he'd given her every opportunity to back out. She let out another sob and covered her face with her hands. She'd been an idiot. A fool. Her heart ached as if a giant fist was squeezing the stupidity out of it.

Cain banged on the door and called, "Ten minutes, Harlow."

She straightened and took a deep breath. She needed to forget Cain, the amazing sex they'd just had, and the connection they obviously *didn't* have. She had to figure out a way to stay. They'd only gotten this far because of her. She'd make sure they didn't forget it.

Ten minutes later, she was dressed and ready to take on Cain, but it was Nick who walked into the room. "Harlow," he said. "How are you feeling after last night?"

She blinked and stared at him for a minute. Was he asking about her and Cain? "Um…" Then it hit her…the beach. "I'm fine. It was a bit scary, but we made it and we learned who the banker is. What's going on with that?"

Nick smiled. "I have some people working on background and Axe is following him this morning, so I think we're good. Are you ready to go?"

"About that—"

Nick held up his hand. "I'm putting you on that airplane, Harlow. You've done amazing things on your own and you got us here, but you can only cheat death so many times. It's something we live with and accept when we sign up. Your brother knew it, too. You have been lucky more times than I can count. Your luck will run out, and I know Cain will not survive if he has to tell your parents that another one of their children didn't make it. If anything happens to you, it would crush us all."

She wanted to argue, but his words took the wind out of

her sails and guilt bloomed in the void. Maybe it was time to go home. She did not want to die. She didn't want to hurt her family any more than she already had. Maybe she wasn't always so sure about moving forward, but this whole thing had awakened something in her, and now she wanted… more. A new career, a new life. That's what waited for her when she went home. She just needed to find a way to create it. And forget Cain ever existed.

"Okay, Nick, I'll go, but I want to be kept in the loop. I want phone calls and emails. I'd wear an earbud if it worked that far away."

He smiled. "Deal."

She took a couple of minutes to pack her new clothes and then they headed out. Nick put on a faded ball cap and large sunglasses. Harlow wore a pair of shorts and a sky-blue T-shirt with her new pair of sneakers. She might as well be comfortable on the ride home.

They moved very quickly out of the lobby and climbed into the waiting SUV. Cain was driving. Seeing him gave her a jolt, but she kept her glance trained out the window and her mouth shut. He was equally silent. The ride to the airport took no time, and soon they were pulling up to the curb. Nick had turned in his seat to hand Harlow her ticket when his cell went off.

"Taggert." There was a long silence, and then Nick started looking around. "I've got him. Shit." There was more silence and then, "Yeah." Nick listened for a few more minutes before saying, "You're here? Okay meet us at the hotel." Nick supplied the name of the hotel where they were staying and then hung up. "Foley." He nodded toward a man coming out of the last doors of the terminal. He had his own bodyguard with him.

"I know him," Harlow said. "He was there the day they

dug up the money. There was tension between him and Vance, or that's what it seemed like."

Nick glanced back at her. "You're saying you saw Foley in Iraq when they pulled the money out of the ground?"

"Uh-huh. Didn't I mention that before? Vance had a brick of money in his hand and when Foley came over and spoke to him, the brick disappeared. Foley had his back turned toward me so I couldn't see what happened, but I always assumed Foley took the money. Vance didn't have it when the men moved apart."

He turned to Cain. "She can link Foley and Vance directly to the money."

"All the more reason to get her out of here," Cain reasoned.

"True, but one of us will have to go with her. She can't be left alone on a regular flight."

Cain frowned. "Do you think he knows about her?"

"By now, he probably knows she was in the container but is still alive. He probably doesn't know the rest, but that was enough to go after her folks. Now the stakes are even higher since the other two shipments are gone."

Foley got into a black SUV that was standing at the curb.

Cain swore. "This is going down today."

Nick agreed. "If Foley is risking being here and being seen with Vance and the money then, yeah, it's a good bet that it's going down today. Or they'll at least start to transfer the money into the bank today."

"Shit. We aren't ready for that. We haven't even found the money yet." Cain's knuckles whitened where his hands gripped the steering wheel.

"Yeah, but I'm betting Foley will lead us to it. And now we have help."

Cain looked at him. "What help?"

"The Callahans are here. I asked them to do some

digging for us and set them up to follow Foley. I needed someone outside Washington who we could trust."

"That makes it a bit better. Still, we're not nearly set up. Too many unknowns."

"Agreed," Nick said. "Let's go back to our hotel and hash this out."

"What about Foley?" Cain asked.

"We'll follow him for now and then hand him off to Finn and Axe. Elias can stay at the resort and keep an eye on Vance."

"What about her?" Cain gestured toward the back seat.

Harlow sat quietly in the back of the vehicle. She was going to interrupt, but she quickly realized Nick was making her case for her. If she spoke, it might just piss Cain off again and he would force her to go. Better to sit quietly and see what happened. Not her usual temperament, but she was desperate and willing to try anything at this point.

Nick glanced back at her. "She'll have to come with us now. With Foley here, I feel like the stakes have gone up, and she's the only link between Foley and Vance with the money. I'm not sure I want to trust anyone else to take care of her."

Cain nodded once, but the muscle in his jaw was jumping.

Harlow sat back as they watched Foley's SUV pull away from the curb. Cain did the same but kept several cars between them. She ducked her head and allowed a small smile to bloom on her lips. Cain might not be happy, but she didn't care.

Nick's words came floating back to the surface. She'd been lucky and cheated death a few times now. He was right. But odds were her luck was going to run out sooner rather than later and she wasn't going to make it. She said a small prayer that she managed to take Vance and Foley down before Lady Luck deserted her.

CHAPTER EIGHTEEN

C ain pulled to the curb behind a box truck and shoved the SUV's gearshift into park. Tense silence dominated the cab of the vehicle as they watched Foley climb out of his SUV in the marina parking lot. His bodyguard alighted with him, and the driver emerged a moment later. A minute later, two other SUVs pulled up. Vance, Patel, and Daughtry got out of the first one and the men Harlow had previously identified got out of the second.

"Hail, hail the gang's all here," Harlow murmured from the back seat.

Nick's cell went off. He put it on speaker. "Axe, Finn, where are you two?"

"Look in your side mirror," Finn said.

Cain glanced in the mirror and saw them parked a little bit down the street. Then he looked back through the windshield and saw Elias parking about half a block away on the other side of the marina parking lot. He lifted his chin, and Nick nodded.

"Give me a sec, guys. I'll patch Elias in." Nick asked, "Everybody hear me?"

There was a chorus of yesses.

"Let me bring you up to date. Foley arrived when we were at the airport. We think the money transfer is going to start today. It's almost ten-thirty. I'm thinking they are going to bring it to the bank in chunks. It will have to be counted so it's a time-consuming task. The whole thing, if they do it smartly, will probably take them a month or so, but I'm guessing Foley may try and rush it."

"Is that why Foley is here?" Finn asked.

"It's all supposition, but yeah," Nick said. "I think he's here because the rest of the money is gone. He needs to make sure this one gets to the bank. The cartel has to be breathing down his neck on this."

Cain watched as the men climbed aboard two different tenders and headed out of the marina into the bay. "Do we have any way to find out where they're going? If they have the money on another island, we won't find it."

Axe piped up. "It's not going to an island. It's going to a boat."

"Why do you say that, Axe?" Cain asked.

"Because they need something close by so they don't have to travel far to get it from the resort. I'm guessing the money is on a yacht we can see from the beach. They can keep an eye on it the whole time without drawing any attention to it."

"Shit," Cain mumbled. "And we didn't even twig to it. You're right. Makes perfect sense."

"Also means there are more Silverstone guys here than we thought," Elias added. There was a lot of rustling from Elias's phone. "I'm going to see if I can keep them in sight." They saw him exit his vehicle and head across to the marina. Then he disappeared around the side of the building.

Harlow cleared her throat. "How many more do you think, men that is?"

"Good question," Nick said. He counted off on his fingers. I'm thinking an even dozen. What do you guys think?"

Cain nodded and then said "yes" out loud for the rest of the guys. The number sounded right to him.

Finn sighed. "That means they have more than twice our number of fully trained operatives and a strong likelihood that there are more."

"We have some back up," Nick stated.

"We do?" Axe asked.

"The Callahans are here. They were following Foley for me, so they flew down when he did. We're going to go back to our hotel and meet them. Axe, you and Finn stay here and back up Elias. See if you can figure out which boat they're on. Follow the main players. Let us know when they hit shore again."

"Roger that." They all clicked off the call.

Cain pulled away from the curb and headed to the hotel. He was trying to keep his anxiety about Harlow in check, but it was like sticking your thumb into a dike to hold back the flood… Damn hard. He needed her gone so he could concentrate fully on this op. With that many tier-one operators involved, it was going to be messy no matter what they did.

Ten minutes later, they pulled into the hotel parking lot and climbed out. The Callahans got out of their SUV as well. Nick walked over to them. "Mitch." He offered his hand to the blond guy, and they bumped shoulders.

Mitch smiled. "Good to see you, Nick. These are my brothers, Gage"—he pointed to a tall well-built dark-haired guy—"and Logan." The other brother was similar in height and coloring but was leaner in build.

"Nice to finally meet you in person." Nick extended his

hand, and the men shook. He turned. "This is Cain Maddox and Harlow Moretti."

They all shook and then headed up the stairs to the suite Nick had organized for them. Nick let everyone in, and they all found a spot to sit or stand. "So, what do you know?" asked Mitch.

Nick laid it out for them. Cain listened intently. Sometimes, it was in these moments that something stuck out to him that they'd missed. It was like rereading a file several times and then finally seeing something new. But this time, nothing jumped out at him.

"So, you think it's going to happen today?" Gage asked. "Makes sense."

Logan spoke up. "I think you're right. Foley is here to make sure things go smoothly."

Cain leaned against the doorjamb to the bathroom. "The cartel has to be breathing down his neck as well. He will have to get the money sorted quick time. They may already have people on the island. All this doesn't put Jesus Espinoza in the best light." Not, Cain thought, that there was ever a good light on the leader of a cartel.

"About that," Gage said. "I spoke to some friends in the intelligence community, and you guys were right, the whole kidnapping of Congressman Lamston was a hoax perpetrated by Foley and Espinoza. It's a well-known secret. Espinoza, however, has been in a power struggle for the leadership of the cartel for the last year or so. That money would have come in handy. Probably would have put him on top."

"That's why Foley had to move the money and why he killed Perry and the rest of the team. He couldn't wait it out any longer. Only their deaths caused more issues, and he ended up not being able to get the money out until recently." Cain ground his teeth. *Fucking Foley and his cartel asshole friend.*

Gage nodded. "I think that's likely. We're sorry about your former team. That's tough."

"Thanks." Cain glanced at Harlow, who was sitting on the desk where he usually sat, being unusually silent. It was worrying, but he couldn't think about her now and still focus.

"So how are we going to do this?" Mitch asked.

"I have no fucking clue." Nick shook his head. "We just figured out who all the players were yesterday, so we're way behind the eight ball on this. I wish we could slow it down. Even if we could slow it by a day, it would be good. I think once they start moving the money, it's going to be really hard to stop them. We could call in Treasury or the FBI but Bertrand is being cagey about that. He seems to want us to do this on our own."

Logan was sitting on a bed leaning against the headboard. "Washington politics are always sketchy. You're right about one thing though. Once the money is in the system, it's done. All the banker has to do is hit a few keystrokes and the money exists, and then it can be sent all over the world." He frowned. "If I were the banker, I would have them deposit a substantial amount of cash on the first trip so I knew they weren't lying about the transaction. Then, in actual fact, he could start spreading it around immediately. Yes, you're right, once this starts, it's too late to collect the evidence and make a case. They'll just keep moving the money."

Logan climbed off the bed. "I guess we should fill you in a bit. While we all run Callahan Security, I'm the more business-slash-money manager type. Mitch manages the personal security side of things, and Gage manages everything else. Why that's relevant is, I'm going to get changed out of my jeans into an expensive suit and go down to the bank and stall the banker, whose name, incidentally, is Wilbur Fortescue. I will attempt to bog Fortescue down so that he won't be able to deal with Foley today. That buys us twenty-four hours if we're lucky. I'm sure you can come up with something in that amount of time."

"Sounds good," Nick said.

Logan grabbed a bag and disappeared into the bathroom.

"Now, does anyone have any ideas on how this assault should go?" Nick asked.

Cain straightened and folded his arms across his chest. "I've been thinking about it, and since they're on a yacht, I think we need to sink it."

"Come again?" Nick said.

"Scuttle the damn thing. Do it just after daybreak. We sink the yacht and then they'll all be in the water. Fish in a barrel. We can pick them out and arrest them."

Axe frowned. "Ah, but won't the money go down with the ship?"

"With any luck, yes," Cain confirmed.

Nick scratched his chin. "I'm not following your thinking."

Elias hooted and slapped his fist on his thigh. "I am. And I think it's fucking brilliant. What Cain's suggesting is, if we sink the boat fast, they'll have time to save themselves, but not the money. We arrest them and then dive for the bags of money. We can dry it out, or DHS can dry it out. Someone will make sure the money is dry. Either way, the point is they can't get away. Take their boat out, and they literally have to swim for it. The money is way too heavy for them to swim away with. So as long as the money is on the boat like we think, then we're golden."

Nick nodded slowly. "I see where you're going with this, but it sort of leaves the door open in a way. They won't be caught with the money. There might be some wiggle room for them."

Cain cocked his head. "That's where Harlow comes in. She can place both at the scene where they dug the money up. She can place Daughtry in the container, and it's hardly believable some mysterious person put a hundred million dollars on a boat to frame Foley and Vance."

He hated the idea that Harlow would have to testify against these men. They were animals, and her life would no doubt be in danger, but it seemed to be the only card they could play. They needed her to make the link. And knowing Washington, it may never get that far. His stomach churned just thinking they might get away with it, but he knew it was possible. Foley had way too many friends in Washington. Too much dirty laundry to air if he was given the opportunity.

He glanced at Harlow. She looked tired and a bit lost. She was in so far over her head, and she didn't even realize it. He wanted to protect her. To wrap her in his arms and never let her go. Maybe after this was over.

No. It was never going to work because after this there was still his father. No. Better to sever ties now.

Mitch pointed at Cain. "I like the way you think. Totally outside the box. They won't see it coming. Smart."

Gage nodded. "I gotta say, I think it will work."

"Agreed," Nick said. "Now, how do we blow up the boat?"

The late afternoon sun was reflecting off the water as Cain re-entered the suite. He'd come back for his stuff, and if he were being honest, some time away from Harlow. It was damn hard to keep her at a distance. Being icy to her was draining and soul crushing. She'd been so hurt this morning when he'd told her to get dressed because she was leaving. It had cost his heart deeply to keep pushing her away. He wanted nothing more than to crawl back into bed with her and stay there forever.

He flicked his hair out of his eyes, grabbed his bag, and started shoving clothing into it. Get Vance and Foley, and then get back to Miami and normal life. Of course, there was his father to deal with. Who the fuck knew how that was going to go? And even though Nick hadn't said anything, he knew there was something going on with Bertrand. Nick was keeping the admiral informed every step of the way, but there was a lot of hushed tones in those conversations and Nick was stressed. Something was definitely up.

He finished packing his bag and glanced around the room. An image of Harlow riding him floated into his mind, head thrown back, back arched. God, she was so damn sexy. He was getting hard just thinking about her.

"Fuck," he mumbled. This wasn't going to work.

Now that Foley was here, everything had changed. They were moving from the resort back to the hotel. They didn't need to be here anymore, which was a damn good thing because every time he looked at the bed, he saw Harlow in it, and he lost focus all over again.

He double-checked that he had everything. It was time to get back to the other hotel and see what progress was made on the op. He thought they had a good plan outlined. They still needed a few more details in place, but it should work.

Logan Callahan was a magician. He'd tied Fortescue up in knots about something and succeeded in buying them a day. That was all they needed. Perry was going to get his justice soon, and Harlow was going to go home and back to a normal life. His chest hurt at the thought of not being in that life, but she needed stability, a chance to heal. He couldn't offer her that. Not with his family situation and his job. His world was always in flux.

He opened the room door and stepped out into the hallway. There was a slight sound to his left. When he started to turn, someone placed a gun to his head. The barrel was cold against his temple. He saw the weapon in his peripheral vision, but he couldn't see the person behind it. "No sudden moves, or I'll drop you right here."

Cain didn't recognize the voice. Then another man behind him grabbed the bag out of his hand while the gun was still to his head. There were definitely two of them, but they were keeping out of his line of sight. The second man took the gun from his waistband and his ankle.

"Now, you're gonna walk down this hallway and not give me any trouble," said the first man with the gun to Cain's head.

Cain turned and started toward the elevators. He thought about how he could disarm the gunman and fight off two men. He knew their skill set was probably similar to his, so they would know his moves. Was there something he could do that they wouldn't expect?

As they approached the elevators, Cain decided that he'd make a play for the gun as soon as the doors started to open. He mentally got himself ready to move. They stopped in front of the elevators but at the ding, the world suddenly went black.

Cain became aware that he was swaying slightly. No, not swaying; he was on water. It was the movement of the waves. He was on a ship. His head throbbed. The gunman must have smacked him on the back of the head with the gun. He didn't move or open his eyes. Better not to alert anyone he was awake.

The waves were calm, so they must still be in the bay by the resort. That was his best guess. The smell of salt reached him as did the sound of gulls and people chatting. There was laughter and music. Another sign they hadn't moved the boat from the bay. That meant he was on a yacht called *Summer's Dream*. He tried to recall if Elias had shared any details about the yacht at the afternoon briefing, but nothing sprung to mind. Only that it was about a hundred-and-fifty-foot cruiser with big engines and lots of room.

The floor underneath him was soft. Carpeted. That meant they hadn't dumped him in the engine room. Smart. The engine room or mechanicals was a rookie mistake. If the person had any skill at all and woke up, then they could do damage to the boat.

These guys weren't amateurs, for sure. They knew he'd strike when the elevator doors opened, so they hit first. He really needed to remember to think outside the box. *More Giancarlo and less Cain.* Where the hell had that thought come from? He took a minute to assess his body. Was he in pain? Other than his head, no. His feet were bound as were his hands, secured behind his back. Zip ties most likely.

He rolled his head, but a wave of wooziness spun around his brain, and he stopped moving. Alright, not just a bump on the head, but drugged as well. He mentally went over his body again. Was there anything that didn't feel right? His shoulder, the left one. He was lying on it, but there was slight pain. They'd drugged him. That meant it was later than he thought. It had to be after sunset. He paused one last time before opening his eyes to make sure no one was in the room. No. He was alone. Of course, they could be watching him on camera, but he couldn't do anything about that.

He slowly opened his eyes. Just a slit at first. The room was dark. He was on carpet, staring at the built-in base of a bed. He opened his eyes fully. There was a wall behind him and a built-in nightstand by his head. The door was at his feet.

He heard footsteps.

They grew closer, and the door opened. "On your feet, sunshine."

CHAPTER NINETEEN

"But how do we know he's okay?" she asked Nick as they drove to the marina.

He grimaced. "We don't."

That was not the answer she wanted to hear. She'd said she wanted the truth but now she wasn't so sure. The truth scared the shit out of her. She stared out the window as they passed through the palm tree lined streets. The moon was full and the sky clear. That was a bad thing, apparently, because it made it harder to sneak up on the Silverstone guys. She rubbed her head.

"Do you think they'll kill him?" she asked, keeping her voice quiet.

Finn spoke up. "Harlow, you followed these men for months. What do you think they'll do?"

Her breath hitched. They were all trying to get her to see the reality of the situation without telling her. No one wanted to say it. He was their friend, their brother. He was the love of her life. No one wanted to lose him.

Axe grunted, "Yes."

"Yes what?" Finn asked.

"Yes, they will kill him."

Icy fingers gripped Harlow's heart. Axe was telling her the truth, the one she needed to hear. Her stomach rolled and bile rose sharply. She fought the need to purge the contents of her stomach.

"But not immediately," Axe continued. "They'll want to see what we know first. Once he breaks and tells them, *then* they'll kill him. It just means we have to be fast about this. Cain knows the plan. He'll know how to react. We've moved up our timeline. They know we're coming, but they'll think we'll do it in the middle of the night. No one will expect us to show up at ten at night. It's practically happy hour. It's the best we can do. Cain will just have to hang on 'til we get there. He can do that."

Axe spoke with confidence, but Harlow heard the fear in his voice. She sensed it in all of them. They wanted to save their brother. They were all terrified this whole thing was on the downward slope into the shitter. So was she.

"One last check, Elias. Anything?"

"No. If they're watching this place, it's with a drone."

They pulled into the marina. It wasn't the same one from earlier in the day. This one was several miles down the coastline. They didn't want to be seen. It was also a small, family run place. The owner was happy to take their money and keep his mouth shut.

"Do you think they have drones?" she asked Nick.

"Harlow, get your shit together. You followed these assholes all over Iraq. You can do this. We agreed to let you come because, quite frankly, we have nowhere else to put you, and we can't spare anyone to watch you. But we have a job to do. Cain is one of us, and if we have any hope of saving his ass, we need to fully focus. I need you to stop asking questions none of us can answer and get your head in the game. Can you do that?"

Heat burned up her neck and into her face. He was right. She was being an ass. No, worse. She was being a…a ninny. A hand-wringing idiot. It was Cain's fault. He'd turned her into a mess. If she hadn't been so in love with him, then she'd be fine. She closed her fists and clamped her jaws together.

"You're right," she said. "Sorry. Won't happen again. What can I do to help?"

"Just do what we say and don't get in the way."

She nodded once.

They all got out of the SUV, and Elias walked over to meet them. They were already all decked out in tactical gear. Elias helped Axe unload the bags from the trunk. They'd brought some stuff with them, but luckily the Callahans had brought more when they'd flown down. Easier to do when you come by private jet.

"Okay, you all know the plan. Axe, you and Finn take the smaller speedboat and head out. Harlow, Elias, and I will be right behind you in the larger one. Harlow, I want you below deck at all times and out of sight."

She nodded.

"When we get into position, I'll give the signal. I haven't heard back from Bertrand yet about the *Walton*. He's unavailable." He paused. "There's definitely something going on with Bertrand, so I'm not sure we're gonna get much help on this one. It's up to us to save Cain's ass. Let's go get our boy. Stay sharp. Watch each other's six."

Everyone dispersed to their boats. She climbed in after Nick and immediately went below as instructed. Nick leaned in the hatch and handed her an earbud. She nodded once and put it in her right ear. The engines started, and they were moving out in no time.

Harlow leaned back on the little built-in couch she was sitting on. Her heart pounded against her rib cage. Cain just had to be okay. He could not be dead. They could not kill him. She wouldn't survive it.

CHAPTER TWENTY

"Have no idea," Cain said and then braced himself for the coming punch. Daughtry pounded his knuckles into Cain's left kidney.

He grunted and tried to absorb the pain by breathing shallowly. He'd be peeing red for the next good while if he managed to get out of this. He lifted his head once more and glanced around the room. They were in the yacht's salon. They'd tied him to a chair in the middle of the room. Foley was sitting on the couch to his left, reading a document of some kind and drinking scotch. Patel was sitting on the couch on the right with his feet up on the coffee table, watching the interrogation.

Vance strolled into the room. "Any progress?"

"No," Daughtry said. "But the night is young. I plan on getting my tools out in a bit. This is just softening him up a bit."

Great. Tools for torture. Cain tried to move his hands, but the zip ties were tight. He had no illusions that he could withstand any great amount of torture. Once that started, the countdown was on. Everyone broke under torture. It was just a question of how long.

The original plan had been to get in and out as quickly as possible and do it during daylight hours. Now, it was much more complicated. Not only would they have to attempt to blow up the boat in the dark, but they'd have to get him off the ship first.

On the other hand, if they just left him, it would improve their odds dramatically. He would hold on as long as he possibly could under whatever torture Daughtry would dish out. He hoped that would be enough time for Team RECON to get in place and ride in like the fucking cavalry. If not, maybe he'd get lucky and die. He would rather that than tell these motherfuckers anything about his teammates.

He looked over at Vance. "When did you recognize me?"

Vance glanced up at him from his spot behind the bar. "It wasn't until I saw you walk across the lobby this morning that it clicked. You looked familiar, but I couldn't place you. The blonde was distracting. Nice touch, by the way. But this morning you were…serious. All business. And you'd pulled your hair back. It clicked then. I knew if you came back to the resort, we could grab you. We didn't have a chance to put a tail on you before you were gone."

"Why the fuck are you telling him anything?" Daughtry snarled.

He shrugged. "Why not? He's a dead man. If it were me, I'd want to know."

"How many of you are there?" Daughtry demanded of Cain.

Cain braced himself before he said, "Just me. Like I said. I'm on vacation. This is just one big coincidence. The blonde will be worried right about now."

Daughtry hit him again.

When he'd caught his breath, he asked, "Patel, did you kill Omar Balik?"

Patel raised his eyebrows. He looked over at Foley, who looked at Cain and then nodded at Patel.

"Yes," Patel confirmed.

Axe would like to hear that. Omar had caused the Suez to be blocked and Axe's girlfriend to be trapped on board the barricading cargo container. Silverstone people kidnapped and tried to kill her. They'd suspected Patel, known now as Kapoor, of killing Omar, but there was never any proof.

"His father hired you?" Cain asked. Maybe if he kept asking questions, he could postpone the inevitable a bit longer.

Patel nodded. "I enjoyed the irony of it. The son hiring us to tip the scales in his direction and the father hiring us to deal with the problem his son had become. There's symmetry in that."

Yeah, Patel would find out about symmetry if Salvatore Ricci ever found out about this. Cain might not love his father, but the old man would never let his son's death go unavenged. That thought brought him a slight bit of comfort. If all else failed tonight, his father would make sure these men paid with blood.

Daughtry snarled, "Enough," and then hit Cain on the right kidney without warning.

Cain doubled over as far as he could. That one hurt. He shook his head and blinked his eyes to try to clear the haze the pain had created. He needed to keep them talking. What else did he want to know?

"Do you have any connection to the Russians and Santiago in Miami?" he asked. His voice was weaker to his own ears.

Foley looked up from his papers. "Now why would you ask that?"

Cain shrugged. "Call it curiosity. We just had dealings with Santiago." Elias had to go undercover to get Santiago. It had been a rough go since his girlfriend was also undercover with them. Santiago had killed Elias's childhood best friend so the whole thing had been a nightmare.

Foley studied him and then threw the paperwork on the table. "We were aware of the Russians working with Santiago before he died. We've heard they're looking for another contact." Foley leaned back on the couch. "Put that under 'possible business ventures.'"

Daughtry moved forward again, but Foley waved him off. "Give him a drink of water." Daughtry sneered but went and got a cold bottle of water from the mini fridge behind the bar. He held the bottle while Cain drank.

"Do you have any other questions?" Foley asked.

"How involved were you with Josh Hargate and Greyscale?"

Foley's eyebrows went up. "You do ask the most interesting questions. What do you know about Greyscale?"

Cain cocked his head. "We know what Hargate was up to with a certain group of senators."

"Huh. Yeah, I helped Josh a bit there. Provided some men and equipment. He managed the rest. He still owes me some money. You wouldn't happen to know where he is, would you?"

"CIA black site is my best guess."

Foley stood up. "Well, that *is* interesting. Was your team part of that takedown? I heard it involved the Coast Guard."

Cain remained silent. There was no point in confirming it. Foley was just trying to get him talking about his team, and that just wasn't going to happen. He glanced at the clock on the wall. It was nine fifty-five. He assessed where he was physically and knew, in a heartbeat, he wouldn't make it until morning.

"You and your friends certainly get around," Foley said as he went behind the bar. Crystal clinked against a bottle as he poured himself a drink. "You've fucked up several of my operations, and you've been dogging my every move. It's too bad for you the bullet Vance put in your leg didn't have a more lasting effect. Then you wouldn't be here. Because this is when it's about to get nasty." He took a swig of his drink. "I've answered your questions, and now it's time you answered mine."

Cain said, "Okay, ask me a question. So far, only your goon here has asked anything, and it's always the same one."

Foley studied Cain over the rim of his glass. "What happened to the woman who was in the container? Is she the same woman at the hotel with you?"

Cain shook his head. He was doing his best not to think about Harlow. He regretted not being with her sooner. On the other hand, he knew the idea of a future with her was bleak. Never going to happen, even if he did find a way out of this. "Sorry, can't answer that one. I don't know where she is at this moment."

Foley laughed. "Nice try. So, yes, she's the same woman. Good to know."

Cain kept his face impassive, but inside he was screaming. He wanted to rip Foley's throat out just for asking about Harlow.

"What happened to my money in Belize?"

Cain met Foley's gaze. "I have no idea. The container blew up when we were there. The locals said you had it rigged to blow in case anyone found it."

Foley rattled the ice in his glass. "We didn't have it rigged. Someone stole the container, took the money, and killed my people. I thought maybe some Coasties thought this might be their retirement plan."

"If that were true, do you think we'd be down here going

after you now? We'd all be drinking margaritas on a beach somewhere with no extradition treaty with the U.S."

Foley nodded as he poured himself another drink. "Makes sense. So someone else out there has my money."

"It would appear so," Cain agreed. And he knew who, too, but that would have to keep.

"One last question for you," Foley said. "What's your endgame?"

"Excuse me?" Cain stared at Foley. What did that mean?

"Your endgame. What do you expect will happen at the end of this?"

Cain attempted to shrug, but it hurt so he just leaned back in his chair. "I expect you'll go to jail, and the government will get its money back."

"Come on," he said with a harsh chuckle. "You don't believe that. Not really. What do you really think is going to happen?"

Foley was right. That was not what he thought would happen. He thought he would probably die, and Foley and his cronies would get off because they had too many friends in Washington. But the money might get back to the government. He told Foley as much.

"I like that you're realistic." Foley downed the last of his drink. "You are right. You are going to die, and even if your little friends show up and somehow arrest me, I do have friends in high places. I wouldn't see one day of jail time. But you're wrong about the money. That is mine." His eyes turned flat as he said it. "Daughtry. Go get your tools. I'm done dicking around. Find out what this guy knows."

CHAPTER TWENTY-ONE

Harlow sat on the cushioned seat in the boat. She was feeling quite nauseous, but she wasn't sure it was because of the waves or because of the situation. Every minute out here was another minute Cain might be living through torture. Maybe he was dead already. *No.* She couldn't think that way. She wouldn't. Cain was going to be fine. They all were.

She'd tried to keep calm, but her stomach was at her feet and her brain was going a mile a minute down dark paths. She took in a deep breath and glanced at her watch. They were behind schedule. It was taking everyone longer to get into place than they thought it would.

They were sitting in the bay not too far from the yacht but not too close either. They had several boats between the two for camouflage purposes or so Nick said. She shivered. The breeze was warm but the dampness and the cold block of fear in the pit of her stomach made her skin icy.

Elias still hadn't gotten back from placing the explosives on the hull of the yacht. It did not help that, apparently, Cain was the group's explosives expert. Elias said he'd manage, but if he got it wrong, well…she wouldn't think about that.

Nick looked down the stairs at her. "How are you holding up?"

"Shitty," she said. "How's Elias doing? Is it set yet?"

"Almost."

She stood up. "This is nerve-wracking."

"Yup," Nick agreed. "We're in good shape, though. I promise. Things are coming together. We got the explosives from an old friend of Gage Callahan's, so we know they're good. Elias knows what he's doing. He'll be back any minute. Then we'll go." He sat down on the top of the stairs. "I want to talk to you about what will happen."

She clenched her hands into fists. "I'm ready."

He smiled. "I know. You are going to stay here. I want you to keep down and stay out of sight. If things go according to plan, we'll bring Cain back here. We'll take the Silverstone guys on the other boat."

"Okay, got it. I'll stay low and keep watch."

"Harlow, if things don't go well…" He paused. "If they don't go well, take the boat into a marina and call for help. The emergency number for the Caymans is the same as the States, nine-one-one."

She frowned. "You mean, if it all goes to hell and you guys…don't come back, you want me to save myself and go for help."

He nodded. "This is going to be ugly. The chances of us all getting out are pretty slim. I just want you to be prepared. If I shoot the flare gun, go for help. You're gonna need to be closer to shore for the phone to work."

"But I—"

"Harlow, if I shoot the flare gun, it means run. Go as fast as you can to shore and get help. Your life is in danger here just like ours. Please don't wait. The flare is the signal. We'll do our best to bring Cain back to you, but you have to help us and do what I say."

"Nick, I… please bring him back." She didn't want to live without him. Even if he ended things once this night was over, at least she'd know he was alive. The back of her eyes prickled and she bit hard on her lip.

"We'll do our damnedest." The sympathy and under-standing in his eyes were her undoing. She sniffed. Nick's lips clamped in a tight seam and then he said, "This is a dangerous situation, Harlow. Cain will want you to be safe. He might not know it yet, but you're someone to him. So help a brother out…repeat after me… If I see the flare I'll get out of here."

She stifled a sob. Nick was telling her if they were going to die…*if Cain was going to die,* he'd send up a flare so she could escape.

She cleared her throat. "I'll go if I see the flare."

He nodded and gave her shoulder a squeeze. He stood up and went to stand beside Axe at the stern of the upper deck. Harlow climbed the ladder a couple of steps but stayed low. She needed some air. She felt sick. All that time following them in Iraq, and she never once felt like she was gonna puke. She didn't care then. About herself or anyone else. Now it was different. Now she understood better the worry that her parents must have suffered through, not only over Perry and his job, but also over her. She was suffering now. Cain was on that yacht, and he was being beaten. She knew it because they could see in the windows with binoculars. It made her heart hurt.

"Nick," she called. He turned and came back to her. "They're beating him upstairs in the salon in front of the windows. Why would they do that on purpose? People can see in. We can see it. Aren't they worried someone will call the police?"

He crouched down beside her. "They know we're watching. That's why they're doing it. They want us to see. They're hoping we get upset enough to make a mistake. If you look around out here, there aren't many people on the boats. They all go into town and come back later. It's pretty quiet out here now. They know the risks, but they think psyching us out is worth it."

"Oh." They were right. She was totally psyched out.

Nick went back to his lookout. Axe handed the binoculars to Nick. He spoke softly, but the wind carried his words to her. "Daughtry stopped hitting him. He brought out some sort of kit. He's getting tools out. We need to move now."

She stumbled off the stairs and sat down heavily on the cushion. They had moved from beating to torture. She curled into a ball, her head on the back of the couch. As she wrapped her arms around her knees, an agonized groan escaped her lips. She said a prayer. *Please God, don't let him die.*

Then, suddenly, there was a scuffling sound on deck. She was off the couch and up two steps to see what was going on. Nick and Axe were helping Elias over the side of the speedboat. He sat down hard on the deck and pulled off his mask. The other two helped him out of his SCUBA tanks.

"Are we good?" Nick asked.

Elias gave the thumbs up. Nick spoke into his earbud. "We're a go. Repeat, we're a go."

Elias peeled off the wet suit and got into his tactical gear. Nick helped him as Axe got the boat going. Harlow stayed perched on the stairs, watching them. This was it. The moment of truth. Elias looked over at her, and their eyes locked. He nodded at her. She tried to take heart in that, but her whole body seemed to be shutting down. She'd never been so scared in her entire life.

CHAPTER TWENTY-TWO

"Anything?" Foley asked.

The man Harlow had called Hugo shook his head. "Nothing yet. No movement. Jonas and Mosley are going to go in the water and do a sweep shortly just in case."

Cain's gut rolled. If Foley sent guys into the water to check, it might make it impossible for their plan to work. Elias would have to be very fuckin' careful to get by them, or he'd have to take them out.

"Okay," Foley said. "Make sure they're thorough. I want them in every hour or so."

Vance sat heavily on the couch across from Patel. "I'll be glad when this fucking mess is over."

Cain shared that sentiment. His head ached from the hit by the gun butt and then the punches to the face. His left eye was swelling, as was his lip. His kidneys were on fire. Daughtry was laying out tools. It looked to Cain like he was about to lose a tooth or two. That was going to hurt like a motherfucker.

He turned his head to study Vance. It seemed odd to him that Vance was so quiet. He struck Cain as the type that usually liked to be the cock of the walk. So why was he silent? Was it because Foley was there?

Vance shot a look at Daughtry, who gave him a small single nod.

Sonofabitch! Was Vance turning on Foley?

Time to stir the pot. Cain cleared his throat. "So how much do you all stand to make on this deal? Is it an even split, or are some of you getting more for your efforts?"

Vance glanced at Daughtry but kept quiet. Foley was back behind the bar, making another drink. "What the fuck does that matter to you? It's not like you're gonna see any of it." He rattled the ice cubes in his glass.

"Just curious. It's a lot of money. A lot less now, though, since you lost two of the containers. I hear the Cortez Cartel is not so pleased with you at the moment. Espinoza wanted the money to guarantee his place at the top. Now he's gotta fight for it. I'm thinkin' it's not such a good idea to have the Cortez Cartel pissed at you."

"Shut your fucking mouth." Foley slammed his drink down on the bar countertop.

Landed that one right across the bow! Cain smiled. "Someone is a might touchy. Espinoza called, did he? Wants his money? How's that gonna work? If you give him what you owe him, will there be anything left for your guys? And if you don't pay Espinoza, then you'll be running for the rest of your life."

Foley nodded at Daughtry, and Cain only had a second to prepare for the blow. This one was a direct hit in the stomach. It was like being hit by a bull. Cain doubled over and coughed repeatedly. Fuck, it hurt. He tried to catch his breath.

At least now he knew it was a sore spot with Foley. If he could get Vance and Foley to get into it, he might have a chance. To do what, he didn't know, but maybe it would give him some kind of opening. "Vance, how much do you get out of this? You've been waiting almost, what, twenty years? A million a year? Two? Five? I bet it's a lot less now than it was."

Vance's face flushed, and he got to his feet. "Daughtry, kill this asshole."

"No. Get him to talk first," Foley instructed.

"Why?" Vance demanded. "Why does it matter? We know they're coming, and we know how they think. We're on top of it. Why do you think he'd tell us the truth anyway? Torturing him seems like a waste of time to me."

Shit. Cain flexed his wrists again. He wasn't sure if being killed quickly or being slowly tortured with the hope of rescue was better. Neither one sounded appealing. He strained against the zip ties, but they just refused to give.

Foley ignored Vance. *Big mistake.* Vance glanced at Daughtry again. The two were either secret lovers or they were plotting a takeover. He guessed the latter, although he'd been surprised before. He chuckled. The time in the chair was starting to get to him. He was losing it.

Be calm. Focus. Ice.

"What are you laughing at?" Vance snarled.

Cain cocked his head. What about Patel? Where did he fit into this mess? Whose side was he on? "So, do you need his contact at the bank? Is that why Foley is still alive?" he asked Vance.

Vance's eyes widened slightly, and he set his jaw.

Bull's-eye. "Did you know that Vance here and Daughtry, and probably a few other men, are planning a coup, Foley? You're a dead man as soon as you take the first load of money to the bank. Then they don't need you anymore. With two-thirds of the money gone, one less person means more for them."

"Bullshit." Foley eyed Vance and Daughtry. "These men

are loyal to me. We came up together. We're a team. They would not betray me."

Cain snorted. "I wouldn't be so sure."

Patel glanced back and forth between Foley and Vance, a look of unease on his face. Foley had the same look. Cain smiled. So Patel wasn't involved. Interesting. He'd set a cat amongst the pigeons. Maybe he could get them to turn on each other.

"All that money—" Cain started.

But then there was a sudden rumble. A vibration went through the ship. The cavalry had arrived. There was now a small hole in the hull. It would take a while for the boat to sink, but the guys were on board. *Thank God.*

"Kapoor, see what that was," Foley demanded. "Daughtry, cut him loose," he said, pointing to Cain. "If his buddies are here, we need him front and center."

No sooner did he utter the words when gunfire erupted. It sounded like it came from the flybridge. Foley's men were shooting at his team. There was answering gunfire and a scream, then a splash. Then more gunfire and another splash.

Two down. Cain tensed. Vance was pointing his gun at Cain's chest as Daughtry cut the zip ties. Daughtry pulled Cain to his feet, but Cain twisted and knocked Daughtry off balance. Daughtry struggled to regain his footing, but Cain crashed his shoulder into Daughtry's windpipe. It collapsed under his weight. The man fell back, clawing at his throat, mouth opened wide like a fish out of water. He wasn't getting any air. Foley moved out of the way as Daughtry stumbled into the bar area. A half dozen bottles toppled over with a crash. Daughtry fell to his knees and then fell face first onto the carpet. *Three.* He felt zero remorse for killing Daughtry. The man had tried to rape Harlow. He was only sorry that it had been so quick.

Cain's gaze locked with Vance's. He was surprised the

man hadn't shot him. Foley, too, for that matter. *One less man to pay.*

The muffled sound of gunfire came from below this time. Only one shooter, but Cain guessed that his team was using suppressors so he couldn't hear their shots. At least, he hoped that was the case.

Vance still had the gun aimed at Cain's chest, but he still hadn't pulled the trigger. "I don't give a shit about him, but I want you alive." He came closer to Cain and signaled him to walk out onto the deck. "Your boys need to see that you will die if they keep coming."

Foley came out from behind the bar with a gun in his hand as well. He was lining up with Vance so they were both behind Cain.

Patel came back into the salon. "A hole in the hull. Too big to patch. There are four dead down there. His team came in via the ramp by the wave runners and took out our guys down there. I shut them up in the engine room, but it won't hold."

Seven. Five left and three of them were with Cain.

"Go," Foley said and shoved Cain out the door onto the deck. He made Cain walk to the end of the deck and turn around. Foley stayed with his back to the wall by the ladder to the flybridge. He extended his arm. "Your people try and take me out, and you die. Do you understand?"

Cain had his hands up. "I hear you."

"Kapoor, get the tender ready. We're leaving."

Patel came out of the salon and took a few steps down to the back of the deck. "The tender is gone. The only way off is to swim."

"Fucking hell! I thought you had this all sorted, Vance? I thought your men knew what the fuck they were doing!"

Vance came out of the salon as well. "They did, and

they're your men, not mine." Vance was much calmer than Foley.

Cain's adrenaline was pumping, and his heart rate was off the charts, so it took a second for it all to click, but then it did. There was something off about Vance's reaction. He knew something. Something that made him relaxed.

"The money. Not all of it is here." Cain studied Vance's face, and a telltale flush started up his neck. He raised his gun.

"What do you mean?" Foley demanded. "What's he talking about?" He swung his gun around to Vance.

Cain tensed and was about to make a move when Patel put his gun against Cain's head. "Don't even think about it."

CHAPTER TWENTY-THREE

Harlow had moved from the hull on to the deck but stayed low in the boat, watching over the side. The guys had left what seemed like an eternity ago. They'd gone in through the door at the back that led to the engine room. Or, at least, that had been the plan. She'd heard the rumble that must have been the charge going off and then gunfire from the flybridge.

The sound of sirens was growing louder. She looked toward the shoreline. Police cars were arriving at the pier. They wouldn't have much time before the cops would be out here in their boats. She had no idea if that was a good thing or a bad thing in the current situation. There was so much going on that she didn't fully understand. At this point, all she cared about was getting Cain back in one piece.

She popped up her head like a gopher and took a peek at the yacht. It looked like everything had gone quiet. She reached over and grabbed the binoculars that the guys had been using earlier. She raised them to her eyes and put them into focus. The flybridge was empty. She looked lower and bit her lip. Cain was being held at gunpoint by Foley. It looked like Vance and Kapoor were there as well. Did that mean that Daughtry was dead? She fervently hoped so.

She looked over the rest of the yacht and then back to the deck where Cain was being held. What was going on? Where was Nick? "Come on, come on," she mumbled.

There was movement in the water off to the left by the bow of the boat. Two heads bobbed in the water. She focused in on them. Yes, two men wearing SCUBA gear. The two men disappeared around the bow. Did Nick and the rest know they were there?

She watched until the men disappeared. Hitting her earbud, she tried to tell the team about the guys at the back of the boat, but there was no response. Was she too far away? Was there interference? She dropped the binoculars and scanned the water around the boat, but it was hard to see through the darkness.

Should she pull up anchor and drive the speedboat alongside Vance's yacht? Or was it better if she stayed where she was? She knew they would want her to stay where she was and out of danger, but Cain was being held at gunpoint, and she had no clue what the others were doing. The two men at the bow, if they managed to get on board again, then what?

It was all too much. Harlow turned and went to the controls of the boat. She turned on the engines and raised the automatic anchor. She just couldn't let Cain and the rest of them be blindsided. She'd come this far. She might as well go all the way. The hell with being safe.

CHAPTER TWENTY-FOUR

"What's he talking about? Where's the money?" Foley demanded again.

Vance shook his head. "Why would you believe this asshole?"

"Because you're too calm. What the fuck is going on, Vance? Where's my money?" Foley fumed.

Vance snarled, "Your money is down in the engine room, currently getting wet."

"Where's *your* money?" Cain asked.

Vance turned to glare at him. "Shut the fuck up!"

"Put down your weapons," Nick said as he came out of the salon. Vance and Foley both stepped behind Cain and Patel.

"Why should we?" Foley asked. "What are you gonna do, shoot all of us? I don't fucking think so."

"Don't be so sure." Nick nodded to Cain. "You okay?"

"Yeah. Good timing." He started to move, but Patel pressed his gun into Cain's head.

"You move and you die," Patel said.

Cain smiled. "I think you've got that wrong."

Patel frowned and put his finger on the trigger. It was the last action he ever made. His head disappeared in a cloud of red mist a second later. The report of the rifle sounded as Patel's body hit the deck.

Foley and Vance ducked and scrambled for cover looking to see where the shot came from.

What the… Cain hadn't seen that coming. Where had that shot come from? He must be more disoriented than he thought from the beating he'd taken from Daughtry.

"Now, assholes, drop your weapons!" Nick said one more time. He pointed his gun at Foley.

Cain blinked to clear his head, then swept Patel's gun up the deck and pointed it at Vance.

Foley and Vance both slowly dropped their weapons to the deck. Then they straightened and raised their hands.

"Good. Now, you two are going to get down on your knees with your hands behind your head."

He threw Cain some zip ties. "Make 'em nice and tight."

Cain grinned. "Don't mind if I do."

Harlow brought the speed boat close to the yacht, which was now sitting low in the water. It was definitely starting to sink. She hit her earbud. "Nick? Elias?"

Nothing.

She tried again. "Finn? Axe?"

Still nothing.

She finally spotted Elias at the back of the yacht in the wave runner bay. He was helping Finn, who seemed to be cradling his arm. Axe was there, stacking the bags in the tender. Cain was on the deck above. She brought the speed boat in as close as she dared.

Elias looked up. *What the fuck?* his face said.

She pointed upward. *They need help.* She mouthed the words. There was light coming off the yacht, but she wasn't sure they could see her. She pointed up again and then held up two fingers.

Elias shook his head.

Fuck! She looked around frantically. There. She let go of the controls and went to the back of the boat and grabbed Elias's mask from his dive earlier. She ran back and held it up. Then she held up two fingers and pointed toward the front of the boat.

Elias stared at her a second but then nodded vigorously. He said something to Finn and took off. She looked over to Axe, who smiled suddenly. He also said something to Finn and then dove into the water and started swimming toward her.

Cain had leaned over Vance to zip tie his hands when a voice said. "Drop it, motherfuckers."

Cain looked up. Mosley and Jonas were standing in the salon with their guns trained on Nick. They were wearing swim trunks and holding guns. They must have been in the water when the guys boarded. *Shit.*

Nick glanced over his shoulder. "Fuck." He slowly bent down and put his gun on the deck. He stayed crouched down.

Mosley came out on to the deck. He glanced at Patel's body but said nothing. Foley and Vance got to their feet. Mosley asked, "Foley, what do you want to do with these assholes?"

The sound of sirens hit Cain's ears. The cops were coming. He had the sinking feeling that wouldn't improve things.

"Shoot 'em. We need to get out of here." Foley looked at Vance. "Shoot him, too."

Jonas raised his gun. "You want Vance dead as well?"

"Yeah, after you shoot the other two," Foley rasped.

Jonas shrugged. He raised his gun and aimed it at Nick. There were two quick spitting noises and Jonas fell forward hitting the floor face-first. Elias aimed at Mosley. Before Cain had a chance to warn Elias, Mosley opened fire, but his shots went wide and Elias dropped him with two in the chest.

Nick stood, gun in hand. "Thanks."

Elias nodded.

Cain let out the breath he'd been holding. That had been fucking close. Too close for comfort.

Nick waved Foley and Vance over to the side of the boat.

Cain came to stand in front of them. Nick handed him a weapon. "Okay, this is what's gonna happen. You are going to tell us everything we want to know, and then we're gonna drop you in a dark hole somewhere."

Foley started laughing. "You think so? I don't." His laughter died. "I have friends in Washington. I'm not going in a hole. They'll bail me out. No one wants their dirty little secrets to come out."

"You think you can get away with killing a team of Navy SEALs because you have friends?" Cain snarled.

"I don't think. I know it," Foley said. "Besides, he was the one who killed that team," he said, pointing to Vance. "He's gonna go down for that. Me, I'm gonna apologize for hiring a bad actor and keep a low profile for a little while, and then I'm gonna come back bigger and stronger than before."

A sinking feeling started in Cain's gut and went all the way to his shoes. This asshole was right. He was gonna get away with it.

Vance said, "I have proof that Foley ordered the hit. If I

go down, he goes down, so I'm not going down either. No one wants us to tell the world Washington's secrets."

Cain glanced at Nick. He hadn't been present for the final game plan, so he didn't know what rabbit Nick was going to pull out of the hat to fix this fucked up situation. Nick almost imperceptibly tipped his head out to sea. Okay —that explained where the shot that killed Patel had come from.

Nick lifted his left arm, palm open, with most of his fingers curled up, but his forefinger pointing between Vance and Foley for a nanosecond before flattening out his digits.

Given the circumstance, Cain knew this was Nick's way of communicating the plan. Somewhere out there, on a boat Cain didn't dare shift his gaze to look for, they had back up.

Cain extended his left arm the same way, palm open as if entreating Vance and Foley to surrender.

Then he addressed the men they were holding at gunpoint. "Here's the thing," Cain said. "You could be right. You could get off for all the murders and atrocities you committed. Or we could kill you right now."

The sirens were getting louder. They'd be here in the next couple of minutes. The yacht was taking on more water now and was already half submerged.

Foley laughed. "You won't do that because you're Coast Guard. You don't have it in you."

Cain stepped forward. "You killed my team in Iraq, and you betrayed Nick"—Cain motioned to his team captain standing next to him—"so he ended up getting sliced by a machete. I wouldn't be too sure about what we're willing or not willing to do."

Vance's eyes narrowed. "That's right. I'd forgotten all about that. Taggert. That's your name. I remember now. I thought you were pissed about that whole Panama thing, but it's about the thing in Yemen."

Cain's gut rolled. These men were responsible for a pile of bodies in Panama as well as so much more carnage, and the idea that they might get away with it was mind-blowing.

Nick snarled, "You two are the biggest pieces of scum I have ever seen. You don't deserve to live."

"Save it," Foley snapped. "We'll be out of here in no time. And then we'll come for you and your families."

Cain looked at the police boat. It was slowing down off their port side. He turned to Nick. Their gazes locked. They fisted their hands simultaneously. Vance and Foley's heads disappeared in a veil of pink mist. The sound of the rifle reports hit their ears a few seconds later.

CHAPTER TWENTY-FIVE

Harlow stood on the pier and waited. Where the hell was Cain? Why wouldn't the police let her see him? She paced back and forth. Cain was on the police boat. Nick was there, too. The two were being questioned at opposite ends.

"He's fine," Finn said as he came to stand beside her. His arm was in a sling.

She frowned. "What about you? What happened to your shoulder?"

He winced. "To avoid getting shot, I zigged when I should have zagged and whacked my shoulder on the engine. Minor inconvenience. No permanent damage. Damn good thing you came with the boat, though. There was no way Axe could have gotten all the money off on his own." He grinned at her.

Being in a sling didn't seem like a 'minor inconvenience' to her, but they were military. She was sure they'd experienced worse. "I was worried about those divers."

Footsteps sounded on the dock, and she looked up. Cain and Nick were walking toward them. Cain's eyes were practically swollen shut, and the left side of his mouth was cut and puffed up. He was holding his right arm tight to his side. Bruised and battered, she was still happy to see him.

She hurried over to stand in front of him. "Oh, my God, are you okay?" She wanted to put her arms around him and hug him close, but one look told her he wouldn't let her. The pulse in his jaw vibrated. His eyes were flat.

"I'm fine. It'll heal." That was it. That was all he said.

Nick shot him a look. "We're free to go. The *Walton* is offshore. Gerhart is sending a bunch of guardsmen to get the money and pick up the few remaining Silverstone men. Once we do the hand off, we can leave." He turned to Cain. "Why don't you go now to the hotel and clean up?"

Logan Callahan joined the group along with Elias and Axe. "Actually, I've taken the liberty of moving you all to the resort. Jameson Drake, the owner, is a very good client of ours, and he said to offer you all rooms and whatever else you need. He's impressed that you brought down the Silverstone Group. He's had run-ins with Foley over security issues in his hotels and doesn't… or, I guess I should say didn't think very highly of the man.

"Axe helped me pack your things." Logan handed each man a key and then turned and smiled at Harlow. "I thought after everything you've been through, you could use a bath so I gave you the room with the biggest bathtub."

She smiled up at him. "You're fabulous!"

He grinned at her. "So my fiancée tells me."

"She's a lucky woman," Harlow added.

"So I tell her." Logan winked.

Harlow tried to remain smiling and happy, but inside she was a mess. Cain was okay, but he wouldn't even look at her. Vance and Foley were dead. It was all so…confusing. She thought she'd be so happy when this was all over, but she just felt numb.

"Can I ask a couple of questions before we all disappear?" Harlow said.

Nick tipped up his chin, signaling her to proceed.

"What happened to Kapoor, Foley, Daughtry, and Vance? I mean, I know they're dead, but how?"

"Not sure what happened with Daughtry. He was dead when I got there," Nick said. "But the rest of them were aiming to kill me and Cain out on the deck." He pointed to the two Callahan brothers. "Gage and Mitch were stationed not far away with sniper rifles. They took out the other men." Cain and Nick didn't look at each other, and there was something about what had *not* been said that vibrated the air with tension.

She turned and stared at the two Callahan brothers. There was more to the story. She knew it in her bones, but no one was going to tell her. Her brother always said there were certain things that happened on the battlefield that no one would ever talk about. She would just have to live with the knowledge that the bastards responsible for her brother's death were gone. It would have to be enough.

Cain spoke in a low voice. "I smashed Daughtry in the throat with my shoulder when he untied me. Crushed his windpipe." He met Harlow's gaze for the first time all night. "He died a painful death."

She nodded. He wanted her to know that the monster that had attacked her was dead. He'd made sure of it. Relief flooded her. Hearing the man who tried to rape her was dead was one thing; knowing it was quite another. She owed Cain for the fact that she was going to sleep well tonight. The monsters were all dead.

"How did you come to get the money in your boat, Harlow?" Nick asked. "As I recall, you weren't supposed to move."

Chagrined, she grimaced at Nick. "*Weeeell*...when I was

watching everything unfold, I saw two heads bobbing in the waves. They were at the front of the boat. I knew none of you guys saw them, so I went and got Elias's attention and told him, in a manner of speaking."

"So that's how you came upstairs." Nick nodded to Elias. "Thanks for that."

Harlow continued, "And since I was already there, Axe swam out to meet me, and we brought the boat in closer. Then we loaded it with the rest of the bags of money. Although"—she cocked her head—"it seemed a bit light to me. Are you guys sure that was all of it?"

"Ah, about that," Logan said. "Nick overheard Cain ask Vance where his share of the money was, so he asked me if I could figure out where it might be. Turns out Vance stored half the cash in a separate room here at the resort. I found it and the two men guarding it. They are now with the Coast Guard as well."

"So…are we all good?" Nick asked.

Everyone nodded.

"Let's head to the resort then." Nick motioned for the guys to go ahead.

Harlow was anything but good, but there was nothing much to say. She tried to catch Cain's eye, but he moved around her and went up the pier. Nick gave her a sympathetic smile, which just made her feel worse. Well, he'd done as he'd promised and brought Cain back. It wasn't Nick's fault that Cain was freezing her out.

She turned and walked slowly up the pier to the resort. Every step was painful. Her body hurt in ways she hadn't anticipated. The money had been heavier than she'd thought possible, and the fact that it had gotten wet, well, it had made it that much worse. Axe had done the bulk of the lifting, but she'd dragged the bags to the edge for him to get them in the boat.

She smiled as she walked with the group to the inviting resort. They were all tired, but the relief was palpable. They got their man back. Sadly, it didn't look like she could say the same.

She made her way through the fancy resort, her wet jeans and navy T-shirt clinging to her. People gave them all types of looks, but no one said a word. The concierge came over and asked if he could do anything to help. Logan took him aside and began making requests. She was too damn tired to think.

She got in the elevator with Axe, Cain, and Elias. They were all on the same floor. The doors opened, and they walked out into the hallway. Axe and Elias were off to the right, and she and Cain had rooms to the left. She wanted to say something to him, but the entire way he carried himself said "*Don't even try it.*"

She let out a breath. "Do you need help?"

He gave her a tired glance. "No."

"I meant because you were hurt. Do you need any help getting changed or getting some meds or something?" His face softened slightly, but he still shook his head. "Okay then. See you in Nick's room shortly."

He nodded once and disappeared into his room.

"Great talking to you," she mumbled as she fought with the key and finally managed to get her door open. The suite was similar to the one she and Cain had shared except for the bathroom. Logan hadn't been kidding. It had a deep soaking tub with jets. She looked at it longingly, but if she had a soak now, she'd never get through the call with her folks.

It was just going on two a.m. She was exhausted, but she knew she needed to fill her parents in as soon as possible so they could stop worrying. She sat down on the toilet seat and put her head in her hands. It had been a year since her brother's death. She'd spent most of it tracking his killers. They were dead. She was numb. What the hell was she supposed to do now?

Tears threatened to fall. No. She wasn't going to do that either. If she started, she wouldn't stop. Instead, she got up again and looked for her cell phone. Logan had her stuff neatly packed in a new suitcase on the bed. She opened the bag, and her cell phone was on top. She pulled out the number Nick had given her before and dialed her parents. They deserved to know it was over.

It took a couple of minutes to get them on the phone. "Sweetheart?" Her mom's voice came down the line.

"It's me," Harlow forced out through a tight throat.

"Daddy is here with me."

"Hi, honey. Are you okay?"

Her eyes filled with tears again, and this time she let them fall. "I'm fine, Daddy. It's over."

There was a long pause. "You got him? The man who killed Perry?"

"He's dead, Dad, and so is the man that organized the whole thing. We got them all."

"Oh, my God," her mother said and then let out a sob.

Harlow cried right along with both her parents. Ten minutes later, she had calmed herself and rang off with promises to be home soon. She loved her folks. It would be nice to be back on the small hobby farm they had in New Jersey. She'd given up her apartment when she went to Iraq. She'd have to find a new place when she got back. Maybe a place in one of the small towns around her folks. She'd have to find a job, too, not that she was too worried about that for the moment.

She stood up and dragged herself into the bathroom. She turned on the taps and started to fill the tub, adding a bit of the pricey bubble bath that was on the shelf, compliments of the resort.

While the water filled, she stood in front of the mirror. She'd aged since this all began. There were little lines by the corners of her eyes and around her mouth. Exhaustion was written all over her face. She was definitely changing her hair back. The blond reminded her too much of Cain. Of their time together.

She stripped down and crawled into the hot water. Everything hurt. Her arms, her legs, her heart. She started to cry and didn't stop for a long time.

CHAPTER TWENTY-SIX

Sunshine filled the room as Cain lay in bed and stared at the ceiling. Everything hurt. It was going to be a while before his kidneys healed completely. The EMTs had taken a look at him and recommended he go to the hospital for a full checkup, but Cain just couldn't stomach the idea, so he'd promised Nick he'd go see his doctor when they got back to Miami.

He'd been beaten up before. He knew the drill. It would take a while, but his body would heal. Not his heart, though. His heart was forever damaged. He'd realized it while he was getting hit by Daughtry.

He was in love with Harlow.

Had been since the moment he'd seen her, but he could never make it work with her. His job was dangerous. She would worry about him. After seeing what it was like to worry about the woman he loved getting hurt, he refused to inflict that on her. No way. Plus, he'd promised her brother that he'd stay away from her. Perry knew. He knew what being with someone like them would be like for her. The worry. The anxiety. How could they have a family if she was always worried about him?

Then there was his father. How was he supposed to be with her when his father was a mobster? That would mark her forever.

He touched his face gingerly and winced and then rolled over and sat up with an exaggerated groan.

Life just sucked. He'd gotten the bad guys, but he didn't get the girl. Why couldn't life be like fairy tales? He stood up and went into the bathroom. A couple minutes later, he was pulling on a pair of cargo pants when there was a knock at his door. He opened it to find Nick standing there. He moved back, and Nick walked in, handing Cain a cup of coffee.

Nick crashed down on the sofa, and Cain eased himself gingerly into the chair across from him. "Thanks for this," Cain said, holding up the coffee cup.

"I figured you'd need some. How are you holdin' up? Are you sure you don't want to go to the hospital?" He eyed Cain's bruised lats, which were colorful in an unwanted way. "That looks painful as hell."

"Yeah, but I'll heal. I promise, once we're back in Miami, I'll see someone."

Nick eyed him as if he wasn't quite sure Cain would go. Finally, he said, "Look, I want to talk about the whole Foley and Vance thing."

"What's there to say?" Cain had no regrets. None whatsoever. "Those men were the scum of the earth. Killing them was the only answer as far as I'm concerned."

Nick nodded once. "Good. We're on the same page. I just wanted to make sure you had no regrets."

"What about the Callahans? Are Mitch and Gage okay with it?"

"Yes. Both of them have seen a lot of shit. I explained the

whole thing to all three of them before I asked them to come along on this. They got it. Not one of them has second thoughts."

"Good," Cain said. He knew in his heart of hearts if he had to make the decision again, he'd make the same one every time. He was willing to face his maker about it when it was his time to be judged.

"Harlow." Nick said nothing else.

"What?"

"You were a little harsh with her last night." Nick took a sip of coffee.

"I told her what she needed to know. Daughtry was dead. He paid for what he did to her. End of story."

"You could have given her a hug. Told her you were fine. That everything had worked out."

"Nick, I had Patel, Vance and Foley's brains splashed all over my body. Hugging her was totally out of the question. She knew the rest. She didn't need to hear it from me."

"But she wanted to hear it from you."

Cain shook his head. "That's her problem, not mine."

Nick frowned. "What the fuck is holding you back?"

"I…I just don't know if I can do it. There's so much… and I promised her brother…my father…"

"Just don't do anything stupid. Give yourself some time to get your head right and then make your decision." Nick's cell went off. He looked at the screen. "Bertrand." He stood up. "Remember what I said." He walked out of the room.

Cain sighed. What he hadn't said to Nick was he just wasn't ready. He wasn't sure he'd ever be ready to have that kind of intense relationship. He finished his cup of coffee on the bed, then pulled on a forest green T-shirt. He left the room and headed for the lobby. He wanted breakfast.

Five minutes later, he was exiting the elevator when

Logan Callahan and Harlow were just about to get on. "Cain," Logan said, "how are you feeling?"

Cain nodded. "I'll live."

Logan smiled. "Glad to hear it."

"Harlow," Cain said. "You got a minute?"

She stepped out of the elevator again and turned back to Logan. "I'll meet you there in a bit."

He nodded, and the doors closed.

Why was she meeting Logan? Didn't he say he had a fiancée? Jealousy burned through his gut that he tried to tamp down. It wasn't his business. They moved over to stand by a low sofa in the lobby. "I want to apologize for…leading you on. I should never have spent the night with you. I promised your brother, and I broke that promise. It—"

"I understand," she said, completely composed. "It wasn't the wisest of moves for either of us. Let's just let it go and forget it ever happened."

Forget? Was she out of her fucking mind? He'd never be able to forget her. Not. Ever.

"Right, well, um, take care of yourself."

She looked up at him, her face devoid of expression. "You, too."

He was fighting the need to grab her and kiss her, no matter how much it hurt him to do it at that moment, and she was just standing there as cool as a cucumber. It wasn't fucking fair.

"If that's all, I have to go. Logan is helping me replace my passport so I can go home."

"Er, right."

"Take care, Cain," she said. Back straight and rigid, she crossed the lobby, got into an elevator, and disappeared.

"Sonofabitch," Cain muttered and went to find breakfast.

CHAPTER TWENTY-SEVEN

Two weeks later

"What the hell happened to your face?" his father snarled.

Cain shrugged. "Work." He wasn't getting into it with his dad.

Salvatore Ricci studied his son. They were sitting in the same restaurant at the same table, but it was obvious to both of them Cain was not the same man.

"I'm glad you are healing."

Cain nodded. His father was trying, but Cain was tired and would rather just get to the point. "What is it you wanted to see me about?"

Ricci's lips thinned. "Fine. To business then, Giancarlo. Your sister Sophia's fiancée, Angelo, is angling to take over from me."

Cain kept his face blank. "I see."

"I don't like Angelo much. He's too…mercurial."

Interesting choice of words. Cain smiled slightly. "Okay."

"There are factions in the family that support Angelo. It's

the only reason he is allowed to marry Sophia. It's more of a business arrangement. Still, I do not like him."

"I would think it's more whether Sophia likes him or not that matters. She's the one marrying him."

His father waved his hand. "Don't be so naive. Sophia does what I tell her."

Cain frowned. Where was this going? "I'm not sure what this has to do with me."

"I want you to come and work with me. I want you to take over the family business."

"No." Cain didn't even have to think about it. He was not the heir apparent. He did not want to be a part of that life.

His father leaned forward. "You owe me. This is what I want in return."

Cain shook his head. He stood, and his father followed suit. "I don't owe you."

"You do. You asked all kinds of favors, and I did them all. You owe me, and I want you by my side in the family. It's where you belong."

"No, Salvatore. I don't belong here, and the way I see it, you owe me. Not that I plan on collecting."

"What do you mean?" his father demanded.

"Do you think I'm an idiot?" Cain leaned in. "I know you stole that money in Belize. Your fingerprints were all over it. You took my request for help and used it to your advantage. You made yourself a few hundred million as far as I can tell. That makes us even. Beyond even. You fucking owe *me*."

His father's eyes narrowed. "So, you think you're the big man because you figured it out."

Cain shook his head. "No, I think you're a manipulative bastard. The only reason I don't turn you in is because they'll think I'm a part of it. That I hatched the plan with you." He tapped his father on the chest. "But listen up, old man. We're done. You used any last bit of credit you had with me. It's over. Don't reach out to me ever again. If I need you, I'll call you, and you better come running because if you think Tiny and the rest of your guys can protect you from me, you've got another thing coming." He whirled around and left the restaurant.

He was not going down for something his father did. It wasn't until he'd gotten back to dry land that he'd realized the leverage he now had over his father. This was the thing he could use to get his father out of his life for good. The man would not risk losing hundreds of millions of dollars. Not at all. He could finally get his father out of his life. It was over. He was done. His life was finally his own.

CHAPTER TWENTY-EIGHT

"Gentlemen," Admiral Bertrand said as he sat behind his large ornate wooden desk at Coast Guard headquarters in D.C., "at ease." The team immediately relaxed but still stood on the opposite side of the desk. He glanced over at Cain. "Nice haircut." There was a twinkle in his eye as he said it.

Cain stifled a grin. "Sir."

It was nice to know the old guy had a sense of humor. He'd yelled at Cain about his hair the last time they'd met face-to-face, so Cain had made sure to have it cut before this meeting. Something big was coming, and Cain didn't want to do anything to upset his commanding officer.

The admiral took a deep breath and let it out. "As you know, Burns the XO of the *Jones*, has caused us some… issues. By blaming the team for what happened on board the *Jones*, he has effectively put a spotlight on you all that no one wants there."

Cain's stomach knotted. They'd all hoped it wouldn't come to this. They'd all hoped Bertrand could fix things, but his tone left little doubt where this conversation was going.

"Sir, if I may," Nick started, but Bertrand just held up his hand.

"I know. It wasn't your fault. None of it was. I read your reports, both what was written in there and what wasn't. Burns…mishandled the situation, but the captain of the *Jones*, Artie Cross, has backed up Burns' account of what happened. Publicly. Privately, he admits the fault was with Burns and, because he's the top of the food chain on the vessel, with himself."

"Cross is at retirement age, so he's happy to go quietly. Burns is not, and he will not go quietly. He is also well connected here in Washington. There is a feeling with the higher-ups that Burns is going to make a big deal over this publicly if he is censured in any way." Bertrand frowned. "Normally, the top brass wouldn't care, but there's a lot of… change going on in Washington at the moment. No one wants to rock the boat any more than absolutely necessary."

Cain's heart slammed against his ribs. This was his family. His chosen brothers. He did not want to lose this. He knew they'd always be his brothers but having family close was what life was about. He needed the team. It grounded him to be part of it. Harlow wasn't with him, and he felt that loss with every fiber of his being. He needed grounding more than ever. He needed to be part of a team.

"What does that mean exactly, sir?" Cain asked.

Bertrand heaved a huge sigh again. "It means that your team will be broken up. At least temporarily."

All the air rushed out of Cain's lungs. It was happening again. More people leaving his life, not permanently but leaving his *daily* life.

"Maddox," Bertrand barked, "are you alright?"

Cain realized he must have made a sound and was now swaying on his feet. "Sir." It came out rather strangled. He tried to clear his throat.

"Get him a chair. All of you, get chairs." Bertrand hit a button on his desk. "Ensign King, bring coffee. Lots of it."

"Yes, sir," came from the speakerphone.

"Didn't he get checked out after he came back?" the admiral demanded. "I know he took quite a beating before you all got to him."

"I believe he did, sir," Nick said as he pushed Cain into one of the chairs in front of the Admiral's desk and then took the other one. The guys went into the outer office and got other chairs and brought them in. The ensign came in with a pot of coffee and mugs. A few minutes later, everyone was settled again with coffee. The door to the office closed.

Cain took a sip of his. Hot and sweet. He usually drank it just black, but Nick had given this one to him on purpose. Shock sucked, and since he couldn't have an alcoholic drink, sugar was the next best thing. He was trying to focus, but he felt like his entire world was coming apart. First Harlow and now his team. How was a man supposed to survive this? He took another sip of coffee before he became untethered. That was never good in his world.

"Better?" the admiral asked.

He nodded. He actually was. His heart hurt, but his head was clearing.

The admiral nodded. "Under normal circumstances I would not do this but…since you gentlemen have been through so much and, quite frankly, have done so much for me, I feel I owe you the truth." He leaned back in his chair. "There's a war in the Coast Guard upper echelon. I am on one side. Burns and a great many others, including an admiral or two, are on the other. The goal is to sway the top at Homeland to a certain point of view since they are our parent organization. Currently, Burns' side is winning, but they haven't won."

The admiral sipped his coffee and then set the cup on a

coaster on the desk. "I think"—he raised his finger—"I cannot predict the future, but I think the tide is going to turn. You don't need to know all the details, but within the Coast Guard, as it is within Washington, there are two very different camps. The fact that you all brought home that money, well, it made a huge difference. As a matter of fact, the incredible success rate of your team is now a matter of record. People are talking. People are paying attention. The right people. There are many factors, but as I said, they are starting to line up. The outcome looks…promising."

"That's why you didn't want to bring in Treasury and the FBI," Nick stated. "This helped your side and losing the win to another department would have been costly."

The admiral nodded his head. "I am sorry I left you out there on your own, gentlemen, but to be blunt, my side needed the win."

"Sir, why do we have to be dismantled then?" Finn asked. "Is this other side demanding it?"

The admiral narrowed his eyes and then shrugged. "It's been suggested that we dismantle the team *for now* to…" As his gaze went skyward, he seemed to be searching for words.

"To make the other side think they have a win," Cain supplied. The whole plan suddenly clicked into place. "You dismantle us, and they think they're making great progress. Then you obviously have something else you want them to concede on that they will because they need to look magnanimous. 'Of course, we'll accommodate you. We're all on the same side here' bullshit. And that's the Trojan horse."

The admiral studied him and then gave a small nod. "Indeed. That is the broad strokes of the plan." He looked over the whole group of them. "I want you to know how much I appreciate all of your hard work. You have done wonders for the reputation of the Coast Guard, as well as saved a lot of lives. You all are a credit to the Coast Guard, and we are damn lucky to have you. All of you.

"That said, I do have to reassign you, at least temporarily. I am hopeful that this will really be only a temporary situation. Six months with any luck."

Nick spoke up. "We understand, sir."

But did he? Cain recognized the need for this move, but knowledge didn't lessen the pain he feared with the team being torn apart. It seemed to be the story of his life. Every time he settled into a new family, they were ripped away from him somehow. Without Harlow, and now the team, life seemed pointless. Maybe it was better to quit the Coast Guard.

The instant he had the thought, he squashed it. What the hell would he do if he left? No, he had to stay. He just had to open his mind up to different possibilities, no matter how bleak it seemed at the moment. Become *Mr. Freeze* once more until such a time when it all just…hurt less.

The admiral tapped the folders that were on his blotter. "These are your new assignments." He picked them up and started to hand them out.

"Sir, if you wouldn't mind just telling us, I think that would work best," Elias said. "It's not like we're not going to immediately tell one another anyway."

Bertrand nodded and dropped the folders back down on his desk. "Taggert, I have moved you to Schinnen in the Netherlands. You'll be working on our European activities. I know that puts you significantly closer to Dr. Alvarez. Hopefully, that works for you."

"Yes, sir!" Nick grinned. "She'll be thrilled."

The admiral nodded. "Cantor, believe it or not, you are going to the White House."

"The White House, sir?" His voice cracked on the last word. He was stunned. They all were.

"They rotate through all the military services for certain jobs, like overseeing all the servers at state dinners etc. It's our turn. I'm not sure yet what job it will be, but you will report to the White House. Hopefully, Ms. Bishop will find that the White House is much more interesting than we are and write about them instead."

Axe snorted. "I'm sure she will, sir."

"Mason, you are going to be an instructor at the Coast Guard Academy in Connecticut."

"Um. Me, sir?" Elias blinked.

"Yes. You will be molding the hearts and minds of new Coast Guard cadets. God help us all."

"Yes, sir." Elias grinned.

"Walsh, you are going to work here with me."

Finn's head snapped up and his eyes widened. He'd been making an ostrich out of his napkin and he tore a corner of the paper. "Uh, here, sir?"

"Here, Walsh. I need an extra body, and you are it. You seem to be able to remain calm and make your little animals in the most trying of circumstances. Mrs. Bertrand tells me I need to learn to be calm, so you will be here."

Cain's heart pounded against his ribs. He'd listened quietly to where his friends would be, and with the exception of Nick, they'd all be close together. Maybe he wouldn't be too far away.

"Maddox," the admiral said and then stopped. He let out a huge sigh.

Cain's stomach knotted as fear gnawed at him. Adrenaline shot through his system as he waited for the admiral's next words, the pronouncement of Cain's future.

"Maddox—" he met Cain's gaze—"you have always been different than the rest of the team. When the whole idea for this team was started, I asked for a list of men who were the best at what they did, but they were injured. Your name was not on the list. You were never listed as injured.

"Your superior at the time came to me personally and said that you would be perfect for the team. Your injuries were on the inside and not something he was willing to put down on paper. I took a chance. He was right. You were a perfect fit.

"Now, however, you're healed from the gunshot wound and all the other scrapes and bruises. Even your latest injury won't cause you to be out of action for long. There is no record of any permanent damage. In the current climate, I can't put you in the same type of position that I can put the rest of the team in. I tried to keep you close, but there are others who want you out completely, to be frank. They don't like the fact that your father is the head of a mafia family or that you lied on your application."

Cain's lungs froze. They knew. Bertrand knew. The thing he'd been afraid of for years had finally happened. "Sir, I can explain," he managed to choke out.

"No explanation necessary, son. I understand why you did what you did. Like I said before, you are a credit to the Coast Guard. I would like to have twenty more like you, but I don't get to have that say. So, with the idea of out-of-sight out-of-mind, I have found you a position that's a little bit out of the way, but I think might work. I've assigned you to Coast Guard base in Honolulu."

"Hawaii?" Axe said. "He gets to go to Hawaii?" There was general laughter.

"Maddox," the admiral continued, "I know you would prefer to be next to your teammates, but this is the best I can do under the circumstances. Oh, and it also comes with a promotion. Congratulations, Senior Chief."

"Um, thank you, sir. I am…grateful to be allowed to continue to be a guardsman, sir. It is an honor and a privilege." Hawaii. The other side of the country, and then some, but a promotion instead of being dismissed. It was probably Bertrand getting some of his own back.

Bertrand stacked each of Team RECON's files in a neat pile in front of him. "Your job will be a little different than the rest, as I said. It turns out there are a few injured guardsmen out on the west coast. Since you have experience in rehabilitation, I thought you could see what you could do with that lot." He paused. "I'm giving you your own team, son."

Cain was speechless once more. His *own* team. The idea that he would be in charge of a group of men…maybe women too, was terrifying. He'd always thought of himself as a team member, not a leader. Shit. This was scarier than he thought.

He met Bertrand's gaze once more. "Thank you for your confidence in me, sir. I will do my best to not let you down."

Bertrand nodded. "I'm counting on it. Whip those people into shape for me, and in six months, we'll see where we are. I could use a couple more Team RECONs."

He then handed out the folders. "Well, that's it, gentlemen. The details are in your folder. Cain, you will have to hustle. You have seventy-two hours before you report to Honolulu, and I know you need to go back to Miami to get your stuff."

"Yes, sir. Thank you," Cain said as he stood up.

Then they all got out of their chairs and stood at attention. Nick spoke for them. "Sir, we would like to offer our thanks to you for having faith and trust in us. I speak for the whole team when I say you saved our asses."

Admiral Bertrand also rose so that he faced each of them. "No, Taggert. You saved your own asses through a lot of hard work. I merely gave you the opportunity." He nodded at them once. "Dismissed. Walsh, report here oh-seven-hundred Monday morning."

"Sir," Finn said and then opened the door. They all filed out of the office. Everyone was quiet in the elevator on the way down. They exited and then headed for the parking lot. "Dinner," Cain said, "on me. Steaks if I remember correctly. Sorry the girls can't be here."

Axe grinned. "You're on."

Twenty minutes later, they all pulled into one of the top steak houses in Washington. Axe knew someone and got them in. They sat down in the large booth and quickly ordered. With beers in front of them all, Nick raised his glass. "To the admiral."

"The admiral," they all said and took a sip of their beers.

"How thrilled is Carolina that you'll be in Europe?" Axe asked.

Nick looked over at him. "What makes you think I told her already?"

Axe laughed. "The huge grin on your face."

Nick shrugged. "You got me. She's excited. Already making plans for the stuff she wants to do together. Sloan has to be excited you're assigned to the White House."

"Excited might be the understatement of the century. She's already started packing. She's creating a list of people she wants me to get to know so she can get the inside scoop on things." He shook his head.

"This is gonna make your life difficult," Finn stated.

"Yup. No question. But I wouldn't have it any other way."

Cain was jealous of the relationships the guys had. He really wanted that with Harlow, but even if he could get over her being Perry's sister, she'd be painted with his father's brush. Mobbed up. Or that's the assumption. It didn't matter that he'd broken ties with his father. It would always be there. It wasn't fair to do that to her.

"Finn, how are you gonna like working with the admiral?"

Finn grunted. "God knows, but Tory's very happy. She wants to start looking for a larger house immediately, one that has space for both of us." He frowned. "You know, none of these placements are by chance, right? They all fit into the admiral's plan somehow."

Elias nodded. "My guess is he put us in places that he wants eyes and ears." Elias counted off his fingers. "The Academy, the White House, Coast Guard Headquarters, European Coast Guard Headquarters and Cain gets a new Team RECON in Hawaii. The man has plans. Make no mistake." He took a sip of his beer. "Not that I'm complaining. Andrea is happy about the move. She's been wanting to make the switch to the FBI, and there's a job at Quantico she has a good shot at getting. Plus, I love my family, but I do not want to babysit my nephews anymore. They're terrors."

The guys all laughed.

Cain sighed. "I'm gonna miss Mrs. Jimenez's stuffed peppers." And he would, along with the poker and pizza nights at Elias's apartment, Finn's animals, Axe's connections to everyone and everything, and Nick's calm, steady demeanor. They all saw him as the calm laid-back one, but he could only be that way because he knew they had his back and he had theirs. He was already getting tense just thinking about having a new team.

"It will be good, Cain," Nick said.

Cain looked over at his team leader and brother in arms. "I keep telling myself that but...I don't know. I never saw myself as a team leader."

"Then you're the only one who hasn't," Elias stated. "You

are a born leader. We all look up to you. We trust what you say and ask you for help."

Nick nodded. "Elias is right. You're gonna do great. Don't get me wrong, it will suck at times, and it takes a while to build a rapport, but it will gel for you. You're too good at what you do for it not to happen."

Axe lifted his beer. "To Cain, our new Senior Chief."

They all drank. Cain's chest ached. He loved these guys. It was going to really suck to be a world away from them. "Thanks, guys."

"Now, when are you gonna fix this shit with Harlow?" Finn leaned on the table. "You can give me the death stare all you want, bro, but we all know you're in love with her, and she's definitely in love with you, so what the hell is your problem?"

He ground his teeth. He shouldn't need to explain this. "My family is the problem. If she is with me, then she's tarnished by the same brush. Plus, I promised her brother."

Finn shook his head. "So? It's not like it will affect her job as a dental hygienist."

"I'm not mobbed up. She wouldn't be mobbed up," Cain argued.

Finn grinned. "Precisely my point. You aren't your father, Cain. You've chosen a different life. Tell her about it and give her a choice, too."

Nick sipped his beer and then set the glass on the table. "Perry is dead. He warned you off because he didn't want his little sister to get hurt. You're not going to hurt her. Perry would be fine with it."

Axe shook his head. "But for fuck's sake, do it quick before you lose her. None of us can take the level of pissed off you've been lately. Your new team will not survive if you show up like this."

"He's right," Elias chimed in. "You've been a bear lately.

Don't screw this up because of your unfortunate genetics. Don't let *dear old dad* screw up your life any more than he has already. Go find Harlow and make her see reason."

Nick reached over and snatched Cain's beer out of his hand. "No time like the present."

Cain growled, "Gimme my beer back."

Nick shook his head. "No. Go talk to Harlow. If it doesn't work out, we'll still be in town for another twenty-four hours. New Jersey is close. Leave your credit card. You're paying for this."

"This is stupid," Cain started. "Why—?"

"Yup, it is. Stupid that you're still sitting here. Go." Axe pointed toward the door.

Cain looked around the table. His teammates, his brothers, were all telling him the same thing. He needed to listen to them. That was the point of family. But what if they were wrong and she wouldn't accept him? At least he would know for sure. Anything was better than the hell he was in now. He stood up. "Wish me luck." They all cheered him on as he walked out of the restaurant.

"Sir, I know it's late, but I was wondering if I could come in and talk with you for a minute?" Cain asked.

Howard Moretti stepped back from the screen door. "Come on in, son." He was a big man. Maybe an inch or two taller than Cain. He probably had been well built back in the day, but now his belly hung over his jeans a bit. Fair enough. He had to be in his late sixties. Harlow got her blue eyes from her dad and her red hair from her mom.

Cain opened the door and entered the Moretti's kitchen.

"If you're looking for Harlow, she's at her place in town."

"Yes, sir. It's you I actually need to speak to."

Howard nodded and pointed toward the kitchen table. "Take a seat."

Cain sat down, and Howard sat across from him.

"Can I get you anything?"

"No, sir." Cain took a minute to formulate what he wanted to say. "Mr. Moretti, I came to apologize to you and your wife. I… It should have been me chasing down the men that killed your son. I let Perry and you down when I didn't stop Harlow from going to Iraq."

He chuckled. "That's rich. Young man, Harlow is her own woman, and there was nothing you could have done to stop her. Her mother and I tried. I know you tried, too. It didn't matter. She needed to do it."

"Still, I should have at least been there with her. When I think about her doing it on her own…" He swallowed hard. Everything they'd been through still made his stomach knot and forced bile up his throat.

"Perry liked you. He said you were one of the finest men he'd had the privilege to know." Howard's voice cracked, as though he were choking up.

"I felt the same about him."

"You did what you could at the time. You were hurting. We all were. Hindsight is always twenty-twenty. You did what you could. And when push came to shove, well, you got it done." He paused and blinked. "My boy can rest in peace now, and so can we, knowing the men responsible are taken care of. I thank you for that. You owe us nothing, son."

Cain felt like a hundred-pound weight had been lifted off his chest. "I appreciate that, sir."

Howard looked at him closely. "I'm guessing that wasn't the only thing you came here to say."

"No, sir. I want to ask for your permission to ask Harlow to marry me. Perry didn't want me to date your daughter, and I promised him I wouldn't but...I'm in love with her, sir."

Howard leaned back in his chair. "I see. Does Harlow know you're here asking me this?"

"Um, no. I haven't seen her...yet," he finished lamely. "I have some apologizing to do on that front. I'm not so sure she'll have me, but I thought I better get my ducks in a row first." He met the older man's gaze. "I feel like I screwed up a good many things, and I want to get this one right."

Howard nodded. "First, Perry wouldn't let anyone date his sister. In my son's eyes, no one was good enough, so don't feel bad about that. But son, I've gotta tell you, living with Harlow is gonna be challenging. She's impetuous and stubborn as hell. She gets that from her mother. She's also loyal and fierce. It's a hell of a combination."

Cain smiled, at ease for the first time since he'd walked into the Moretti house. "I know that, sir, and I'm sure there will be moments, but when I think about the future, I just can't picture mine without her in it." The thought of that terrified him. He needed her to be there with him. Otherwise, it felt like life had no point.

Howard crossed his arms over his chest. "Well then, son, I will offer you one piece of advice. Get a hobby. Something you can do outside the house."

Cain frowned. "Er, I'm not sure I understand."

"Son, living with Harlow means there's gonna be a lot of fighting. You need a hobby so you can go out and putter at something while you work out how you're gonna not strangle her. And then work out how you're going to apologize for something whether you did it or not because, in the end, son, it's just easier that way."

Cain grinned. "Yeah, I kind of figured that one out already."

"Smart man. Get a hobby. It will help keep you sane."

"So does that mean I have your permission, sir?"

Howard stood up and Cain followed suit. "Perry liked you right away. He told me that you were meant to be part of his team, his family. I expect he was right about that, just maybe off slightly on *which* family." He offered his hand. "You have my permission. Cain."

Cain shook his father-in-law-to-be's hand.

"Good luck, son," Howard said. "You're gonna need it."

Cain stood outside of Harlow's door with a backpack slung over one shoulder. It was going on midnight. There was light coming from her apartment windows, so he assumed she was still awake. He touched the ring box in his pocket, took a deep breath, and hit her buzzer.

There was no response. He hit it again and waited. Nothing. Maybe she was asleep. Or maybe she wasn't answering the door because it was midnight and she wasn't expecting anyone.

He pulled out his cell and texted her.

Harlow it's me. I'm downstairs. Let me in.

Me who?

Cain.

There was a long pause, and then the door buzzed. Cain let out the breath he'd been holding. So far so good. He went up the stairs to her landing and knocked on her door. It took a minute, but he finally heard the door unlock, and it opened.

Harlow was standing there wearing a pair of boxer shorts and a tank top. Her hair was auburn again.

He smiled at her. "I like the red better than the blond."

Her face remained impassive. "What do you want, Cain?"

"Can I come in?"

Her eyes narrowed, but she nodded and stepped out of the way so he could enter. Her apartment was cozy. There was a galley kitchen off to the right and a living room area in front of that. She also had a balcony with a view of a lake.

"You got a new place. Nice. I thought you were gonna stay with your folks for a while."

"Yeah, I couldn't take all the fussing. It's better for all of us if I have my own space." She moved into the living room and stood across from the couch with her arms folded across her chest. "Why are you here, Cain?"

He followed her until he was standing only a few feet away. She looked amazing. Her blue eyes were guarded, and he didn't blame her one bit.

"I came to apologize. I…fucked up."

Saying nothing, she stared at him, her face impassive.

"I hurt you, and I'm so sorry, Harlow." She stayed silent, which was not what he expected. He knew how to deal if she yelled at him or got sarcastic, but silence was new, and he didn't like it. "I pushed you away because I needed to focus, and you were so damned distracting. All my focus was on you, worrying that you might get hurt. I…needed space so I could do my job."

"And when the job was over? You didn't change. In fact, you were colder." She set her jaw, and her blue eyes shot sparks at him. This was the Harlow he knew. "So, you can see why I'm not buying your little story here. What do you really want, Cain?" She put her hands on her hips. "Are you feeling guilt about Perry or something? You want my forgiveness so you can let go of the idea that you betrayed Perry? Great. I forgive you. Now, get out."

"No. That's not it. I don't want your forgiveness. Well…I do, but not for Perry. I want you to forgive me for fucking up so badly."

"Fine. I forgive you." She let out a long sigh. "Just get out, Cain. I'm tired and want to be done with this whole thing."

His heart stuttered in his chest, and his stomach knotted. She wanted to be done with him. *No.* Just no fucking way.

"Harlow, I'm not doing this well." When he ran a hand through his hair, he was still startled that it was short. "I came because I can't get you out of my mind. Because I'm absolutely miserable without you. I came because I was an ass, and I thought pushing you away would make it easier for me to do my job, to support my team, but it just made it harder. And then I thought it was better if you weren't with me because then I wouldn't worry about you constantly, but that didn't work either. I still thought about you and worried about you every damn day. I came because I need you in my life. Because I love you, Harlow."

There, he'd said it. He'd laid it out there for her. Well, most of it.

She stood staring at him. Then her eyes narrowed slightly. "Why?"

"Why do I love you? Fuck if I know. You're annoying and stubborn and way too impulsive. You don't listen and you hate being told what to do. But, goddammit, Harlow, I've been in love with you since I first saw you in that bar. I did my best to stay away from you like Perry asked, but it just didn't work.

"And then at the resort, spending the night with you, I thought maybe if we had sex, it would get you out of my system, but it just made things worse. Okay I didn't mean worse... because you know how it was. The chemistry between us is off the charts. But I thought I could get over you with that one night." He shook his head and gripped the back of his neck. "Now I know I'll never get over you, in this lifetime or the next. I'm never getting over you. I can't stop thinking about you, wanting you, loving you. You are my addiction. I can't be without you. It's too damn hard."

She started to speak, but he cut her off. "There's something else I need to tell you. Another reason I pushed you away. One that won't change, and it would affect you if you're in my life." *Please, God, let her be in my life.* "My father's name is Salvatore Ricci. He's the head of one of the largest mafia families in the world. My real name is Giancarlo Ricci. I've broken ties with him, but I'm still his son. There's nothing I can do to change that."

———

Of all the things Cain could have said to her, that he was a mobster's son, was not even in the top ten of her list. She was speechless. Actually, since Cain had walked in the door, she'd found it hard to speak. He looked so damn good, even with his short hair. Those beautiful green eyes glowed at her, and she was powerless to stop herself from loving him. He'd hurt her. Badly. And yet, she still loved him. Still wanted him in her life. The fact that he was here now was astounding. The miracle that he loved her was just too much to take in.

"I... Cain... Giancarlo?" She smiled at that one. "That would take some getting used to." Her smile faded. How did she say all the things going through her mind? "I... You hurt me. Like really hurt me." The anguish in his eyes was real, and she knew in that minute that he regretted his actions more than anything, but it didn't change the facts.

She held up her hands to forestall anything he might say. "I've had all this time to think about it, Cain. To think about what happened with Vance and us. I've realized a couple of things. I went to Iraq because I was lost. Not just because Perry was dead, but I was lost in life. I had no clue what I was doing. I was miserable.

"This whole thing has made me realize that I want to start again. Create a new life for myself. I don't want to be a dental hygienist forever. I think I want to try something else. I'm not quite sure yet what, but I'm determined to create the life I want, not the life I had. I won't put up with being hurt. I'm putting me first. You need to understand that."

"I get it." He nodded. "You need to do you. That's fair. I have broken off ties with my father but he's still my father. You would have to be okay with that. I don't tell people but chances are good, someone somewhere will find out. There's nothing I can do about that. I wish I could completely shield you from that, but I can't. I'm trying to be honest with you, Harlow. I don't want any secrets between us."

She nodded slowly. "I appreciate your honesty."

He swung the backpack off his shoulder and offered it to her. "This might help."

She frowned. "What is it?" She reached for the backpack and unzipped it. The money. "Holy shit! Where did you get this?"

"You left it at the hotel when you flew home. I grabbed it and brought it back." He smiled. "I cleared it with the Admiral. You are allowed to keep it as a finder's fee since you were the one that led us to the money in the first place."

She grinned. "This will certainly help me build a new life." Then she frowned. "But maybe I should share it with the families of the men on Perry's team." She dropped the backpack on the floor.

He smiled. "I'm sure you'll do good with it whatever you decide. But Harlow, is there any room for *us* in your new life? Are you willing to give me another chance to show you that I do love you and I want to treat you the way you deserve to be treated? To love you the way you deserve to be loved?" His gaze captured hers. His voice seemed lower to her. It rumbled out of his chest and sent shivers down her spine.

"I…" She wanted to play it cool, set boundaries, be an adult, but she also desperately wanted to jump into his arms. Yes, he'd hurt her but if she was being fair, she also had to acknowledge that he'd been hurting too. Not only was he there when Perry and the team were killed but he had to live with the fact he couldn't save any of them. He also had survivor's guilt. It was a lot. She knew he carried all that guilt and pain deep in his soul. That would make anyone angry enough to lash out. The question was, would he change going forward?

She closed her eyes and took a breath. When she opened them again, Cain was down on one knee, holding a box with a gorgeous solitaire diamond ring in it.

"Will you marry me, Harlow? Will you let me be a part of the life you want to build?"

Tears sprung to her eyes, and she blinked rapidly. Every fiber in her being wanted to scream 'Yes!" but something held her back. A question that demanded an answer. "Cain, I need to know that you're willing to change. To work on not being so angry. You need to find a way to deal with your emotions and your guilt about the team's deaths."

"I know. I'm working on it. I'll go into therapy if it means you'll give me another chance. I'll do whatever it takes Harlow."

Fuck being an adult. "Hell, yes!" she grinned.

Cain's eyes widened in surprise, and then he burst out laughing. In the next second, he was on his feet and she was in his arms. He captured her mouth and kissed her hard. She wound her arms around his neck and deepened the kiss. She wasn't letting him go. Not ever again.

Cain finally broke off the kiss. "Um, Harlow, there's one more thing. Would you mind if we built our life together in Hawaii? I just got transferred. It will be far away from my father so that's a bonus but it will be far from your family too. They can come visit whenever you want."

She let out a whoop of joy. "I'm all about it. Hawaii! Ooh, beach wedding." She laughed until he swooped down and kissed her again.

The End

Exciting News!
Coast Guard Hawaii is coming in 2023.
Turn the page for a sneak peek at the pulse-pounding adventures of the Coast Guard Special Ops teams.

You can sign up for my newsletter to get updates as the stories of Cain's team come available, along with all my other writing news.
https://lorimatthewsbooks.com

KEEP READING FOR A SNEAK PEEK OF A LETHAL BETRAYAL

BOOK 1 OF THE COAST GUARD HAWAI'I SERIES

Chief Petty Officer Dane Landry is injured and burning through his last chance with the US Coast Guard. His new team is tasked with finding stolen military-grade technology, but he finds himself in the crosshairs of an investigation as the prime suspect in the murder of a former teammate. With his career and freedom on the line, his top priority should be clearing his name while navigating the complex web of suspicion and betrayal that surrounds him. Being thrown together with the beautiful investigator is a distraction he doesn't need.

Coast Guard Investigative Service Special Agent McKenna Rankin is determined to find out who killed the Senior Chief, but it soon becomes obvious there's so much more at stake. Her attraction to the prime suspect is an obstacle she hadn't anticipated, but one she isn't sure she wants to overcome. As her investigation heats up and tensions run high, Dane and Mac must find a way to reconcile personal feelings with professional obligations while racing against the clock to uncover the true culprit before it's too late.

Filled with pulse-pounding action and heart-wrenching drama, "A Lethal Betrayal" is a thrilling ride through the high-stakes world of the US Coast Guard, where loyalty and duty are put to the ultimate test.

A LETHAL BETRAYAL

Chapter 1

"They're late," a voice said in his earbud.

Chief Petty Officer Dane Landry had been thinking the same thing. It was zero-zero-forty-five hours. Cain Maddox, his team leader, wasn't impatient. He was just stating a fact, one that made Dane's gut tighten.

"You sure your guy had the right spot?" Cain asked.

"Yes, Senior Chief," Koa Kilani responded.

Cain swore. The entire team knew how much the senior chief hated being called by his title.

Dane smiled in the darkness. Koa didn't like to be questioned. Using Cain's rank was his little revenge. *Hilarious.*

Hidden in the bluff of the beach, Dane was lying in some grass and keeping his eyes on the shoreline. He shifted his position to reduce the pressure on his back. It was starting to ache ever so slightly, and he wanted to stop it before it got unbearable.

The night was quiet. The smell of the ocean and spring flowers drifted to him on a light wind. The breeze also kept the bugs at bay. Plenty of those on Oahu. The sound of their chirping and clicking came from the nearby bushes.

Their new team was coming together. The fact that they were already needling each other was a good sign. When he'd hurt his back, he'd thought his career was over. He'd never see action again. Being number two on a team like this was a dream he didn't think was in his grasp. He was so damn glad he'd been wrong about that.

"Anybody got anything?" Jace asked. "My ass is going numb."

"You were the one that wanted to sit on the rocks," Chief Petty Officer Tacitus—Tac—Holden reminded him.

Jace growled, "Sand. I hate the way it gets into every nook and cranny."

Chief Petty Officer Cassidy St. James snorted. "This could be interesting. Exactly how many nooks and crannies have you got?"

A few muffled guffaws came through the earbud before the night got quiet again. Yeah, it was shaping up to be a good team and Cassidy, being the only woman, added a whole new dimension to things. As a crack shot, she was the team sniper and even he had to admit as much as they were all good, she was the best by a wide margin. It didn't hurt that she had a great sense of humor and was tough as nails. A killer combination. She could also be cold and scary as hell. Dane ranked her as the second scariest member of the team. The first place was a tie between Cain and Koa. Those two took badass to another level. He was so glad they were on his side.

Dane scanned the horizon once more. Nothing. Then movement. Way out on the waves. He couldn't be sure yet, but he thought there was a boat. "On my two o'clock."

Silence and then, "I see it," Tac said.

"Got it," Jace agreed.

Cassidy chimed in, "Pickup truck coming down the road."

"Look lively." Cain wasn't big on commands unless absolutely necessary. That was about as command-like as he got.

"Roger that," they all responded in turn.

The pickup pulled into the lot and turned off its lights. Then instead of parking, it drove onto the sand past the bluff.

That was unexpected.

"Shit," Tac mumbled, who was forced to scramble to get out of the way.

Dane held his breath. Tac had been damn lucky that the pickup didn't have its lights on. The driver didn't slow, so it was a safe bet he didn't see Tac crabwalk out of his way. He turned and focused on the approaching speedboat. It was slowing as it approached the shoreline. "Incoming at the beach."

"Roger." Cain's voice was soft. "Four, you good?"

"Yeah. I'm awake now," Tac grumbled.

The night was a bright one. The moon was three-quarters full, which made it easier to see; good for them on the one hand but bad on the other. Sure, they could see better, but they could also be seen. Not ideal.

The team had spread out across the bluff and on some rocks that marched out into the water. Cass had been on the far side of the car park but was moving quickly to a new position by the beach. She ducked behind some palm trees and then flattened on her belly in the sand.

"Who's got sand in their nooks and crannies now?" Jace mumbled.

Dane cracked a grin. *Love this team.*

The pickup did a wide circle and then backed up to the waterline. The powerboat shut down its engines and coasted in with the tide. The pickup driver hopped out and waved a high-powered flashlight. The guy in the powerboat signaled back.

Dane squinted into the darkness. His gut tensed. *No fucking way.* He brought his binoculars up and flicked on the night vision. He zoomed in and made the images as clear as possible. *Sonofabitch.* He closed his eyes for a brief second. This could not be happening. His stomach lurched.

Dane's biggest nightmare just pulled his boat up onto the beach.

"Got visual," Cass said. "Boat man has bags. Multiple backpacks. It looks like three in total."

"Pickup driver getting something out of the back of his truck," Tac reported.

Cain confirmed. "An exchange, like your guy said, Three."

"Roger that," Koa responded.

Cass stated, "Driver handing duffel over and taking backpacks. Wait… They seem to be arguing. The pickup driver is shaking his head. He's taking back the duffel."

Dane's throat closed over. He was struggling to hear what his teammates were saying over the sound of his pounding heart.

"Is he opening it?" Jace asked and then answered his own question, "He is. He's taking something out. Too fast. I didn't get the shot. He stuffed it in his jacket. Now he's handing over the duffel. The boat driver doesn't look happy. Exchange complete. Got the pictures."

Dane finally managed to make his vocal cords work. "We have a problem."

"Repeat, Two," Cain demanded.

"We have a problem," Dane said again.

The guy in the pickup put the backpacks in the cab of his truck behind the driver's seat.

The boat's engine revved and eased away from the shore.

Cain demanded, "What problem?"

"The guy in the boat is one of us." Dane finally managed to get the words out.

"Coast Guard?" Tac asked.

"Yes, MSRT. My former team leader, Craig Owens."

"You sure?" The sudden tension in Cain's tone crackled through the comms.

"Positive."

"Well, shit."

"Yeah." And that didn't cover the half of it. Dane let out a breath as he watched the boat pull away. "We don't need to follow the boat, not that we were planning on it. I know where to find it. But we've got to abort the rest of the plan."

Tac swore. "You think he has guys watching."

"Affirmative. We've just been damn lucky they haven't spotted us." They were at a secluded beach off a nature preserve on Oahu's north shore. They'd come early to get into position and then stayed in place. That had worked in their favor. If they'd moved around, then Owens's scouts would have seen them. The fact that the handoff had happened meant that no one had seen Tac or Cass move. But it also meant Dane's team hadn't seen Owens's men arrive. How had they come? Where were they?

Dane swore. "They're behind us on the left. They have to be. That's the only place they could be where they wouldn't have seen Four and Six move."

On the other side of the road was just a rocky cliff front. If they were on top of it, they would have a great view of the beach, but the palm trees would block Owens's team's view of the road and give them only keyhole views of the beach parking lot, including most of the bluff.

Dane resisted the urge to turn and scan the surroundings in that direction. "Five—"

"On it," Jace whispered.

He had the best view because he was out on the rock jetty that curved slightly on the right side of the beach, facing the rest of the team. Owens's team was in front of him, off to his right. Dane held his breath.

Jace's voice vibrated in his ear. "Shit. Got one at my two o'clock. Another on my four."

Fuck. They were stuck until those guys moved. The pickup drove up the beach and over the bluff. He went back through the parking lot and made a left back onto the road. A few seconds later, his taillights disappeared. Nobody moved.

Damn. He hated that the guy got away with the drugs. Tension vibrated along his body like tight guitar strings. Pins and needles stung his back, but he didn't move. He brought the binoculars up slowly. Owens stayed just off the beach in the speedboat. He hadn't left yet. *Why?*

"Two, got any insight into why he's hanging around?" Cain asked.

"None." What the fuck was Owens waiting for? A sound reached his ears. A buzzing. "Shit. Drone." Dane froze. Moving even slightly now would give them away.

The drone swooped in over the boat and hovered. It was carrying something, some sort of basket. *What the fuck?* It wasn't looking for them. It seemed to be looking for Owens. Maybe confirming he was there? The drone did a swooping circle and then came to a stop chest-height, hovering above the beach.

Owens brought the boat in and dropped the anchor on the sand. He hopped out and then reached over the side of the basket. He pulled out a small, black square box, the size of carry-on luggage, only square.

"Five, are you getting this?" Dane whispered through his comms.

"Yes. Lots of shots."

Owens put the square bag back into the basket and stepped back. The drone dipped, almost like a bow, and then took off, first over the water, and then back over the trees. It was gone from view in seconds.

"Some sort of handoff," Tac mused.

Owens got back in his boat and turned out to sea.

Dane stayed still. The churn in his gut matched the burn in his back. This was not how this night was supposed to turn out. They were supposed to follow the pickup and arrest the guy for drug smuggling, but he was long gone. Jace probably had pictures of the truck's license plate, but the likelihood of it being legit was small.

Jace's voice broke into his thoughts. "Watchers are bugging out."

Dane heard the distant sound of a motor. Thirty seconds later, an SUV went down the road to the left. They all stayed where they were for another couple of minutes. Satisfied they were alone, Cain called it.

Dane got up and swore. His back had stiffened up so much that he moved like a one-hundred-year-old man. He was also crunching sand in his teeth. Jace hadn't been wrong about the nooks and crannies part.

They rallied in a parking lot three-quarters of a mile away. Dane was the last to arrive. His back was too stiff to move quickly if it wasn't necessary. He walked up to Cain's vehicle, a black pickup ironically enough, where the rest of the team was waiting.

"So, what the fuck?" Jace asked. "Your old boss?"

Dane blew a breath through his clenched teeth. "Senior Chief Craig Owens. I knew that guy was up to no good. I even spoke to base command about it, but I was told to talk to CGIS. I did, but they screwed me. Owens found out, and then I…had my…incident." He couldn't bring himself to call it an accident because he was sure it wasn't. He knew in the pit of his stomach that Owens had been behind the shit that happened the night Dane suffered his back injury...the reason for his persistent pain, but there was no proof.

"Cass, you're Tactical Law Enforcement. What do we do?" Cain asked.

Cass leaned her slender frame against the truck. "We don't have enough to charge him with anything at this moment. We have to see what the pictures captured. For all we know, he could have had rocks in that box and the duffel bag could've been full of laundry." She held up her hands to stave off any kind of argument. "I'm not saying it's likely. I'm saying what we know and what we can prove are worlds apart. We need more."

"What do we know?" Koa asked. "Cass is right. We were told there would be a drug deal. That's what we saw, but we don't know for sure that drugs changed hands. Zero proof on that. We know Owens is involved, but in what? And we know he gave three backpacks in exchange for a duffel bag and then he put a black case in a basket of a drone. We can fill in the blanks, but it's supposition, not fact."

Tac leaned on the side of the truck. "So, again, what do we do?"

Cass sighed. "Realistically, we're supposed to hand something like this off to the Coast Guard Investigative Services unit."

"No fucking way," Dane said bluntly. "I tried them last time. I just told you what happened. I put Owens on their radar, and they shut me down and then offered me up on a platter." He clamped his jaw shut. It was a long story, and he didn't want to get into it, but he could tell by the looks he was getting he was going to have to at some point. It just wasn't going to be on this beach in the middle of the night.

Cain unstrapped his body armor. "We start poking around."

"You mean we're going to stay on this?" Dane asked. He didn't want to get his hopes up. Nailing Owens was something he'd been dreaming about.

"We're the Coast Guard. Our job is drug interdiction. We just watched a man presumably bring drugs onshore. That falls under our purview. I will confirm with Admiral Bertrand since he's our direct boss, but I think he'll go along with it. One of our own is the man in question. I don't know about you all, but I hate the thought that someone, who took an oath to protect and defend, is bringing drugs onto our shores. It pisses me off."

That was probably one of the longer speeches Cain had ever given, and Dane found himself agreeing. However, his doubts rose when they started to talk about the next steps.

Cain tucked one of his weapons into the gun locker on the back of his pickup. "Jace, get those pictures uploaded and let's see what we have. Cass, run the plate and see what pops. Cross-reference the names that come up with names of Guardsmen just in case. I don't think the guy in the pickup was one of us, but you never know. Koa, see if you can find out anything else from your friend who gave you the details of this meet." He ran a hand through his hair. "Tac, see if you can come up with a best guess of what could be in that square case. I got a bad feeling about that one."

Dane waited. Cain looked at him. "Go home and take care of your back."

Fuck.

"I need you in the best shape possible. Figure out what you have to do to get yourself there and do it. That's an order." Cain tapped into his phone and studied something on the screen. A clear dismissal of the topic.

Dane's heart thumped like a damn rabbit, and heat crawled up his neck. Cain hadn't assigned him a task other than "get stronger," which seemed like an insult. Hell, he was trying. It just wasn't working out.

"Now, go home. I just got word that the container ship will be available tomorrow for training. See you at oh-five hundred. This opportunity doesn't come up very often, and I want to take advantage. You'll be tired and pissed, the perfect way to board suspected drug ships. Dane, it's your turn to bring the coffee and food." With that, Cain climbed into his truck.

Dane walked over to his SUV and let out a string of curses as he hoisted himself in. Koa pulled alongside on his Ducati motorcycle. He flipped up his visor.

Dane put down his window.

Koa, true to form, didn't mince words. "He didn't give you a job because he can't have you too closely involved. You have history with Owens and the CGIS. You're pissed about it. That could affect things."

Dane paused and stared at Koa. He hadn't thought of that. *Shit.*

Did this mean he was going to be detrimental to the unit? He started to say something, but Koa drove off. Typical Koa. A man of few words, but what he did say was usually spot-on. He'd understood what Cain was doing while Dane still had his head up his ass. Ego was blinding him to the realities of life.

Koa was right. He did have history with Owens, and none of it good.

Love it?
Grab your copy here

Have you checked out the Callahan Security Series yet?
A page-turning series guaranteed to keep you up past your bedtime.

KEEP READING FOR A SNEAK PEEK
AT CATCH AND RELEASE

From the Amazon and Barnes & Noble Bestselling Author of the Coast Guard RECON series

While in Italy for a forensic accounting project, Madison Montgomery discovers she is being followed through the streets of Florence by a Russian who seems to have ties with the local Polizia. But why is he following her? Absolutely nothing is making sense to Monty, other than she is scared to death.

Executive protection expert, Jacob Boxer, is in Florence when one of Callahan Security's biggest clients, Jameson Drake, calls in a favor. His lead accountant is in trouble and needs protection. Unfortunately, no one seems sure from who or what. When he gets to know Madison, Jake loses the fight to hold fast to the cardinal rule of personal security: never bed the client. While their pleasure-filled night was worth breaking the rules for, Madison's situation goes from bad to worse when they learn not only does someone want to frame her for theft, they want her dead.

Being on the wrong side of both the Russian and Italian

mafias could be a death sentence. On the run through Tuscany and the streets of Florence, every turn takes Monty and Jake farther from safety and closer to disaster.

CATCH AND RELEASE
CALLAHAN SECURITY BOOK 5

CHAPTER ONE

Madison Montgomery stopped and pressed herself flat against the stone wall. She listened, but the footsteps stopped as well. She waited. Nothing. The sound of far-off traffic reached her ears, but she could barely hear it over her own harsh breathing. Maybe she was imagining things. Who would follow her? She shouldered her bag and crossed a narrow cobblestone street from one lane to the next.

The sun was just setting, but it was dark in the lane. The old Florentine buildings blocked the light so effectively she was having trouble seeing. She moved as quickly as she dared but running on cobblestones in high-heeled boots was not something she wanted to try unless absolutely necessary.

The darkness got thicker the deeper she moved into the small lane. Was that the sound of footsteps again?

Not for the first time, she regretted taking this assignment from Jameson Drake. If she'd just said no, she could have been back in her cozy New York apartment on the

Upper West Side. But she wasn't good at saying no, at least not to Drake.

A pebble rolled along the street, but she hadn't kicked anything. She stopped again. The person following her wasn't as quick this time, and a few more steps echoed off the buildings before silence fell. There was only another twenty feet before she rounded the corner into an even narrower lane that the smallest cars couldn't go down. She didn't have a choice. She couldn't go back. She went forward and turned onto the tiny lane. Screw it. She broke out into a run. Her shoulder bag banged against her as her boots clomped over the cobblestones. She raced down the lane, fear chasing her every step.

She burst from the lane into the piazza, startling a few passersby so she immediately resumed a more sedate pace. She kept her head down and stood close to a large group of tourists that were gathered in the piazza. They were taking pictures and listening to a guide who held a white flag with an *Adventure Travel* logo.

Glancing back over her shoulder, Madison glimpsed a man emerging from the lane she had just exited. She left the tour group and quickly joined a queue of customers waiting outside one of the restaurants. Hiding behind a group of American tourists, she watched as the man searched the square for her. He was tall, over six feet, and lean. His face was pockmarked, and he looked to be in his late forties. Russian or Ukrainian or possibly some other former Eastern Bloc country. Probably Russian. He just had that look.

Why the hell would some Russian be following her? She moved forward with the crowd. They were only two groups away from the seating hostess. The smell of tomato sauce and cheese wafted over. Her stomach churned. If the guy didn't move soon, he would see her when she didn't enter the restaurant. Madison bit her lip and watched as the man moved toward the middle of the square. Once there, he turned in a slow circle.

She stepped behind the group so they were between her and the man. She waited, minutes ticking by. When the line moved, she hazarded a quick glance. The man was gone. Madison peered around the square. Where did he go? In the far corner of the piazza, he was just disappearing down another narrow lane.

Madison's shoulders sagged in relief. She stepped around the Americans and hurried along the perimeter of the square until she came to another street. This one was bigger and two over from the smaller lane the Russian had gone down.

She kept pace with the crowd, shuffling along with another group of tourists, this group Asian. Luckily, she had dark hair and blended with the rest of them. It was only a five-minute walk to her place from here, but she didn't want to increase her pace and stick out in anyway. A shiver danced across her skin. She wanted to go home. Back to the relative safety of New York. No one ever followed her *there*.

Florence had seemed like just what she had needed to get her out of her funk. She normally loved to travel with her job but, lately, it was all getting on her nerves. Florence, however, was one of her favorite cities, and who didn't like pasta?

When Drake had asked her to take the assignment, she'd accepted. Getting the opportunity to have an up-close look at the account logs of a fashion company was good for her, since her ultimate goal was to get into the fashion business herself.

Madison loved numbers, and forensic accounting was usually so interesting. She liked the investigative edge it brought to regular accounting. Doing it in the fashion world in Italy seemed like a dream come true. Now it was just a nightmare.

She needed to call Drake and tell him of her suspicions.

But what did she suspect? She wasn't sure. Madison shook her head. She knew the spreadsheets looked good. Too good maybe? The numbers just didn't feel right, and she trusted her instincts. They hadn't let her down yet.

She turned the last corner onto her street and came to an abrupt halt. The Russian was standing in front of her Airbnb, talking to Mrs. Rover, the British woman who looked after the building. She spun around and went back around the corner. Leaning on the adjacent building, she struggled to pull oxygen into her lungs. What the hell was going on?

She adjusted her bag one more time, from one shoulder to the other, wondering why it felt so heavy. She had her laptop and her wallet and keys, but she always carried that stuff. The clutch. The damned clutch purse that Giovanni had given her. It wasn't even her taste. It was black with rhinestones and huge rivets. Not her style at all. It was also frickin' heavy. She'd planned on giving it back to him first thing in the morning. Now she wondered if she'd get the chance.

She peeked back around the corner. The Russian was still speaking with her landlady, only now the *Polizia* were beside him. The officer said something, and the Russian pointed. Then he turned and pointed to another officer that was back by the car. While the man was nearly facing her direction, she pulled out her phone and opened her camera. As he gestured for him to follow the other officer into her building, she snapped a picture. The Russian was a cop?

She watched as the cops entered her building. They must be going to search her apartment, but why? What were they looking for? What could they possibly want from her?

She eased back around the corner and leaned against the wall. She should just walk over there and ask what was going on. That was what a reasonable person would do, and she had always considered herself reasonable above all else. But she was in a foreign country, and she didn't speak the language. Worse yet, she was unfamiliar with the legal system in Italy. Did she have the same rights as she would at home?

She ran a shaky hand through her shoulder-length hair. This was all so surreal. She reached into her bag and pulled out her cell phone. She started to make a call, but then stopped. Should she really call Drake? He'd helped her so much already. She didn't want him to think she couldn't take care of herself.

Then another thought hit her. Could the people after her be tracking her? She half-choked on a laugh. If they *were* tracking her, she wouldn't still be standing a few hundred feet down the street from the people that wanted to speak to her. She touched the screen on her phone as she turned and walked away from her street. She put the phone to her ear and said a silent prayer.

She had the distinct feeling she was going to need all the help she could get.

Coming in October 2022!
Follow me on social media to keep up with release dates, contests and more.

Pre-order your copy today!

READ THE FIRST BOOK IN THE SERIES-BREAK AND ENTER

CALLAHAN SECURITY BOOK 1

Callahan Security is on the brink of disaster. Mitch Callahan pushed his brothers to expand the family business into private security, and their first major client is a complete pain in the ass. It's no wonder the man has a target on his back, but nothing could prepare Mitch for how seductive his adversary is.

Love hurts. No one knows that better than Alexandra Buchannan, so she uses her talents as a thief to equalize the scales of romantic justice. Your ex still has your favorite painting? Not for long. Alex's latest job is her biggest challenge yet. Her target just hired a new security company, and the team leader is as smart as he is sexy.

Mitch knows he's jeopardizing not only this job but the future of Callahan Security. If only he didn't find Alex so damn irresistible. Soon their game of cat and mouse explodes into a million pieces. Unbeknownst to them, there's another player in the game, and his intentions are far deadlier.

Buy the book here: Break And Enter

ALSO BY LORI MATTHEWS

Visit my website to sign up for my newsletter

ABOUT LORI MATTHEWS

I grew up in a house filled with books and readers. Some of my fondest memories are of reading in the same room with my mother and sisters, arguing about whose turn it was to make tea. No one wanted to put their book down!

I was introduced to romance because of my mom's habit of leaving books all over the house. One day I picked one up. I still remember the cover. It was a Harlequin by Janet Daily. Little did I know at the time that it would set the stage for my future. I went on to discover mystery novels. Agatha Christie was my favorite. And then suspense with Wilber Smith and Ian Fleming.

I loved the thought of combining my favorite genres, and during high school, I attempted to write my first romantic suspense novel. I wrote the first four chapters and then exams happened and that was the end of that. I desperately hope that book died a quiet death somewhere in a computer recycling facility.

A few years later, (okay, quite a few) after two degrees, a husband and two kids, I attended a workshop in Tuscany that lit that spark for writing again. I have been pounding the keyboard ever since here in New Jersey, where I live with my children—who are thrilled with my writing as it means they get to eat more pizza—and my very supportive husband.

Please visit my webpage at https://lorimatthewsbooks.com to keep up on my news.